Monique Charlesworth was
was a journalist before she
published in 1986. She now

LIFE CLASS

Monique Charlesworth

SPHERE BOOKS LTD

Published by the Penguin Group
27 Wrights Lane, London W8 5TZ, England
Viking Penguin Inc., 40 West 23rd Street, New York, New York 10010, USA
Penguin Books Australia Ltd, Ringwood, Victoria, Australia
Penguin Books Canada Ltd, 2801 John Street, Markham, Ontario, Canada L3R 1B4
Penguin Books (NZ) Ltd, 182–190 Wairau Road, Auckland 10, New Zealand

Penguin Books Ltd, Registered Offices: Harmondsworth, Middlesex, England

First published in Great Britain by Hamish Hamilton Ltd 1988
Published in Abacus by Sphere Books Ltd 1989

Printed and bound in Great Britain by
Richard Clay Ltd, Bungay, Suffolk

For Alex

1

One man stood silent and apart from the group, failing to offer the nod which seemed to be the minimum greeting due for such a place, for such an early hour. At the sight of the horses there were comic groans and laughter, a pantomime of disbelief that the mounts could be so small. The man looked around intently. He was bearded and in his late twenties, wrapped in some cloth that could have been a bedcover and which gave him the look of a hippie.

It was four in the morning. Here, high in the mountains, there was no electricity, no plumbing, nothing but the stone-paved road leading inexorably up. Behind us lay little col-oured bungalows, the homes of peasant families. They, who rose at first light to till their plots, were prepared to vacate their rooms for a few coins when the hotel at the top was full.

All that night we had listened to the old man coughing in the lean-to at the back, heard the mother shush the baby through the wattle and daub and felt ashamed that we should lie in such proud discomfort. The rusting bed filled the whole of the room and had an uneasy hump which served as a Dutch wife. Its dispossessed occupants had presented us with their lantern and brought us cups of sweet tea with smiles and nods; we had sipped uneasily, for the water might not have been boiled. Later we had cursed at the knock on the window, which woke us from the deepest of finally attained sleeps, and made skimpy ablutions with icy water over the earth pit at the rear. We had grimaced at each other in the dim light at the impossibility of dressing in the space, at the noise we made and the twanging of the bed-base as we sat to fumble at shoe-laces.

The horses, jittering on the steep road, gave out a strong smell. Smiling incomprehensibly, the boys had led us up to the only place in that blackness where there were lights and, among the gaudy trappings of a bar, a dozen tourists on wicker chairs. Not, to be sure, a packaged group, but people who had slept in relative comfort and now drank coffee and debated the worth of eggs that were still queasily glutinous after five minutes' boiling. Affluent people with cameras, chattering and joking and laughing at the way their long European legs dangled, ridiculously, below the stirrups. One by one the pack was hoisted onto the mounts by the mountain men. They, in stoic silence, trudged up carrying lanterns and leading the horses. To warm themselves, they had wrapped faded sarongs around their arms and chests, with an elegance we could not hope to equal.

With a certain instinct for separating individuals out from the mass, our boys ran ahead, tugging at the bridles, to make sure that we headed the procession. All the way up the rocky slope and down the inside of the first crater, the horses were strung out at distances of twenty metres from each other and we preserved the illusion of being alone. As we jolted painfully on the saddles, the chill of the night and the early start silenced us. Looking back, I saw a caravan of tiny dots of light flicker across the sandy plain. Here the horses' hooves were quiet and the only noise the occasional shout as man or boy urged a beast on. It was a weird and beautiful place, a lunar landscape against which the central crater emerged from the blackness and turned misty grey. By the time we reached its base we could see each other and streaks of yellow and crimson hung in the sky to the east. Here we dismounted and started the last climb up a hundred almost perpendicular concrete steps, these and the well-made road sure signs of past industry and another in the making. Perhaps, now, it is only possible to greet the dawn at Bromo with all the hurdy-gurdy of a souvenir market.

Only the tourists climbed up. Below, the boys and men crouched and talked and even the horses huddled in groups. Our guides would not be so foolish as to climb even one more step for pleasure. I was halfway up when Ridinghouse overtook me, leaping ahead and moving some distance along the rim of the crater with a loping stride. There was a path of sorts which led in both directions from the steps to points where jutting tongues of lava gave way to dizzying drops into the void. He clambered over one of these and disappeared beyond; behind us the others struggled up, they, too, silent as the sky turned pink behind the undulating, encircling mountains.

Down below, bright gobbets of orange showed where the fires still raged and clouds of smoke puffed up. The inner walls, furrowed as by a giant fork, bore a white blight. Now the air was losing a little of its chill. Some distance away, where the path was broad, cameras were being pointed and clicked, there was a revival of chatter, lost in the hiss and rumble of the volcano. We breathed in the characteristic stench of sulphur, the smell of rotten eggs.

I do not know why I followed him, at my age, but I did. I clambered over with some difficulty to the point where I saw him standing at the furthermost rim, facing the sun. Under the cloth he was wearing shorts and climbing boots; his brown legs must have been cold. He had closed his eyes and swayed a little, backwards and forwards, as though he were saying some mantra to himself. He opened his eyes, he alone not looking through a lens. Now he moved forward to stand at the very edge and stood perfectly still, unaware of my telescopic eye trained upon him, looking down into the cauldron of boiling rock. After some moments he let the bright blanket drop and it fell at his feet and coiled itself and hung over the edge and he made no move to retrieve it. We both watched as it slithered a foot and then, gathering momentum, scuttled like a beetle down a further twenty feet, coming to rest on a small ledge. A man can climb into Mount Bromo and many do, but where he stood the rock had bunched itself into an overhanging hump. He leant forwards and stretched out his arms and hung, now, like an eagle against the thin blue sky.

Slowly, he began to lean forwards into the void, inch by inch, to the point where the slightest touch would have sent him tumbling over. I focused upon his face, which had the concentration of a man willing himself to undertake a great act, and I realised with a sick horror that he intended to jump. There was a long moment while I gazed in stupefaction and then, with a sudden scrambling together of wits, of arms and legs, plunged painfully down the rocks, started towards him with that ungainly run I have and now the tense head turned with infinite slowness and the deep-set eyes took in my presence. Very, very calmly, he brought down his arms and turned, sliding down from his perch and, perfectly collected, walked towards me. He was past and gone, back towards the others, without our having exchanged a word. I stood, panting in a sudden access of warmth from the exertion and with no doubt a stupid gape upon my face, and watched him go. That look, again, of distaste, a thinning of the mouth, as though I had committed an unforgivable social solecism, lay on his face. His blanket had vanished under a thick white cloud.

With a view to their postponed breakfast, the others had already descended and I was the last there. There was merriment below as the little people hoisted the overgrown adults onto their steeds. I could not see my wife among them and, made suddenly more solicitous by what had occurred, I hurried down to plague her, old fool, with my needless anxieties and she laughed at me and, clucking at the horse, urged it on. Now the sun was fully up and the crater gold, its smaller neighbour dazzling with brilliantly green grassy clumps. Across the Sand Sea I remained at the rear, lagging behind watching the elongated shadow of the horse, myself the hump upon its back. I became aware that I had scraped my good leg quite badly. He was far at the front now, recognisably erect upon the horse and beginning to scale the outer crater and I had the urge, impossible to achieve, of catching up and saying something, though I scarcely knew what. I remember, too, thinking with a kind of irritation that he would probably only have broken his leg, that the climb down to retrieve him would have been an awkward one and visualising with angry clarity the jolting journey back and the impossibility of improvising a stretcher in an area utterly devoid of trees. I thought, too, that he should have chosen Merapi, so much more dangerous and inaccessible than Bromo, if that was what he wanted. Merapi was the perfect suicide spot, a seven-hour trek from Solo on foot and not for the faint-hearted. I had rejected it as unsuitable for Annette and, if truth be told, I could no longer have managed the climb myself.

So down we went again on the rocky path to the hotel and on again to the bottom of the mountain, this time with a third horse added to take our cumbersome baggage. My bad temper evaporated at the brilliant green and silver of the neatly terraced mountain, the rows of cabbages and onions, cauliflowers, leeks and maize. They sat dewy-prim, in ground as perfectly weeded as any flower bed in Kew.

As we descended, the air warmed and turned, eventually, into the heat and dust of any road in Indonesia. The bus for Probolinggo was designed for nine people but actually accommodated sixteen, plus a load of boxes and baskets teetering on the roof. The ride down was spine-jolting; nevertheless I slept against Annette's shoulder while she, avid for experience, took it all in. That penetrating gaze of hers had not, however, noted my bearded friend, for we spoke of him briefly and she looked a little askance at me, as though I was perhaps elaborating for effect. Critics always remark upon the vividness of my imagination as though that were out of place in a man my age. They seem to think that discoveries should cease with maturity, that my awareness of and pleasure in the absurdities of life is rather the province of the young.

The journey took two hours and by the time we reached the little town Annette's cheeks were flushed a delicate rose from the heat and the sandpapering caused by my stubble. I sat her down in the dusty bank where the business of changing money was accomplished. Then came the yet more irksome business of finding transport to Surabaya, where there was an airport. Armed with a tight wad of Rupiah, I bargained in the market-place among the crowds of bus drivers for exclusive use of a conveyance. Two smiling youths eventually picked me, for it was certainly not the other way around: one to drive at breakneck speed, the other to hang dangerously from the open door, gesticulating and shouting at would-be travellers along the way who might have had the notion of sharing our vehicle.

We wound up into the hills to Tretes, south of Surabaya, with the intention of spending the night in the resort and Annette who, no seasoned traveller, had not yet acquired the knack of sleeping anywhere, lay luxuriously across the long seat at the rear. There was a large hotel there, supposedly the best, though I forget its name, a place at that time of year almost deserted and boasting a number of concrete cottages and a garden full of coloured concrete animals which were unaccountably depressing. No, we would not stay there, for there was nothing to indicate that we were in Java and we were the type of travellers who, appreciating comfort, would nevertheless willingly sacrifice it for the smells, sounds and discomforts of the real place. The driver, for whom this palace was infinitely enticing, shook his head at us and began to worry about his fare.

Down we drove at the same rattling pace and up the winding road to Surabaya. At the airport, the driver of the bus, receiving his money after all and a tip far too generous given the jolting and buffeting he had subjected us to, now grew entrepreneurial. He offered to drive us about the whole country at a rate of payment that would have grounded us long before Jakarta.

No, I had decided that we would fly to Solo, I said, my reward the teasing smile Annette bestowed upon me in recognition of a mutual unspoken wish for ease. A man could marry merely to be the beneficiary of that sweet and silent telegraphese.

We ventured forth, the next day, from the Mangkunegaran Palace Hotel. Despite its grand name and corresponding tariff, it had a modern greenish dampness and an uninhabited air. We went to wander around the Pasar Triwindu, which lies almost at the hotel's gates, its labyrinthine jumble a happy contrast. The market is a collection of little stalls setting out a cornucopia of bric à brac. They sell junk, household utensils, 1930s tea sets, all manner of purportedly royal artifacts and some rather nasty oil lamps for the tourists to buy and break on the way home. I had found a gleaming cave of hub caps and was busily photographing it and its proprietor, an old man whose wrinkled face suffered the invasion patiently. The ritual was nearly complete and I was bowing my thanks when I saw Annette's blue dress at the far, bright end of the alleyway, her hair a halo of gold. The proud husband pointed his camera at the distant figure, taking in the long shadow and just framing the shot with a border of pleasingly coloured objects protruding from the adjoining stands. And then I saw her turn and make an animated gesture and through the lens saw the bearded man, half hidden, saw him take her hand and smile at her and there, in her whole manner and beaming face, was a glowing pleasure which I saw had been absent before. Click, it was recorded, two profiles under a cerulean sky.

I am quite a decent photographer, perhaps too fussy with my lenses and equipment, too anxious always to fix my memories on celluloid before they have had the opportunity to occur. It is possible that if I had not had my camera none of the succeeding events would have happened. Certainly, if I had not spotted them and started down that alleyway, she might not have introduced me – he might have passed on. I could date the whole miserable business from that moment, but I prefer an earlier option. It started at that moment on the crater when I went beyond the reasonable limits of the path. I possess, without a doubt, the impulse always to overstep the limits. It is inbuilt; I have made a career out of it, a marriage even.

Encumbered with my bag of camera equipment, discommoded by my stiff leg, I went to meet Ridinghouse. If not precisely a figure of fun, I must have represented a mildly absurd sight, for I cannot walk without lurching a little and indeed am regularly, unfairly, accused of being drunk. Once I appeared, this fleeting moment solidified, took on a distinctive texture, the tone and rigidity of an event. For two people can meet by chance, can grimace and shrug a thousand meanings in an instant and part with a wave, but three cannot, not when there is an introduction to be made. It is a quorum that at once settles to its work: the inevitable probing of the couple who do not know each other towards a vague comprehension of what the other represents. That is what we call society, that need to know is the tension that glues us all together. It is not enough for us to meet another human being through the kind agency of a third, to shake hands and leave it at that. We have to establish a relationship, a common taste or background, a mutual friend, anything, to breach the natural void which lies between civilised people and which they find so very distressing.

And so this introduction was made and forced through against the better instincts of both men and because I had willed it to happen. I made it happen when I pointed my camera.

'John — John Ridinghouse.' Annette presented me with his name with a particular intonation, a slight stress — sufficient to imply previous mentions. It was both a polite and an uncharacteristic fiction. By way of riposte, I remarked, perhaps abstrusely and certainly a little stiffly that we had, at any rate, *seen* each other before. This observation was left to hang unexplained. Ridinghouse extended his hand, said his dour Englishman's how d'ye do. I would have said more but my wife (who must always leap where others walk) launched into a stream of ideas — the nature of coincidence and that she had nearly not recognised him and that he must now tell her at once what had happened to him, after Bristol, and what had he been doing with himself? All this with a brilliant smile and qualified in the next instant by a triumphant non-sequitur that it was her honeymoon — she was a married woman now. The note of child-like pride, the mild surprise in her voice made me smile, though we had already been married for a year. Ridinghouse replied with none of the information required; with the conventional wisdom that she, on the other hand, had not changed at all and he smiled at me over her head, just as though we knew each other. I had the curious notion that this conversation, devoid as it was of any useful information, was taking place in code. I found myself staring at the two of them as though there would be a clue in the way she stood or as if, by following the complex whorls of his beard, I could follow the empty words to the place where their significance became clear.

'Do you realise that Ruffey knows John Pie?' my wife said and then, veering east and west, a small, changeable weather-vane between us, she informed me that John had been in the professor's department. 'Did you ever finish your degree?' Now a hand flew up in mock dismay. Annette has always voiced what she thinks without due reflection, foot-in-mouth disease, her gaucheries charming rather than giving offence. He, seemingly incapable of taking umbrage, merely drew her arm through his and they moved forwards in an unhurried way.

Bringing up the rear, I heard the names of various acquaintances being pulled out as a session began of that satisfying game of discovering that rising young stars have dimmed to obscurity or that the mediocre have achieved a success their youthful misdemeanours did not herald. I stumped along and listened, the sweat dripping down my back. For all his attentive looks, the man gave away little of the past years. We emerged into the dizzyingly bright street and he surveyed us together. How long were we staying in Solo? He would meet us that evening – would take us out. My new acquaintance was naturally familiar with all those marvellous little restaurants locals frequent which a tourist would never discover; there one might dine for a handful of Rupiah and experience the 'real' Solo, rather than that artificial item I had hitherto been exhibiting to my wife.

I was, in other words, more than a little bad-tempered and unfairly so. For, as it would happen, we had dined the previous evening upon the green banquettes of the Mangkunegaran's restaurant with nothing better to look at than a Dutch salesman, whose blond frizzy head had merged disturbingly with the lace curtains behind. Our chance acquaintance of the empty bar sold building materials and special cements and combined an exceedingly slow mastication rate with an equally wearisome propensity to tell pointless tales. He had married an Indonesian girl, carried her off to Holland and fathered a family on her without acquiring one entertaining anecdote en route. For a third of the year, he had told us, he was a resident of the place; we had already resolved to go out that evening and escape him. So there could be no excuse for my long face, no reason to stay at home, no explanation of my mood that could sound anything but petulant. John Ridinghouse could hardly be worse company than the insufferable Janni, whom I had invited to our table and whose expensive cold beers I had paid for.

We walked back through streets now hotter and less bearable than before, past the rough field where a group of children was marching back and forth. They banged their red drums to a raggedy audience of little boys their own age. We stopped to watch. Their teacher demonstrated how to throw batons into the air, how to catch them, and as soon as he looked away the miscreant cheer-leaders began to laugh and to hurl their sticks about with an exuberance likely to maim. They made me smile until I heard my wife's heavy sigh. Annette, a hitherto fascinated observer of local mores and particularly of children (her experience of them being so minimal as to suggest that she had sprung into the world fully-grown), now fidgeted, she yawned as one does at an infant's dawdling pace and we entered the hotel in a mutually intolerant silence.

We slept too deeply and too long that afternoon, waking more weary than before to one of those tiresome rows about nothing which more experienced couples have learnt to avoid. We, who rowed for the pleasure of making up, were finding barbs to jab at each other. I had been unfriendly. Worse, I had been rude. There was a hint, ridiculously, that I was jealous of this unknown who had known my wife before I had. He had not the conversational or other charms to attract a woman, but it was unwise of me, on such short acquaintance, to suggest as much.

But I was not jealous – it was something else, it was rather that the presence of any third party would have unsettled me. And he, if not precisely a harbinger of doom, had a quality that made me uneasy. His strangeness was as apparent in the market as it had been manifest on the volcano. I could not precisely define it; it was almost an aura, an invisible ectoplasm. There are respectable precedents for such feelings; they are not confined to spinster virgins or the mentally afflicted, not the prerogative of whimsical old age. But I was very careful at that time not to chance any remark which might underline the discrepancy in our ages, not to appear an old woman. By that same token, I would not be the first to complain of fatigue. It was foolish, perhaps, but there is no man more foolish than one with a young wife.

Wanting, simply to be rid of him, I said something else — another variant of the truth — that the imposition of a third person took away from the delight of our previous self-absorption, our little unity of two. And did I not add, generously, that the same would be true of any wholly improbable chance acquaintance of mine who might suddenly manifest himself? I do not believe that this was an unreasonable emotion for a man on his honeymoon.

We had married the previous summer to the amazement of a good many people. Depending on their circumstances, my contemporaries found this alliance laughable or a source of deep envy. No man in his fifties can marry a girl half his age and expect congratulations; both parties are soon burdened with the tentative hopes and explicit fears of their supposed well-wishers. Annette had perhaps had more to bear with. Her numberless girlfriends had accused her of being shockingly mercenary, of, as one such friend had put it, getting on the gravy train.

Such ill-judged remarks had performed the useful function of strengthening our resolve, for neither of us had seen it in quite that light. We had fallen in love, an explanation that seemed far too simple for most people. The age difference, far from guaranteeing the lurid scenarios my peers foresaw with lip-smacking relish, produced rather a determination to live the remaining years as fully as possible. I knew that it was sexual jealousy, never more potent than in the nearly-impotent, that prompted all those hints at future cuckoldry, those visions of horns sprouting among my sparse grey hairs. Shackled, as they generally were, to charming but admittedly mature, if not over-mature women who had seen through the crises of early middle age with tolerant affection, my contemporaries had hitherto consoled themselves for my freedom by predicting a lonely old age. Now they betrayed themselves in their gloomy and strident prophecies.

I had never married, contenting myself instead with a number of long-term affairs which had all seemed, at their zenith at least, to be perfectly satisfactory. When I met Annette, I had had one such long-standing liaison which convenience and habit had prolonged. The thunderbolt, scoring a direct hit, had quite pulverised my ossified rituals and shattered, in the process, all my preconceptions about how my sixth decade was to be spent.

We had met at one of those shuffling gallery parties where the wine is acid and the food grease-tracking missiles. She had introduced herself and, little flatterer, paid me a number of compliments in the most direct and outrageous fashion. I remember that I looked at her as a child might gaze at an ice-cream when its pockets are empty: a delicious and perfectly unaffordable girl, unaffordable, that is, in terms of human resources, of years remaining and virtues to offer, of promises to be made and kept.

This holiday was the first fruit of such a promise. I had wanted to show my wife the country that I love and the place of my birth in Jakarta. I had sentimentally infused the whole event with a sense of bringing together the threads of my life into a coherent whole. I thought ruefully that it was not perhaps a wise notion after all, to take the new love to meet the old.

I heard her singing in the shower. What a mercurial creature she was. One mood succeeded another, sunshine then storm with no apparent cause. She was innocent, unperturbed, as though it was she who was the observer, rather than the instigator of such naughtiness. For these were the qualities of a child: stubbornness in wanting things, a refusal to take no for an answer. She was headstrong, childish indeed: characteristics I found admirable when I was the sole object of her desire.

I watched her through the door: the effortless forwards swoop to dry her toes, the dip and rise of breasts that were wonderfully disproportionate, too large for the small frame. She, lifting her bright head, winked and jutted a provocative hip. She is not beautiful. Her mouth is too wide, teeth slightly uneven, the nose has a bump in it. All her features are a little too much of this, too much of that, it is a mobile, fascinating face, one I never tire of. A jolie-laide with an astonishing appetite for sensuality. That characteristic was no prerogative of youth; it was rare at any age and we had, at least, that in common.

It was she who seduced me. Most persistently, my wife courted me with wine and flowers, such artless artifacts of seduction bestowed in daily profusion in charming reversal of the usual procedure. She came, interrupting my work, to pour wine down me, to feed me delicacies. Her impromptu picnics took their savour, not from the delicatessen, but from her presence. And I, telling myself, that I was just the age to make a fool of myself over a girl, resisted most virginally. The big room filled up with sweet-scented vases, such feminity against my bare boards a constant reminder, so that when she left I could not stop thinking about her. I could not afford the sort of turbulent involvement that would throw work and peace of mind out of the window, its corollary the yet more disturbing break-up which our disparity in age made certain. So, with commendable discipline, I resolved against the passionate but brief liaison this seemed destined to be and began instead to listen for the ring at the door, to wait for the visits that were of no consequence and, in so doing, I gave myself the time to get to know her.

It was a drug, that vital youth of hers, and I became addicted. For all her knowing sexuality — and I could not stop watching her — she often seemed vulnerable, naïve, demonstrating at times an ignorance that was touching. How learned I was in comparison; I talked to her of art and all kinds of things and she paid me the compliment of serious, intelligent attention. And yet, no deferential listener, she could be abrupt and funny and she made me laugh and sometimes — for she was stubborn too — she made me cross. I wondered all the while why she came to visit me. I thought that she wanted a teacher — for she had talent, a minor but not contemptible one — but if that was so, she was strangely reluctant to show me her work. And yet once, when I made some casual reference to our being friends, she took umbrage in a ridiculous way, said I was a bloody idiot and flounced off, all wounded feelings, leaving me baffled. What could she possibly mean by it? And when I asked her out — in the most casual way, for a drink, she refused point-blank, as though I should have known better. Then she did not appear for four days and I was frightened — she knew well how to drive a man mad. I did not understand her at all.

When she reappeared, she brought me a little pot of African violets wrapped in purple paper. I have the paper, somewhere, still. I asked her whether she had been home — the home I knew nothing about for I had neither asked, nor cared. It was a boyfriend that I feared. Then she started to talk about her father. I do not know which pained me more: that she should have concealed so great a part of her life, or that I should never even have inquired before.

Now I understood the lacunae in her education and marvelled, rather, at how much knowledge she had picked up. It was a humble background: her father ran the despatch department of a firm which made extruded plastic items of all kinds, most of them risible. It was, as he never tired of repeating, a good, white-collar job.

Mr Huntley was a man of rigid beliefs, conservative in his ways, a church-goer. He believed in law and order and in 'decent values' and frequently expounded such views, choosing above all to do so at Sunday lunch times when the sanctity of his church hung sweetly about his shoulders. His wife and daughter knew to sit silent as he sermonised; interruptions only lengthened the process. His verbal ruminations started when the meat and gravy were finished — gravy was the touchstone of his humour, its colour, quality and consistency being food for speculation, approbation and derogation, just as the poor sinners were. His soliloquy was always the length of three vegetables, pudding with custard and a cup of coffee.

He neither drank nor smoked; he believed in helping his neighbours and doing as he would be done by. He was always conspicuous in the High Street on a Saturday morning carrying shopping for one or another of his 'old dears' while his wife and daughter shared their burden in the rear. His week never varied. Wednesday was bowls night in summer, darts at a neighbour's in the winter. On Fridays, before tea, he visited 'his' OAPs and carried out an informal check-up on the neighbourhood, boldly walking up paths and knocking on doors where he fancied spying signs of neglect or need. Stoutly he bore the cross of being often misunderstood, sometimes even reviled. On every other night of the year, bar summer holidays, he remained at home. Home was the centre of family life; that was why he had a family. So, after his tea, he would thank his wife for it, remarking comfortably that he was glad he was one of those husbands who knew how to appreciate his blessings. Then he would sink into his armchair, flick through the newspaper and give his daughter the benefit of his commentary on world news before encouraging her to run upstairs and do her homework. As soon as she was gone, he turned on the television and watched it for the remainder of the evening. While his wife sewed and knitted − such homely pursuits being congenial to him − he avidly took in a large and indiscriminate dose, commenting meanwhile on the deterioration of values, the shameful escalation of violence.

Each fine Sunday afternoon in the summer, he would mow the grass and then enter the house, to remark, self-deprecatingly,

'That's looking a bit better, isn't it Mother?'

His wife knew to run to the window, say the lawn was lovely and thank him, for if she didn't, he would repeat the remark until she did. He was a man of extraordinary stubbornness.

I imagined a great, red-necked bull of a man and was surprised, when eventually I met him, to find a small fellow, balding and meek-looking. He was only in his mid-forties but as cautious in his movements, as self-consciously spry, as one decades older. He wore a green polyester suit in my honour. It sparkled with synthetic fibres and had a most unpleasant, cauliflower-like texture. He looked askance at my lack of a tie, pressing his lips into a thin, disapproving line. He told me at least three times that he had decided he should meet me as that seemed 'the least I could do'. He seemed put out when I showed no gratitude. The lips folded again. That implacable line of his remained in force for most of the visit. I would have laughed at the paper tiger, were it not for the anxious, pleading look in his wife's eye.

Susan Huntley was a faded, half-pretty, nervous woman, utterly in his thrall. Her house ran to set rules; cups of coffee were produced at 11am precisely, the tea tray at 3pm, meals on the dot. She looked after the house meticulously. It was one of dozens of small, three-bedroomed semi-detacheds along an endless avenue which, to merit its name, sported a stunted tree every three hundred yards. It lay near the main route from London to the coast and there was always the faint hum of traffic. Life was circumscribed by the great highway of escape which had to be crossed and re-crossed, to get to school, to the shops, to the station, anywhere, out.

Annette was an only child; brought up to be pretty, she turned out to be clever. This was best concealed. She learnt to keep her peace, for her father could not be argued with. Conversation, for Len Huntley, meant a remorseless advance by small promptings and nudgings towards the inexorable recognition of his virtues.

Annette drew and painted well – for the local comprehensive boasted an excellent department – and perceived in that a novel and dizzying freedom of expression; she linked art with escape. Her parents never suspected such a shocking thing. Her father noticed rather the swelling bosom, the remarkable delicacy of her waist and, being as little inclined to impute virtue to others as he was to doubt his own, he kept a strict watch upon her. Annette evaded him with clever schoolgirl stratagems and managed the customary parties and discotheques and the usual number of pop concerts and illicit boyfriends. Her real achievement – a secret kept to the end – was the planned escape to art college. It was astonishing, how the process worked and the making of applications, the seizing of grants; these things were as far-fetched and unattainable as the moon.

Sheer perversity preserved silence and ensured a bombshell announcement that she well knew could, with care, have been defused. She meant to deny him the pleasure of assimilating the notion — of claiming, as he would have done, that it was his idea. She did not even permit her mother to share in it; it was too important. Altogether, it was a fine revenge. He could not — did not — approve of the freedoms, the unsuitability, the arbitrary and asocial nature of the work — the nakedness and immorality. She could not have hit upon a notion that would appal him more. If he was unyielding, why so was she; they discovered something in common. It was provocative of me to assert such a thing. Obdurately she lifted her chin, flashed a flinty eye.

'You don't understand,' she said, flatly. 'Some things you have to keep to yourself or else they lose their power. When I left, do you know what he said? That I'd get a welcome at home, in Christian charity, come what may. And later on he boasted about me being at college — "We've all got to do our bit to help the young ones, haven't we? That's what parents are for".' She said this with an oleaginous smirk.

'He's mean. My mother's not had one proper pair of leather shoes in her life, with leather soles. I used to watch her face when he put a pound in the collection box on Sundays. He'd get a clean note ready beforehand and then make a performance out of finding it — folding it up so it would go in, giving a little shrug, you know, a polite little apology for holding everyone up,' and she mimed the action with a twisted mouth.

After that, I decided that it was a father figure she wanted. I resigned myself to avuncular cheer and all the while I ached, just once, to kiss her as she bent to pour my wine and (quite unnecessarily) allowed her hand to graze my shoulder with electric effect. She knew. She provoked me beyond measure simply by being her own, utterly female self and then yet beyond that by those clinging summer clothes she wore, I thought, to torment me. I found myself putting aside my work to sketch her; the hours of her absence filled up a notebook of studies. Once she fell asleep on the couch, curled up like a kitten, and I spent a happy hour drawing from life and undressing her with my pencil.

I found myself bidding adieu to the old friend who had warmed my back on many a cold night. I could not bring myself to make love to her and that poor cement proved to be all that had held us together – and still I did not admit to myself that I was hopelessly lost.

I reached within a few weeks a pinnacle of conflicting emotions that made any thought of work impossible. I was certain, on the one hand, that I must bed Annette or give her up to achieve any peace of mind – positive, on the other, that she saw me as the father she would have liked to have and that the strong sexual signals emanating from her were innate and therefore neutral. At the same time I could not help feeling that I would prefer not to make love to her at all than to lose the by now necessary pleasure of merely feasting upon her with my eyes. Poor Ruffey, who had no idea that this turmoil was called love, who despite numerous affairs had never been in love and thus, at an age when men are supposed to be in control of their amours, was suffering the torments of much-belated adolescence.

She chose, at precisely this moment of exquisitely pleasurable pain, again to absent herself for a few days, thereby confirming all my best and worst suspicions. Then, one evening she burst in to find upon my easel a nude which, for all its lack of a face, could only be her.

She fixed me with her most mischievous look, the solemn mouth belied by dancing eyes and very slowly began to peel off the T-shirt she often wore which clung so breathtakingly to her naked breasts. Without a word she unfastened her skirt which fell about her feet and, turning around slowly, she offered herself and — for I stood rooted to the spot — came then and entwined her warm, nearly naked self around me.

There was time enough for talking, later; for the exact anatomical comparison which proved I had not done justice to her extraordinary breasts, nor to the exquisite curve of her thighs.

That desire has remained, a constant and miraculous phenomenon. I have fed upon her youth. That she wanted me — what nourishment that gave for vanity to preen itself, each day's awakening bringing with it a fresh surge of elation, so that I wanted to throw my head back and bay like a dog for glee at my good fortune. What I have, I hold. At once I became the instigator, seizing my chance and securing her to myself with all due vows and promises and even, rough old atheist that I am, entering a church for the first time in thirty years. It amused me enormously to deck myself out in that undertaker's regalia, to perform the conventional rite under the baleful glare of her father, younger than I, the rigid stare of her mother, aghast that this wolf should steal her ewe-lamb away. For they had pleaded with her, in their suburban language, rather to live a 'trial marriage', thereby swallowing in one gristly lump the prejudices of a lifetime. It was a rich joke to see their nauseous faces when we insisted upon propriety.

Now she lay, pliant, in my arms and thinking to take advantage of that amenable torpor — for I, too, am nothing if not persistent — I told Annette that her friend was the odd man I had seen on Bromo. It seemed to me remarkable that she had not noticed him there. While I uttered these words, the unpleasant idea suddenly fixed itself in my mind that he had sought her out; that he had followed us to Solo. Even that she – not I – had been the intended witness of the spectacle on the volcano. She sat up in a fury. It was intolerable that I couldn't enjoy myself, that I had (oh unfair, childish accusation) to spoil things by creating mysteries where there were none. No, she had not seen him on Bromo; she had not seen him for years and he could hardly be blamed for turning up here: where else in Java did tourists go? No doubt, she added tersely, he also found it unpleasant to run into 'people' – a category from which she plainly excluded herself – but he had better manners. I kept my thoughts to myself. It was evident that to deny her the pleasure of the evening out would be the action of an irascible, jealous old man. It ended, as such discussions always did, with mutual softening and protestations of love, but I could not help contrasting the unthinking happiness of yesterday with the present situation, even while I promised to be on my best behaviour.

The evening brought the excellent news that Mr Ridinghouse was on his way back to England. A joint expedition to Borobodur was mooted by my precipitate wife; we would proceed thence to Yogyakarta and there our paths must separate. This did something to reconcile me to the man. That process was aided by our affection for the country. Reticent when it came to talking about himself (so much so that that maligned imagination of mine immediately manufactured a disreputable past), he could grow expansive on the subject of Indonesia. His love for the place was paralleled by a knowledge of its history and customs far more thorough than my own. Mine was a rag-bag of memories, anecdotes and images. The collection had had years to form. It was a rich sediment; time had solidified the arbitrary into the very stratum of an existence. My knowledge was sensual, instinctive, personal – communicable not through the recital of facts, but rather by a kind of osmosis, the interchange of good spirits, bonhomie. In short, the very character of the man muzzled me. Mr Ridinghouse, however, had an army of facts, whole regiments of detail to muster. He managed, even, to communicate all this without becoming a bore. I made, then, the connection with my old friend John Pie.

Perhaps it was merely the assumption of superiority that jogged my memory. At any rate, the comparison unleashed a pleasurable train of thought. I wondered if he aped Pie's tone – if the former student of philosophy had acquired both his ideas and his overblown sense of his own value from the master of those genres. There was no opportunity for me to interject anything as ill-natured. The other two were absorbed. Annette drew him out with a barrage of questions, receiving in return his eloquent, knowledgeable replies. Her saté grew cold as he described the Indonesian royal courts; he conjured up a procession of caparisoned elephants bearing silk-wrapped wives. It was the story of the susuhunan moving his entire court to Solo, bringing trees and flowers, gamelan sets and troops, the mass of the people bringing up the rear and dragging his cannon. Ridinghouse described the jewels, the smell of crushed lotus flowers, the ground trembling under the elephants' feet as though he had stood on the marshy ground alongside the monarch two hundred years before; as though he had nodded – yes, here, looking at the river with his dark eyes. I announced, with a natural wish to deflate, that my father had been present at a procession of that type – a royal event in Malaya. It was to celebrate the circumcision of a young prince.

Ridinghouse nodded. He waited for me to say more and my fickle memory drew from the void no detail, not one scrap of substantiation, but a vision of my father swaying and crooning in our little sitting-room. 'God it was boring. And hot, do you remember Joan? Afterwards we went back to old Tommy's place and got out the gramophone and danced under the stars.' He had pulled my mother up and twirled her about the room singing 'Dance, dance, dance, little lady, youth is fleeting to the rhythm beating in your mind' and she, flushed with pleasure, had whirled around lightly, laughing, and I had stared – for I had never seen them dance together, not before, not since.

'That must have been in 1933,' the tiresome man said. 'I think that was the last. In Kota Bahru,' and on he went, neatly marshalling his interminable detail – ah, but he did it well. Curious and inscrutable he might be, but when he exerted himself he had an appeal. I was aware of him watching us with that level of curiosity and interest that is often ranked as charm. It is a quality of attention that both sexes can find bewitching. I, in turn, observed him closely, feeling his spell rather in Annette's breathless attention. Now and then, for they monopolised the talk, she remembered me and turned with a half-apologetic smile, with what I fancy was a trace of guilt.

I did not possess even a third of his store of information, for all my small boy's memories, my hearsay stories. Who was there to teach the pampered child of the 'thirties, that protected and enviable being, about the races among whom he lived? We were born aware of our innate superiority, unable to envisage a future when we would not be the masters. White men learnt customs and languages in order to govern and to trade. The old colonials' pangs of nostalgia and regret for that life are made all the more acute for that lost empire of innate superiority. I, at least, was born early enough to have had that experience. I thought at the time that John Ridinghouse was one of those who sought to escape the modern world, a man born out of his time. Such a simple motive was the one I ascribed to him; the more simpleton I.

He was only twenty-seven, the prime of young manhood. He had thick brown hair, cropped short, but the beard already grew a few grey hairs. His head and face were slightly over-sized and would have fitted a larger man; seated, he was of a height with me, and when, after some hours, he rose, it was a small surprise to rediscover the lean frame. The beard was, I suspect, a symptom of laziness and certainly made him distinctive in a nation which often sports fine, silky mousta-ches, but seldom such luxuriant growth around the chin. There was no weak chin or overlong upper lip hidden there; his profile was even handsome, his elegant nose adorned with the chiselled nostrils of antiquity. He would have been any good-looking young man were it not for the strange eyes, dark and deep-set, which rested for unconscionably long periods on an object or a face. What made him remarkable, I decided, was a quality of repose. He spoke quietly, without ums or verbal tics, in what must be described as an educated voice. He could not be embarrassed by a silence into fidgeting or shifting, nor startled by a noise. He sat perfectly still. His hands were beautiful, slim with long, tapered fingers, their gestures made all the more eloquent by their rarity. As to dress, it was as simple as was commensurate with decency: a white shirt, baggy shorts and sandals which hung together by an effort of will. Impervious, seemingly, to heat and mosquitoes, to crowds or discomforts, he did not appear capable of irritation or anger. He had about him an invisible mantle of perfect self-sufficiency, something so very rare that I have come across it only once or twice in my life. It is a quality some travellers possess.

While I examined him, while he and Annette talked, we

ate a variety of delicacies at a surprisingly low price and he and I exchanged clipped courtesies over the pouring of beer and passing of dishes, and the conversation wandered erratically on through trance dances and the varying skills of different dalangs and episodes of the Ramayana or the Mahabharata – for on all these subjects the wretched fellow had something to say.

I watched and listened and became, by degrees, more and more absorbed in a kind of sub-plot to the main drama – a by-play, which engrossed me a great deal more than the conversation could. It was a ballet of gestures. It began thus: soon after we sat down, I had taken Annette's hand, which lay upon the table. Lightly, a moment later, she drew it away. Lightly, as though the act merely facilitated her study of the rosy little nails, the perfect tiny moons, she clasped her hands (in that defensive manner) in front of her plate. A woman can be reluctant to demonstrate physical closeness to a man for many reasons. I found myself thinking, oddly, that a more worldly woman would have known to lay her arm around me, to smile, to disarm me with a touch – but my wife was too simple for that. And he, meanwhile, had reacted to this tiny – this after all barely noticeable – movement of hers, by turning away. He gave his attention to me; he asked me some question – I think it was about my work. He did not look at her again, although they faced each other, until she said something about my working habits – and then she was rewarded with a glance. When, in due course, she laid her arm across the back of my chair, her recompense was a smile.

So it went on, both fascinating and repelling. We ate and talked and each movement brought, not rebuttal, but confirmation of this odd notion of mine – of this game. I thought that if it were so perfectly unconscious, then they could not have acted with such consistency: for as she advanced, he retreated; she leant towards him across the cloth and, smoothly, he would lean away. Until she made some small, uxorial gesture, he remained distant, his attentions to her the reward for hers towards me. It was perfectly consistent throughout. I could not think it a product of my over-ripe imagination; no, it was a comedy of manners which played itself out for my benefit, which simultaneously unnerved and flattered its spectator-object who could neither comment nor be seen even to notice. Impossible to say anything, then or later.

I knew a corporal in Cyprus, many years ago, a small, hirsute fellow with crooked teeth. He used to wrap half a dozen thick rubber bands around his wrists – would pull them tight, so that they cut deep red weals. He enjoyed that and the way the rubber caught the thick, springy hairs. He would laugh, when somebody noticed. I began deliberately not to notice, to remove his pleasure because there was something ancient and crude in it. This was the same kind of not noticing and the tension at the table as thick, as stretched and painful as those rubber bands.

At last it came to an end. Ridinghouse hailed a becak to take us to Sriwedari Park to hear the wayang wong group and loped alongside while the emaciated driver pedalled furiously to move his burden. Ridinghouse had been pleasant, to be sure, the evening had to be termed a success, but I could not like him. He had exerted himself to obtain tickets for us; he had insisted upon buying us dinner and it would have been ungracious to demur, but I hated feeling beholden to him. It was a perfectly irrational and unreasonable dislike, the only sort I entertain, for genuinely unpleasant people I can laugh at. Ridinghouse had done nothing to provoke me and I had, at least, the minimal sense to refrain from saying anything to my wife. Annette was charmed at the notion of his accompanying us; clearly taken in by his allure.

So she went to bed and I sat over a last drink in the empty bar and, wishing that I possessed John Pie's pyrotechnical ability in insults, pondered the happy issue of which verbal bludgeon he might have used to crush Ridinghouse's pretensions. Must have used; no student could have escaped Pie's even-handed distribution of scorn.

Pie is a philosopher by inclination as by profession; he is an amateur archaeologist, who does not hesitate to assume that his fellow diners must take equal pleasure in his hobby. So he launches, unprovoked, upon descriptions of this or that newly-discovered shard, its relationship to other fragments and likely provenance, offering the whole as the most delightful dinner-table talk. Should the conversation divert to such workaday topics as books or holidays or the theatre, he interrupts without ceremony and resumes his theme. He is more interested by far in the occupations and leisure activities of diners long dead; if recalled to the present, he is in the habit of remarking rudely to his hostess that her treasured Royal Worcester or whatever will reveal little of value about her, should it by some mischance survive. Oddly enough, hostesses love him. They offer him up as a savoury treat and he never fails them, bringing out as his party trick all manner of outrageous assertions and particularly a number of Nietzschean aphorisms he has off by heart. He specialises in German philosophy, Nietzsche in particular, and it has often occurred to me that he apes the great man's peculiarities in life as in conversation, drawing the line, however, at such worldliness as the apocryphal Cologne brothel where the philosopher reputedly caught the clap that addled his brain. Pie, however desirous of emulating that exploit – and certainly he would claim for himself the more pleasantly lubricious aspects – is but an armchair lecher. He is profoundly ill-at-ease with women. Should one dare to enter into a discussion with him, he brings out his favourite maxim — 'That if a woman has scholarly inclinations, there is usually something wrong with her sexuality.'

Pie sprang from a strange set of parents. A withered old pair, they looked like brother and sister, any conjecture as to sexual congress between them being not so much lewd as ludicrous. She was as whiskery sharp as he was rosily benign; both were scientists and had worked together in a biochemical backwater all their lives. When obliged to do so, they viewed their son with the same faint measure of alarm and curiosity that they brought to the observation of a slightly dubious experiment. Pie was not mothered, never nannied. House-maids reared him with no very tender notions about the sex. He is as thorough-going a misogynist as one could hope to find. 'Women destroy creativity': a favourite speech. 'They can't stand it, having none themselves. Walking wombs. An assembly of hormones.' He is frightened of them, of course, and the more beautiful the packaging around the hormones, the further he flees. He would be as awkward, as easily duped in love as his hero, were he ever to dare such an experiment. There is little risk of that. Pie, who in other respects is scrupulously honest, has always claimed to frequent whores — he tells outrageous stories about them. At sixteen he calmly absented himself from a school outing to the National Gallery, walked to Soho and bought a whore. That was his explanation for his absence and he was punished — not for the actual, preposterous crime but for compounding his offence by such bare-faced, smutty lies. I, who was obliged to relay this information to the housemaster, could not believe it either and I have the idea that he has not been near a woman since. It is too late now. Pie grows ever sharper with age, thornier, more abstruse, and my wife's provocations have lessened the frequency of our meetings. I pity him for that bile, but our successes are made no less sweet for the failures of our friends. With this pleasant thought, I went, at last, to bed.

We drove to Buddhist Borobodur in an ancient black Mercedes, a car so proud of its good name that it sported a further three Mercedes stars fixed to the radiator grille. Polished outside to a faintly scoured gloss, tinted windows shut to give the impression of a cool interior, in reality the car was bakingly hot, seats cracking and creaking. We wound down the windows to let the oven cool, receiving in exchange the dust of the roads. It was a pleasant journey, all the same. We left very early and the small, surly driver warmed up alarmingly, as the day did. From ten kilometres away the road began to fill with charabancs overtaking each other recklessly around corners and puffing out black smoke. Our driver would not be humbled by these monsters and squeezed by at the most unlikely places, finally proving his worth by fitting the big car into a parking space on the grass as near to the entrance to the monument as could reasonably be expected. The place was a warren of market stalls and out-buildings and teemed with building workers as with traders.

The crowds were astonishing. Somehow I had expected to see tourists, Europeans, an assumption as ridiculous as expecting to find only Americans at Windsor Safari Park. Families, school parties, children swarmed over the place, crowding up and down the steep stone staircases, hanging from the dagobs and photographing each other in every possible position.

Rising from the jungle a mass of intricate grey, in places covered with lichen and blooming with erosions where the endless work of restoration was not complete, Borobodur suffered the invasion of its calm with the indifference of a monument which had survived eleven centuries, including eight of neglect. It would be proclaiming the path of enlightenment to the empty sky when we were all dust and ashes.

We made our way as rapidly as the crowd permitted up to the topmost terrace representing *arupadhatu* – formlessness and total abstraction. We were, naturally, indebted to Ridinghouse for that information and more besides which he had delivered in the course of the journey. He had expressed, too, polite interest in my work, proving as evasive as ever on the subject of his own. At the summit, my blonde proved a greater attraction than the latticed dagobs with their calm-faced Buddhas inside. We were at once assailed by grinning lads wanting their photographs taken next to Annette; even by a charming little pair of soldiers who posed on each side of her to the appreciation of the gathering crowd. One of them, not quite daring to put his arm around her, held it hovering in the air inches from her back, while attempting both to smile at his friend's ancient brown-box camera and to give me an ingratiating, apologetic look. Against such complex emotions, my wife's face flashed a radiant smile of utter simplicity.

Ridinghouse drifted away and I lost sight of him, fully occupied with the task of fending off her small admirers as politely as possible, since the midday heat was intense now, for all the cool green surrounding us. We drifted around and down the different levels examining the carvings without a sight of him and indeed in that throng even my girl could be invisible in a moment, for all her brightness. I tired at last of the jostling, of the ever-renewed audience which stared in rapt admiration at my cameras and wife alike. Down, then, we went across the fields where women stood in the heat hawking their souvenirs, T-shirts and brilliantly coloured drinks. We drank ice-cold Coke which left us thirstier than before and finally made our way back to the car.

Ridinghouse was not there, nor did he return. We waited; we grew silent. We watched the blue sky with its silly storybook puffs of white cloud as it darkened and streaked with flame. The coaches were leaving. Persuading Annette to wait at the car, I climbed once more to the top and saw how with the fading light the landscape diffused and the greeny grey shapes blended ambiguously. Impossible to say whether the monument had crept back into the jungle or vice versa; they had reclaimed each other. I did not see him.

Stumping back to the car, certain that he would be waiting, and wanting, I suppose, to punish him and make him wait in turn, I loitered in the market. Following to its source a high-pitched humming sound, I found a seller of spinning tops. A diminutive woman crouched in front of half a dozen of the toys laid out on a sheet of newspaper on the bare earth. Each top was a simple bamboo cylinder on a notched stick with a string wound round it to pull; the end of that stick dipped in red, the bamboo notched like a whistle. I tried and couldn't make one work and the woman smiled. Dextrously, she set them all going at once. There was something immensely attractive about their simplicity, their whirring slenderness. She could not afford the paint that would have turned them into something altogether more flamboyant, less eloquent. I bought them all, took them to Annette. Ridinghouse was not there. She lifted her head and saw me coming, looked with a kind of despair at the bamboo sticks which hung in my useless hands.

Our driver was growing impatient to leave, for the arrangement was that he would drive the further forty-odd kilometres to Yogyakarta where we would part company. Annoyance at Ridinghouse's tardiness gave way, then, to anxiety about his well-being and finally, as the monument closed for the night, to a last search, one in which a couple of guards accompanied me. They were reluctant; for all the bright stalls below and the hubbub of the departing crowd, the place was suddenly eerie. Unlit, except at the perimeter, it grew alien and chilly against the darkening sky. The Lilliputians had withdrawn to a safe distance while the giant slept, but it seemed to me that the great grey mass watched us; that somewhere in the intricate crevices of stone an eye stared out, unblinking.

I looked at all the corners for places where a body might have fallen, where a man, leaping from the summit, would have smashed against the stone and the guards, infected with terror, at last hustled me away. I looked, too, in the market – in every little drinks stall, even in the long row of horse-drawn becaks lined up ready for the next day, in case he might have fallen asleep in one of them.

John Ridinghouse had climbed up carrying his small bag which contained, as far as we knew, all his possessions. He had left us no evidence of his having ever been there. Inconceivable as it was that he could, say, have been abducted and ridiculous to speak of foul play, we nevertheless bumped along the road to Yogyakarta prey to lurid speculations. Annette was convinced that he would never have abandoned us without a word voluntarily; it was only the impossibility of finding a place to stay that persuaded her to proceed at all. I do believe she would have stayed and searched again, the next day, if I had permitted it.

In Yogya, at her prompting, we made a missing person report to a policeman who wrote down the name in careful, even capitals and wondered visibly at our concern for a man we hardly knew – for we could not supply a home address, nor next of kin; we knew nothing of his stay and could not even list his occupation.

In Yogya, too, I took a film to be developed and found,

opposite the smiling profile of my wife, a black blurred edge which repeated itself on every slide. The only trace of the man was a small triangular protuberance which must have been his beard; the rest of him was wiped out in a way that seemed uncanny. There was, of course, a perfectly rational explanation: the flap of the battery compartment had flipped open, a failure of the catch which proved to be unique.

He didn't turn up, but he was with us all the same. We could not enter a restaurant or walk down a street without a certain strain: Annette's looking and my consciousness of that. We could not pass the Puri Artha's reception desk without Annette's stopping to inquire whether a message had been left for us. A further stress was imposed by our eventual, mutual embargo on the subject. That did not stop either of us thinking about him; it merely accomplished a retreat into our own heads, into separate and individual ways of dealing with a difficulty. If Annette, each time a traveller's cheque was cashed, was wondering in her practical way if he had had sufficient money, speculating that he might have been attacked for an excess or spitefully murdered for a lack and blaming herself for never having inquired, I, disagreeably aware of that sort of train of thought, was wishing rather that he had never existed. She, in turn, thought me callous and this produced in her that kind of sensitive shrinking that occurs when a person becomes aware of an unpleasant characteristic their partner is exhibiting to a third party; the inevitable corollary was to imagine that she, too, might suffer from it in due course.

And, yes, I think of this as a peculiarly female characteristic, an anticipation of the worst before it happens, which goes a considerable way towards fulfilling the expectation. Women, a lot of them at any rate, are particularly good at this, and not just the simple craft of predicting what types of rotten behaviour are to be expected from a given man. It goes beyond the personal with them and becomes an art form; fuelled by resentment, they manage to feel offended not just on each other's behalf, but in absolute terms, on behalf of womanhood as a whole. It was not exactly that Annette wanted to judge me, or even began to do so, it was more that the possibility of judgment existed, where there had been none before. How apposite, here, one of Pie's Nietzschean sayings: that when we have to change our opinion about someone, we hold the inconvenience that person has caused us greatly to his discredit. The honeymoon was, ipso facto, invalidated; it remained for us to put the suffering beast out of its misery.

We left the Puri Artha Cottages and hurried on to Jakarta, where we stayed at a modern, expensive, ugly hotel where Javanese in business suits ate steak and baked potatoes side by side with Americans picking at desiccated saté. Outside this air-conditioned fairyland, the city manifested countless further excesses in the American mould throughout its sprawling, senseless grid, the whole exacerbated by indigenous dirt, rubbish and poverty. A paradise had been lost, irretrievably. We jolted in a dirty taxi through the steamy night to Old Batavia, perched on seats without springs so loosely secured that every corner threatened to tip us onto the floor. The quarter was dark, threateningly empty, the only signs of life the Vespas flitting and buzzing like fireflies. The taxi drew up and at once a light sprang up inside the cave opposite which purported to be a restaurant and two young men leapt out of the blackness to escort the suckers inside. Even American Month and pumpkin pie seemed better than that.

I suppose it was inevitable that the old house should be gone, replaced by an engorged complex of offices that had swallowed half the avenue. I could hardly be surprised, yet at the sight of this sprawling concrete snake an extraordinary depression settled upon me. It had been hovering in wait as a migraine does, giving nauseating twinges in anticipation of sharper punishments to follow. A day had to be got through in this blackness before we could leave the place. We did not go out. We chose to sink into the anonymity of the hotel, sleeping and reading rather than braving the streets, needing soft security, as a sick man wants his anodyne. I had entered Indonesia with all the joyous expectancy of a homecoming, long-awaited. Now I was slinking away, as from the scene of a crime and, victim or villain, whatever he was, John Ridinghouse's spectre sat between my wife and myself during the long aeroplane journey home.

2

I held the aeroplane on course effortlessly. I am so expert, so vigilant a passenger-seat pilot that it is child's play for me to balance the whole rumbling, shaking machine, to carry out my constant checks, auditory and visual, while I flick through magazines and papers. Unlike the man in the cockpit, I never rest. I do not need a gauge to tell me that we have lost height, or that the throbbing of the engine has changed its tone.

This flight seemed endless. My wife, heartless, was asleep with her head resting on my shoulder, my bad leg was stuck out at its usual peculiar angle. Thus buttressed and braced, one cerebral hemisphere monitored the mechanics while the other surveyed the foibles of mankind.

In Salinas, California, a Korean woman was suing her husband's mistress for a million dollars. This sum did not relate merely to the purloining of the spouse; it was to indemnify her for the little finger that her rival had bitten off. This loss, she claimed, not only interfered with her profession of acupuncuturist, but it prevented her from rejoining her ancestors after she was dead. In the eyes of Korean-Americans, she had lost face as well as a digit, she told the judge.

I found, too, folly of a more lugubrious kind: an ice-cream murder in Manila. The son was killed by an ice-cream vendor twenty years exactly (it is always exact) since his father had suffered the same fate for the same crime, that of supposedly not paying for the cone bought for a small son.

The world was peopled by passionate and dangerous eccentrics, their whims and tragedies compressed into half a dozen lines of small, bold print, the human interest filler. There were men whose job it was to record these stories, to whittle them down into that special simplicity calculated to raise a half-smile, a rueful shrug of the shoulder.

A photograph to record an event in this category: a passsionate, bold man takes his wife up a volcano on their honeymoon. No tame, quiescent one, it is erupting, clouds of gas are being released from the rock, great lumps breaking loose and tumbling down across the lava field. The couple sit, side by side, on horseback – he spine-rigidly erect with a smile of self-satisfaction. She has a curve pasted onto her face, she is determined not to be seen to be afraid. Behind them, steam rises from long fissures in marvellous, sinuous plumes, but it stinks of sulphur and the woman is making that face because she is gagging on it. Did the earth move for you, darling?

There is another photograph of this. An amateurish effort, which supposedly shows a piece of lava being hurled across the field of vision, but it is a blur, impossible to interpret. This is a picture of no interest, one that would have been discarded, were it not for the fact it failed to record – that the blur landed ten feet away from my father. Et in inferne, ego.

It was chic, in the 1920s, to undertake such an excursion; it was daring and avant-garde. Naturally my father, the lover of volcanoes, would seize the opportunity when he chanced upon Bromo in eruption. Of course, six decades later, his sentimental son would emulate the feat, would produce a better set of photographs for fewer pains, would receive for his temerity more than he had bargained for.

My father had tried to pass on his love for this phenomenon without notable success. I was three when he took me to see Krakatoa: someone had told me that there were devils in a volcano and I believed them. It was to be a splendid treat, young Ruffey held up over the railings of the ship, the better to obtain a view of the mushroom cloud bubbling out from below the water. It was a fountain of rock and gas and steam, shooting into the sky as the submerged volcano formed itself anew. The ship went as near as it dared and it was understood that passengers embarked at their own risk. When the little man all starched up in a white sailor suit screamed before they even got near, the father was deeply ashamed — and when the child made himself sick, he was disgusted and passed the little coward to a sailor.

My childhood was recorded in photographs taken in brilliant light, faces either over-exposed or deeply pitted with the shadows of hat or nose. They are all posed. There is always a row of grown-ups standing or sitting and young Ruffey is always correctly attired and, as often as not, is mimicking his father's upright stance.

The most memorable of all are those of the lost Shangri-La, but I do not feature in them; my parents left paradise before I was born. There are several albums of these. My father, too, must have felt the need to record the evanescent moment of glory. There are dozens of the same type: the white man, immaculate in light shirt and breeches, even sporting a small bow tie, cradles his rifle and stands, all nonchalant ease. Around him a semi-circle of dark men in sarongs, solemn-faced, encloses the hunter with the carcase of the beast he has just shot, leopard or tiger. Sometimes it is more dramatic: there is one of my father with his arm around the neck of an orang-utan which he grips while a heavy neck-chain is being put on by a grinning assistant. It is quite safe: the lower half of the animal and its long, strong arms are swaddled in a net. The eyes of the beast stare out of the all-too human face in desperation, mouth open in a giant-toothed, long-gummed rictus in what passes, in humans, for hilarity. They would capture a baby, tether it to a tree and wait for the mother to come — glory indeed, to capture the animal alive.

My father explained it all to me and I, all fired up, would dance about the room and shout bang-bang, aiming at imaginary beasts, a trick to make him smile. He always said that I could go shooting when we went home to Malaya, and that I would have my own gun. There was a tacit understanding that these talks took place when my mother was not in the room, though whether it was Malaya or the shooting that should be kept from her, I did not know.

I knew from the earliest age that we would return, one day. I knew everything about the plantation that was rightfully his, by work if not title. Sometimes my ayah took me to the office to meet him. We walked home together through the dusty heat of Jakarta and while she loitered behind, looking in shop windows, he would transport us back to the jungle. He had come out from England poor and in seven years on a big estate in Kelantan had mastered his trade: only world economics were big enough to defeat him. With pride he told me about the loneliness of it, the bouts of malaria, the way all night he had heard the cracking noise of the nuts splitting and falling, the cries of animals. He was a plantation manager by the age of twenty-five; if the rubber slump hadn't come we would have been millionaires. I was to go back with him, to remake that fortune.

He had a way of talking to me, man to man, that was irresistible. I was his partner, his equal, a secret princeling guarding my secret from my playmates and guarding his, too. Always on the way home he would stop off in a couple of bars for a quick drink, so that by the time we got to the house he was a little flushed and jolly and I, unprimed, knew to say that we'd had to wait for him as he was working late, to explain the time the walk had taken.

'Women are like the tiger,' a favourite remark of my father's. 'Vicious when roused, otherwise domestic. No sense in provoking them.' It seemed to me that he was bent on provoking them, for he made pretty women in the street the object of his gallantry. He was quite a good-looking man, fair in the English style and tall and while there was nothing outstanding about his looks, he had a way of talking to people so directly and personally that they could not resist his magnetism. I try, but cannot think of a single significant remark that he ever made, certainly nothing remotely intellectual, but I remember that at a party he was always surrounded and that people looked at him and that on the street dozens of people would come up and shake his hand.

I understood perfectly that if Mother and I were playing when my father came home, I would always be sent off to the ayah while she gave him her full attention. When he was late home she would sit silently under the lamp in the corner, playing with the fringes of a shawl or turning the cigarette holder in her fingers, restless until he came.

Once a playmate of mine invited us to go to a picnic with his parents in the hills at Puntjak where they lived from Friday to Monday. My mother put on the finely patterned Chinese silk dress she wore for best and a funny little hat. We journeyed interminably in the train that Sunday, for we had no car, no house there, not even the use of one of the absurdly styled chalets. Little Switzerland, they called it. And after lunch, Loek and I were playing together under the table while the men went off for a smoke and a bold, red-headed lady went with them and then I saw my mother's legs following.

'Poor Joan,' one of the women said, which made me pay attention, and then another woman laughed and said, in English, 'Anneke is nutty on Jack.'

When, on the long bumpy ride home, my mother grew tired and cross and said it was the women she couldn't stand and they would never be accepted, I repeated the remark to disprove her, to cheer her up and, little innocence, watched with amazement as she took my father's head in her two hands and pulled it towards her and whispered something that made him colour up.

Unlike my mother, our ayah loved to escape from the house. She would dress me up and parade me through the market showing me off to her friends. We would stop in front of stalls which sold the objects of my greatest desires — peanut biscuits or sticky cakes or brilliant green or pink drinks. My favourite was rose syrup with coconut and shavings of ice, most strictly forbidden. Delving into her net purse, she would buy me one treat after another and stuff them down me. I was made to stand with my neck stretched out, for fear of soiling my clothes, while she held the glutinous mass. I gobbled like a fledgeling, terrified both of her anger, if there were stains, and of being seen, pleasure and humiliation thus so mixed that I did not know myself if I dreaded or longed for these excursions.

My ayah slept in my room, because my mother had once been told a story about a child killed in its own room by a black cobra which came up through the floorboards. I used to believe that she stayed awake all night to protect me. Perhaps she told me that. I have the notion now, thinking very hard about it, that she must have been a practical joker.

It only took the aroma of a *kretek* cigarette to waft me back to that real Indonesia, the one that only existed, now, in my head. There, up ahead, was a chap lighting up. What smokers they all still were. But the packet this one discarded carried a government health warning down one side and was smart and anonymous in burgundy and shiny gold: Gudang Garam International. My father's cigarettes came in a paper pack with a green sunrise on it. They were called Thomas Bear's Elephant Cigarettes and I collected the animal pictures inside. How much more satisfactory they were, memories, like dreams, always more vivid than dull workaday life.

I preserved the memories for years, so that they were set hard, like papier mâché, in my skull. I was a man when my mother began her unceasing monologue, her voice a hammer tapping at my head.

'He was sex-crazed,' she said. 'I wouldn't let him go back to the plantation. Imagine, he even wept – a grown man crying like a baby. But I knew what he was crying for. It was the Chinese girls he was thinking of and a Siamese one he'd had and I think he imagined they'd still be there, waiting for him. They offered him a share of the profits, as though there'd be any, but of course the place was gone to rack and ruin.'

'What year was that?'

'Thirty-five, or six. My boy was very little. As though I'd have taken him to that wild place. But Jack had no sense, he was all dreams and big ideas. He was always going to be a millionaire. Thank heavens I had my own money. Jack would've given his last penny to a beggar.'

It is an idée fixe with her, this imaginary income. She looks at the middle-aged son who pays her bills and hints still at the size of her fortune, smoothing her skirt and smiling provocatively. She decides anew, each visit, that I am too old to flirt with, but habits die hard and every now and then a trembling red hand lifts, to touch the wisps that were once a bob, to tap a delicate cheek that is now whiskery. She will be eighty-four next year and her legs are badly swollen. I do not know whether I am imagining the delicate, nervous woman that my mother was or whether she, in turn, is remoulding the past into a more acceptable format.

'Do you want to know why I married Jack?' She asks every passer-by this question. 'I had the pick of all the young men.' The explanation always differs and sometimes, when the nurses are busy, there is only the wall to listen.

'He had these incredible yellow eyes, tiger's eyes. Jack was famous for bagging tigers and all kinds of game. Of course we girls said we weren't going to be impressed when we saw him at the club. That he wouldn't bag us. We were introduced at last by Jimmy Duane, he was one of my father's managers and sweet on me, and the funniest thing happened. Jack just stood and stared at me and his eyes really were a cat's, I swear the pupils dilated and contracted and I stared back absolutely hypnotised and I thought my God, that is it. That's the one. And we were married three months later.'

My mother thought it a fine thing to go off into the remote districts to live. She was strong, born in Malaya, she had lived all her life there and the isolation held no terrors.

'I can't tell you how happy we were,' she says, 'we didn't want anybody else. But of course we were terribly popular and people were always coming out to shoot and Jack would take them off with a dozen native beaters. They all said he gave them the best shooting in Malaya. And it was fun for me, of course, the only woman for miles and we dressed for dinner every night, everyone did then, and I thought thank heavens for my trousseau, because I really did have a different frock for every visit.'

There is another version.

'There were always noises at night, in the jungle. I kept waking and hearing what sounded like a baby crying and I'd wake Jack and he'd say don't be silly, it's only the trumpet beetles, but they really did sound like a trumpet and they never made any sound after nine o'clock at night. It was a baby, in the cook house, and it was Jack's. Later I used to see a girl playing with it and I knew she was the mother by the insolent way she stared at me, but of course Jack denied it.

'I wanted my child, Jack's real son, so badly. After a year there still was nothing. It preyed on my mind, that it was my fault. He used to get up at five to go to roll-call and then I'd be on my own for hours until he came for breakfast and I used to lie in his warm place in the bed and not get up until he was due back. I couldn't do anything, when he wasn't there. It was worst of all when the rains came and then you really were trapped. I used to spend weeks of my life just sitting around, waiting, reading old copies of the *Straits Produce*. He wasn't safe anywhere. He went to whores in the cities, like a dirty sailor, before we were married. He couldn't leave women alone. He told me everything, on our honeymoon, and of course I said it didn't matter, but I never felt the same after that. I never trusted him. Every time he went off I wondered what he was doing and whether he'd gone to her.'

The slump in the rubber price put an end to plantation life

and sent the European masters home. Many of the dispossessed found a temporary home in Kuala Lumpur, my parents among them. Her father was still there, now a ruined man; they lived in the big house that would soon have to be given up and, while my father scoured the country for work, my mother made different plans.

'Jack was prepared to take a job for no money — it was ridiculous, rubber went down to 30 cents a pound and people stopped tapping altogether. But I started a child in KL — as soon as I was away from that place, everything was all right, you see. And I had a girlfriend who was Dutch and her husband decided that they should go to Java, where she had family connections, and between us we wangled a job there for Jack with a Dutch firm. He knew rubber and he spoke Malay and he was lucky to get it. Poor Jack, he wasn't a businessman, always a dreamer. But I made him go and I was right, because the next year and the one after rubber fell again, it went to 5 cents a pound and we would have starved on that plantation of his.'

I was born in 1930 in Jakarta in a small villa we shared with another family. My father was away at the time on one of his frequent trips. He cried when he learnt that he had a son.

The house had a garden, a frail barrier against the swirling dust of the road. Sometimes in the evenings my father would take me out there while he smoked his cigar, and told me, as always, about Malaya — not the Western side with its ugly cities, but the real country, the untamed, mountainous east. The traffic noises and raised voices from the street jarred on his acute ear, which could distinguish the cries of all animals. There, he would say, I would hear only the tock-tock of insects and birds and there would be no dust, but cool caverns under a dense foliage of trees one or two hundred feet high.

Up above, bright against that green, I would see the brilliance of flowers and butterflies.

My father would walk through the marvels of the city as though it didn't exist. In the bustle of the market, he lamented the crowd and extolled a purely animal kingdom while I half listened, distracted by the patterns of batik, the bright shafts of sun through the thatch that set the mangosteens glowing like rubies. I already inhabited Eden; the smells of spices intoxicated me. I would stop to listen to the gamelans and to stare at the intricately carved wooden frame covered with flowers stained red and overlaid with gold leaf and he would say, wait until you hear the Dayak drums. But I felt my pulse quicken to the melodic bronze one, the tinkling complex harmonies that wove over each other.

'Are they as good as this?'

My father bent down.

'That isn't music. I'll tell you what's music, unforgettable, and that is the chant of the Indian conductors at dawn going through the roll of names while you walk down the long line of coolies.'

I always agreed with him, but I couldn't see how names could be music.

My father was a restless man, always seeking excuses to go somewhere. We never went to the North.

'There is a time for going back,' he said, but it never came.

He grew to hate his pedantic Dutch masters, so different from the English with their thrift, their Little Amsterdam villas with imported roses in the neat gardens and pink embroidered lampshades on the porch. They wore high-buttoned stiff collars; he often expressed the hope that they would choke in them. Once he took us to Bali. He told me that the brave Balinese had fought the Dutch to the very last child. We should honour them; they had been the last

Indonesian people to be conquered and even now, he said, their hated conquerors had barely made their mark.

In Den Pasar he met up with a European who had shot a crocodile with an elephant gun and who hunted tigers and they went drinking together. He was a painter with an easel set up in a cool bamboo house. There he captured the delicate beauty of the girls, their elegant profiles and proud, slanting eyes. They emerged, miraculously, from the flat surface. I watched, entranced; he seemed to me to be a god. With tiny strokes of colour, a squiggle on a piece of paper was transmuted into a real person. I wanted to stay there and watch forever.

It was an evening of miracles; my father said that I could stay up late. The painter called in three cooks from the market to cook saté for us, setting them to compete with each other. Smiling the men crouched down with their charcoal, dashing the skewered pieces of goat and chicken with coconut oil and fanning rapidly with one hand while they made a hot sauce with the other. With extraordinary speed, they presented us with the hot pieces of meat in thick banana leaves, and we ate it with our fingers, dipping it into the sauce. My father and the painter vied to see who could consume more and the three cooks, like magicians, worked faster and faster to feed them, until everyone was laughing and each skewer was greeted with applause, was praised more extravagantly than the last.

They let me taste palm beer, but I preferred the bottle of pink drink they bought for me. It had a wooden stopper in the shape of a bird's head, grooved along the beak so the sweet water could be dripped into an open mouth. It grew later and later. It was only five minutes walk back to the dirty streets, the curio stalls and corrugated-iron roofs, but I refused to go. I didn't want to return to the ugly concrete bungalow and my proper supper, which I knew would come on a plate and wouldn't burn my mouth.

My father carried me, in the end. He stroked my head and said, 'Eat your supper, there's a good boy,' and winked. I hid the bird's head in my pocket. He told me that our host was Dutch, but that he considered him an honorary Englishman.

When the bungalow was in sight, I closed my eyes and pretended to be asleep. From my bed, I could hear my mother's voice raised in jealous anger, saying the man was practically a native and burnt so black that if it weren't for his shoes nobody would take him for a European and that there were standards and that he should dress properly.

My father hired an old Chevrolet to take us to Batur, the volcano at the centre of the island which he wanted to see because it had exploded a few years before, burying the village in boiling rock a hundred feet deep. Along the road there were marvellous little villages with bamboo walls and grass roofs and doves in cages and I heard the delicate, complex harmonies of the gamelan, but he would not stop for those, nor for the market with its cagefuls of green, crimson and white parrots. I watched the solemn-faced children flying kites or wandering around unattended, in straggling procession, carrying their smaller brothers and sisters. I have the impression (but perhaps my mother fabricated this) that he drove more slowly when, now and then, we spotted one of those beautiful girls bathing modestly in a stream and letting water from the coconut-shell dipper smooth the skein of her hair and perhaps that is why we only stayed in Bali for half a dozen days. But I did not measure time then; it was as languorous and infinite as the grey-sand beach where I watched the prahus set their bright sails.

I learnt to mark the passing weeks by Saturday afternoons. When work was over, my father took me out. Often we went to Batavia Zoo, the treat recorded by itinerant photographers, each with their monkey on a long chain. The animal, perched on my shoulder, grips tight and chatters its teeth. (Casually, without needing to look, my mother reaches for the pile of albums, selects one, turns unerringly to the right page to make her point. I wonder that she sees no resemblance between that child and her visitor, but her connections are all internal, her circuit board of memories wired to exclude any new input.)

Once we saw trucks lined up with crates piled high and a small crowd drawn up to watch. Inside were giant lizards; as the front of the box was wrenched open, a man with a stick would pound at the back and shout to encourage them to move into their enclosure. It had a high stone wall around it and a moat below. They were Komodo dragons, fat, meat-eating creatures the length of a man. Harassed, they swarmed and waddled up the steps, their ungainly bodies swaying from side to side, turning their heads as they went. Their thick, two-piece tongues darted out. Men gathered at the wall to tease them, poking sticks. Every now and then, one of the huge creatures, goaded beyond endurance and sense, would simply launch itself at its tormentor from the high rocks, out into the void, and would fall like a stone into the water.

This was not my father's idea of fair play, but I laughed at the funny way they moved and the huge splash they made when they fell. Leaving the zoo, he said that I would have to go home in another year when I was eight or a little older. And I, stupidly, said: 'To Malaya?'

'No,' he said. 'Home is England, old chap. You have to go to school and the only place is England. You must start before you're too old and have missed too much. It'll be great fun, you'll see.'

He did not sound very convincing.

'But I like it here. I can go to school here.'

'Everybody goes back. England's your true home, where you come from. Loek and Pieter really come from Holland, don't they, even though they were born here. Europe is really home to us.'

This outrageous assertion ran counter to everything he'd ever said. Fear gave me cunning.

'You don't like England. I heard you tell Mummy so. It wouldn't be fair on you, would it?'

'I shan't be going,' he said very gently.

'I'm too little. Mummy said I was too little to go to the market and England is much further, it's miles and miles away.' I clung to his hand like a baby.

'Of course you won't go alone. Your mother will take you. Now, what about that ice-cream? You'll be much bigger next year and you'll feel quite differently about it, you'll see.'

The weekly treat was not quite as good as usual and I remember that my father didn't have one, for the first time. He must have been over forty and, desk-bound, was putting on weight. Perhaps that was the first time I saw that he might not be invincible and, with the great maturity of seven years, realised that a grown-up could be unhappy about something and still decide to do it.

That dragon year, my father bought a new camera and determined to become expert. The time was approaching when I, too, would be boxed up and sent far from home, so the camera was always being trained on the small boy and, a touch less frequently, on all manner of boats. Ships were runners-up to volcanoes but more accessible. It was the bustle of going somewhere that he loved, the escape.

He went rushing off to Sumatra when the *Emden* called at Padang and there is a picture of white-ducked legs aligned with military precision while above, sticking out like flag-poles, a couple of hundred arms are raised in a Nazi salute. There is a photograph of me in front of the *Tjisardea*, of the Japan-China-Java line. Behind my upturned face, a whole stream of Chinese refugees is flooding ashore, women in cheongsams, men in shirtsleeves and hats carrying baskets, suitcases, small children, the flow being pointed forwards by a stern-faced officer. No dockside picture marked my departure, in 1939, when so many children were making that journey in reverse. There were many parents who deemed South-East Asia to be a far safer place than Europe.

It was arranged that my mother and I would take the steamer from Jakarta which went right up to Singapore, where the big ocean liners stopped. We waited on the quay and my mother paced backwards and forwards, checking the time constantly. For the hundredth time she rummaged in her bag to check the sheaf of tickets.

'He's been delayed at the office,' she said, not meeting my eye.

We were the last to board. We stood at the stern and my mother took my hand. For once, in deference to the momentousness of the occasion, I did not try to pull it away. With a great shudder, the boat inched away and we saw a man in the distance, running, stumbling, and she started forwards.

'Quick, there, you see? Wave,' and as, with agonising slowness, the steamer chugged ahead, she went through a pantomime of gestures, tugging at me with one hand and waving frantically with the other. As the figure lurched on and right up to the end of the quay, I stood rigid at her side, my hands grasped behind my back, for it was still near enough for me to be certain that that wasn't him.

All the way to Singapore my mother was agitated. She

had wound a scarf around her hair to hide part of her face, but it could not disguise the tears rolling down her cheeks. She never cried. When I asked her what was wrong, she would dab ineffectually at the tears, take a shuddering breath and talk about Singapore and the hotel. I already knew that the expenses were so considerable that it was incumbent upon me to enjoy myself. Wasn't I appreciative enough? I assured her that I was very happy, begged her to stop crying and ran away, roamed about the ship and pretended to be a stowaway.

At the Hôtel de l'Europe I pretended to be a rajah's son, off for a grand education in England. I ordered lemonade with the lordliest of gestures, learnt which were the best rooms, the best tables. My mother was preoccupied with papers and arrangements, packing and re-packing my trunk, checking her lists again and again with a distracted air. I didn't see anything amiss: she was always nervous, she was always worrying about practical things, about eating properly and being clean. My father offered adventure, but it was my mother who made the world safe.

The evening before our departure I was to dine with the grown-ups and downstairs, where our little table for two was not quite so well-placed as I would have wished, she told me that she was not going with me. She had changed her mind; she was sending me to that strange place at the other end of the world quite alone. I was dumbfounded that she could have been taken in by my make-believe maturity.

As soon as that was announced, she became quite incoherent with details of the itinerary, with advice — not to talk to strangers — to tip the purser at the start of the voyage, but not too much — she reeled off the names of people in England whom they knew. But they would all be strangers. Upstairs in the room her nervous hands scattered the tickets and pieces of paper with addresses on them and the times of English trains, taken from a timetable a decade old. Her face wore the incredulous wavering smile of somebody keeping their features in place by an exertion of will-power so great that only one expression could be maintained. I could do nothing against that smile.

'But Daddy said you'd go with me. He promised.' It seemed that my trump card was a joker.

Children travelled on their own, then as now: the crew of the great passenger liners always boasted avuncular types, trained for precisely this function. I would make friends with a boy two years older than me on the boat and, years later in Cyprus, hear his name in a list of servicemen killed when their truck was bombed.

My mother saw me aboard the *Empress of Asia* and put me into the care of a steward and I was grateful that she did her crying in the cabin because her nose turned red and shiny and I didn't want anybody to see her until she had powdered it.

'I wish I could come with you, but I can't,' she said. A betrayal so great could not be discussed. I didn't believe her. I wanted her to go, to leave me alone. I would manage; hadn't my father said so?

In 1946 my mother turned up at school. A few months after VE Day I had had a letter which told me that my father was dead, then another which said she would come as soon as she could. A year passed with no news and then I was hauled out of class for a 'visitor'. That was such a rarity, my housemaster's voice so full of suppressed excitement, that I knew at once. He ushered me into his study and left me with a thin, small woman with badly dyed red hair and high heels, who lit a cigarette with trembly hands before she embraced me. She said, without preamble, 'You have to understand that we knew the Japanese were coming. That's why we had to send you home. You do understand, don't you?'

'Yes.'

I watched her gaze flit about the room, so that we both averted our eyes, politely, when they met. I wondered how to avoid calling her 'Mummy'.

'So many years, I can hardly believe it. We had no idea. I couldn't go with you, darling, I wanted to, but I couldn't. Of course we didn't know it would be like this. Your father used to say there's only one good thing to be said about this war and that's getting Edward to England. It was his great comfort, knowing you were safe.'

I nodded.

'It's a very good school,' she said, 'you must be happy here,' and looking at the rows of books, she nodded her approval.

'They interned children too, you know, in the camps in Singapore. They didn't all get out.'

I knew that they had gone home, to Malaya, as soon as they had got rid of me. I had had that sentence ready for a long time, but I could not bring it out, could not throw the accusation of the abandoned child at this stranger. It was years before I would understand the impossibility, for my mother, of explaining to me, who had loved her, why she had been unable to leave my father, who so patently did not. She could neither apologise nor explain. His loss had scooped her out, left her hollow. I thought her callous, later, when she had her affairs, her men friends to take her out, but she was simply attempting to fill the void. I suppose she is alone with him now, she has, at last, a kind of peace.

'We went to Malaya in 1940 – well you know that.' She fell silent. There had still been letters then, I had them by heart. 'Of course Daddy is volunteering for the war effort,' she had written, and, 'We must *both* feel proud of him.' Another cigarette was lit in that sanctum never before profaned; she used the plant pot as an ashtray with jerky tappings which riveted my attention.

'You have such a look of him,' she said suddenly, 'I didn't think – you'll be the image of him in a year or two. Poor, dear Jack.' That phrase was clearly her commonplace.

'You must go to university, that's what he would have wanted. Well, there'll be time to discuss all that,' and in that glance of faint inquiry I understood that henceforth she would seek my approval. Later I would experience that combination of pity and power that has marked our adult dealings, but at the time I was paralysed by a realisation as sharp as it was ignoble: that she was really rather common.

I had metamorphosed her over the years into one of those pleasant, capable women who came to visit their sons in uniform, or wearing suits that had once been 'good'. Their fingernails were short and unpolished, not these red claws. Even in the little fox cape, my mother was shivering and now I began to let my image of her dissolve and this new one form. Later she would say how incredible the green of the country was and I would hear for the first time the foreign beat in her voice.

'Their war' had not been easy, she said. My father, considered too old to join up and determined never to return to Jakarta, had worried away at the civil defence authorities until at last they gave him permission to return to his old plantation and organise its defence.

'He left me in this dreadful little boarding house in Singapore,' my mother said. 'A shabby little house and we were officially at war – it was just before Christmas and the Japs were bombing and all he wanted to do was get up to Kelantan. Within weeks there were evacuees all over the place with their bundles and prams and people stretched out along the corridors and sleeping on the verandah, because every last soul in Malaya was coming down.' (She meant, of course, every European.)

'Well Jack came with the last of them and he was spitting mad, because he'd got within twenty miles of the place and then was ordered to retreat without firing a single shot. And then we had to share a room with this couple with a baby that screamed all night — well I experienced plenty of hardships, but the baby and the bombs were ear-splitting.

'Well Singapore fell of course and Jack forced me to take a ship out so I ended up in Australia and I could count myself lucky because plenty of those ships were bombed, women and children only on them, those devils didn't care. It was a mad scramble and later I found I had nothing but evening dresses because I'd packed in five minutes and of course, not thinking, I'd only taken the most costly things.' She smiled as one smiles at another life.

'Well, there was no news for a long time, we were all desperate to know, but till the end of the war there was no way of finding out whether our men were dead or alive. As soon as I could I went back to Singapore which was full of walking skeletons, the POWs being sent home, and I kept stopping people and asking and nobody knew a thing and they hadn't got proper lists out — it was chaos, thousands had died in those camps and building roads and the more I heard about it, the more I hoped Jack hadn't gone through all that. He could have been quite safe, all those years, in the jungle, you see. He would have survived that. And then somebody told me about this chap who'd been in the jungle all the time with British intelligence, setting up guerrilla units and I thought at once, that's Jack. It was just his kind of thing, you see. So I started making inquiries and asking every officer

I saw about him and eventually I was sent to a Colonel Smethwick and I was convinced he'd know, but it turned out he was the man they'd talked about and he'd never heard of Jack. Well, I was about to give up and go to England and wait until they'd sorted it all out and then I met a man I knew, a planter, on the steps of the Cathay Building. He recognised me at once and he said, "I'll never forget Jack and the good times. Do you remember those hunting trips we went on together and the time I got a tiger?" — and you see he didn't know I didn't know he was dead, but then he saw my face and he told me.'

This part came out quickly and through the blue cloud of another of her little cigarettes.

'They were together on the last day. There was bombing in some places and quiet in others, so when the British surrendered nobody knew quite what was going on — and they decided to find a boat and get out. They did, too, which Freddie said was a miracle, because anyone with any sense had got out already. It was a sailing boat belonging to a friend of Freddie's that had been overlooked and between them they rigged it up — Jack was a good sailor, you know — and they pushed off. And then suddenly Jack said, "I'm not going. This is my country and I'll never be able to come back and explain that I ran away instead of fighting," and he hopped over the side and into the water and hit his head on a piece of wood and went under. Freddie told me he jumped in and dived for him and swam around, shouting, but he didn't come up. It was dark and the tide was strong and after a time he had to give up and he managed to get back into the boat. He got out all right. Freddie's back in his plantation getting it all going again — well I suppose there's no thinking about things like that.'

'Drowned?' I said, incredulously. 'Drowned?'

'Yes.' She got up and then she smiled at me.

'Term ends in four weeks, doesn't it? Perhaps we should go somewhere together – I thought Scotland, it's beautiful there, isn't it? You could fish and we could spend a little time together.'

'I'd agreed to go to a friend's house,' I said glibly. 'I didn't know you were coming.' It was the truth, but I could have bitten out my tongue. The young have a capacity for cruelty matched in later life only through the most diligent practice.

'Of course you must go with your friend,' she said and gave me a peck on the cheek and then a sort of silly half-wave. I stayed and watched from the window as she crunched lopsidedly down the gravel. When she was nearly fifty yards away and her small silhouette had shrunk to the size of my thumbnail, I flung open the sash and shouted, 'I wrote – every week – for years. I'll send them.'

Did she hear? I hadn't called her name. I didn't know how to address her. A moment later she turned and waved. As I watched her go, I told myself that she couldn't possibly have heard and went upstairs and burnt the letters, so there was no going back. I can see myself in the silent room, holding the flame to each piece of paper, fiercely, wanting to burn my fingers. There are scenes I want to forget but cannot, they present themselves to me like film, they reel through my head with horrible clarity, all details intact.

Thirty years later, I would paint my father. He was floating on fluorescent water under a sky lit by flares. Body turning and circling in an unfathomable orbit, sightless eyes open in a face of waxy calm, he drifted away to oblivion on a glassy river of Lethe green.

3

Safe in London, where an incongruous un-English heat was making the tarmac swoon and the pavements shimmer, where the familiar, faintly musty smell of the closed-up house welcomed us back, we shook ourselves into our lives.

Almost at once I conceived the germ of an idea for new work. It was high time; I had had a year of inactivity. My inspirations – if that is not too grand a word for impulses so random and oblique that it is a wonder they insist so strongly upon reaching maturity – come from only one source. I paint what is real, what I see or know (and they criticise me for my lurid fantasies). It is always some incongruity, some odd juxtaposition of images that sets me off, a glimpse as from a train window. Ruffey in his cups or lured – it is not too difficult – to expatiate on himself, always says that his master is Hitchcock. That impenetrable globe of a man understood exactly how securely the unthinkable roots itself in the everyday.

All my life I have observed things in this way. I need never fear that my well will dry up – no, it is overflowing, and my art is the stemming of its flow, the editing and excluding. I suffer from a surfeit of remembered images. At a distance of forty years I can find in my head one morning the ostrich-shaped birthmark on my maths master's neck, its long legs disappearing under his collar to re-emerge, disturbingly, in the claw pattern of his tweedy tie.

My new work started in the usual royal flush of enthusiasm. This time, it came closer to home than ever before; the muse having been content to stalk doggedly alongside me, always adjuring me to look back, now leapt in front of me and held a mirror to my face.

This time, I worked from life. A tableau vivant prompted me: a hot, lazy Sunday afternoon, a few friends gathered in our garden. The sun was beating down, the paving stones too hot for bare feet. I never take my clothes off in England from a stupid consciousness of the ugliness of my leg, a ban which disappears mysteriously at the Channel, the grey water seemingly dissolving all inhibitions. And yet we have photographs of me on beaches, a tall, middle-aged man in mahogany with something of the spry, wiry look of Picasso at that age and I do not find myself so unpleasing in them.

I had moved back to the shade of the house and contemplated the different positions of the group, the brown and white bodies so expressive of character and attitude, the whole set off by the ordered green of an English garden. Annette lounged between a couple, friends of mine, he as ready to admire as his partner was to find fault. Andrea, in her late thirties, had hitherto figured as the young one in our circle and her nose was severely out of joint. But Robert was an architect, a man much preoccupied with the surfaces of things, their joints and finishes, their sleekness and gloss. He had come to celebrate, had entered wielding a champagne bottle as though it were a club, while his wife brandished a similarly ballistic smile.

Now he hung a little over Annette, admiration evident in a posture that was half an embrace. He was trying to monopolise her while Andrea, perched with formidable elegance on the other side, interjected a deflatory, faintly malicious note. I could see that Annette was amused by them and was glad of it. She had been quiet since our return. There had been a constraint between us, or rather a mutual reluctance to broach a discussion which would only give rise to remarks best left unsaid. Trouble – disquiet – in her was manifest in an untoward passivity, a kind of semi-inertia. Admiration revived her; of whom would that not be true? She looked ridiculously young in her shorts, perfectly natural and a foil to Andrea. It was always a shock to discover how plain Andrea was – for she was so marvellously assembled, so carefully matched and coloured and finished. She was wonderfully elegant; it all resided in a fine little nose, a perfect little chin, in whippet-like thinness – sharp effects, which bright lipstick and her striking pallor enhanced. She sat, curled up, on an old wicker chair, chattering and waving her small hands so bracelets tinkled. In that harsh sun I saw the first crow's feet flocking to the corners of her eyes, noticed faint grooves running from nose to mouth. Time, that master mason, had begun delicately to chisel into her pale flesh. I watched her black eyes rest their wise stare upon my wife's face.

Meanwhile Robert bent towards Annette in that complete oblivion to all else which is the most desperate kind of flattery. He is a big man, there is something raw and shaggy about him. Even his colouring is crude – a thick gingery thatch of hair partnered with pale eyes, with a brickish coloured face and butcher's hands. Yet he is the most courteous of men, gentle in all he does, and I have watched as for an hour he has sat utterly still, perfectly relaxed, to eat a pomegranate with a pin. Behind them lay the symmetry of the flower beds, new little trees. Annette had laboured there, planted her chives and rosemary and clematis and brought order, just as she had tamed me from a selfish old alley cat into a docile pet only too happy to lie in her lap. I fetched crayons and began to execute a neat sketch in pastels, quite unlike my usual style. I felt that stinging happiness that comes to me when I work well. It is a piercing, slightly eerie sensation of mind-body dislocation, as though the hand moved of its own volition while the eye observed with fascination an act of creation that seemed to be coming from a different mind, one in harmony with my own but infinitely more subtle and simultaneously radiantly clear.

A little allegory presented itself to me, quite irresistibly. The other three – aware, naturally, of my labour – became a little self-conscious as people do when observed; they were, however, sophisticated enough to hold their positions without stiffening up – soon I no longer heard them. It was years since I had drawn so accurately and I was absolutely concentrated upon the work, upon the texture of the bear's rippling fur and the deep indigo shade beneath the courtesan's cast-aside hat. It brought back memories of a life class, of a tall room, a model putting on a pink robe in a shaft of sunlight in my preposterous youth. I had lain in wait for that girl and walked her home and, making love, had bruised her delicate thighs with my clumsy roughness so that, the next day, the sight of the greeny-dark mark was extraordinarily erotic. The wine and the heat combined with this memory, that and the deliberately slow rendition of Annette's abandoned pose, her perfect, pink-soled feet emerging in tiny strokes that were themselves a caress, produced a state of arousal so strong that I was almost dizzy; faint with desire all the stronger for the impossibility of its appeasement.

Now the grinning monkey's head was done and its curled-round tail and I sketched as background the walled herb garden of five centuries ago which, as I looked, superimposed itself upon mine. Slowly, delicately, the colours melted and shaded into each other and still this tiny movement of my hand held them all in their involuntary stasis. At last I released them and myself with a black, sprawling smudge of a signature and now I held out the sketch to my wife, with a smile.

The three of them looked at it and Annette winked at me past their bowed heads and I felt the surge of glee of the radio ham who picks up a signal from the crackling void. Andrea looked hard at her monkey self. She said, almost at once, that it was wonderful – marvellous – adding not without a touch of acidity that it was a great pity that the female must always be so passive. And Robert looked from her to Annette to the drawing and then at Annette again and issued a great sigh. I felt light-headed that afternoon, electric with new impulses. Watching my friends, I felt myself unable to imagine them in bed or, rather, I could not prevent myself from visualising their mating. A piquant exercise. It is an old man's game, to gain stimulus from such a source, but I have never spurned the sharpness of experience, whatever its source. Sensual in mood and reckless, rocking on the stairs, I took my wife early to bed. I woke with the expectant feeling of a child on a holiday dawn, savouring a coming treat. For a long time I watched Annette sleeping, the bloom on her cheeks more delectable than the most perfect nectarine, resisting the urge to nibble.

I began a series of oil studies that morning, shaking my head in wonderment that it had never occurred to me to paint her before, not since the first little sketch that had brought her into my arms. The pictures came to half a dozen in the end, each a bright celebration of my wife. The subject, so different from my usual ones, brought about a radical alteration of style. On each right-hand corner lay the inimitable scrawl of a Ruffey who, conscious of a new departure, aware that he might be accused of sentimentality, had made his mark defiantly, glorying in both sins.

They are portraits of a woman dressing. She rises in flirtatious décolletée from mock Gainsborough satins, leans in sculptured near-nakedness under a Roman robe. My wife, mirrored as she clasps jewels in her hair, smiling into the distance with tender irony. Hers is a powerful face, that of a woman conscious of those powers and accepting homage to them. Detailed, precise, realistic, they have a certain quality — the glow of the flesh which is the mark of a woman who is loved. There are secrets in her eyes, a complicity between the painter and his subject.

It became obvious to me, as I worked, that the observer could not be kept out. I kept glimpsing myself in the mirror, seeing the absurdity of the man propped on his canvas sling while the girl lay, a half-clothed Madame Récamier, on her chaise longue. So I am there, the incongruity which gives these compositions their force: the admirer with his leg stuck out stiffly, the middle-aged face peering around the mirror with thick eyebrows raised in self mockery; the presence hulking at the door. They hold in that tension (for she is never looking at me) all the ancient absurdities that the flesh is heir to. I found it curious that I should never have painted myself before. I found charm, even, in the notion that, expecting to rediscover my past in Indonesia, I had instead found my present.

I have always worked early in the day but this time it went

so well that I carried on after Annette was released, painting in the backgrounds. It is a peculiarity of mine that I must work undisturbed and will abandon a picture if it is seen before it is finished. Thus my studio is sacrosanct and a sore trial to our cleaning woman, who sees it only in my fallow times. I like it like that, dusty and cluttered, gathering in itself all of the intensity of the previous day's work. I slip sideways through the door for fear some of that precious environment might leak out. Even my sitters are not allowed to look and especially not Annette, whose curiosity was considerable, whose patience received a commensurate reward. They were a commercial success, these tributes of mine to her powers. They sold, every last one, from a miserable little shared exhibition, the kind that seldom produces results. The critics naturally disliked them, but the public knew better, they saw the heart of the matter.

The work of painting them carried on feverishly for a couple of months and the canvases stacked up with great rapidity. I was very tired — painters seldom get much credit for the physical aspect of their labours. I was also very happy. All creative people are selfish in their work, over-susceptible to its demands and liable to sacrifice too much to its jealous whims. In preparing my works of adoration I had no time to pay attention to the activities of their subject. At the end of this time (she must have been extremely bored) she chose, one weekend, to visit her parents.

In a manic burst of energy I completed a picture and saw, suddenly, that it would be the last. The streak had painted itself out.

I cleaned up the studio, as I always do, put the furniture straight and summoned Mrs Derwent to do her worst. On the Sunday I found myself a little at a loss. I went through the house, idly opening windows, nibbling at crusty cheese pieces and enjoying my solitude in the happy expectation of it being soon banished. Continuing my aimless ambit, I went to open the door of the darkroom and found it locked. It was months since I had even thought of it; I had certainly had no desire to touch the remaining films from Java and had done my best to put the whole experience out of my mind.

The room was put in a decade ago, at a time when I was more serious in my photographic ambitions and even produced photo-collages, which I now felt a little embarrassed about. They had served only as an excuse for the acquisition of some splendid equipment.

I tried the door again, thinking that it must have warped with the heat, looked then for the key which was more usually kept inside the door, where its usefulness was obvious. Impossible for the door of that windowless room to have been locked from the inside, so I searched in all the usual places and then in the less likely ones. I found it at last in one of the little inlaid boxes on Annette's dressing table: an artless place of concealment and yet a good one, for I never touch those little feminine things. I had been searching for nearly an hour by then. She had not locked that door by accident: that was inconceivable. It was inconceivable that I, discovering it, would let it alone. We were well-matched in pig-headedness; mine might be more flamboyant but her laughing persistence was just as pernicious.

The key turned smoothly. A white blob floated directly ahead in the gloom and with a start I saw, as my eyes adjusted, that it was a man's face and one horribly disfigured, eaten away. I groped along the wall for the light switch and then the fluorescent tube flickered into life and threw its glare over walls which seemed, in that first instant, to be pitted and eaten away by some blight.

For a long time I stood in the doorway and looked while

the grey walls composed themselves into images; into grainy blown-up prints of fine tracery which, at another blink, turned into stone carvings. The whole room was a Borobodur, from every angle, with crowds toiling up the walls, up the steep stone steps. Here and there, horribly, against the mass, stood Annette smiling, my wife against a complex carving of gods and death.

The room bore witness to obsessive, meticulous labour. She had enlarged and searched and enlarged again and at last she had found the object of her search. The wall opposite me bore an inverted pyramid with, at its tip, a dark print of the main stupa. Before its mysterious emptiness stood a small knot of people. And then, moving ever outwards and up the walls, that group was ever magnified until the tall figure to the right was unmistakably John Ridinghouse and then he, ever more detached, climbed the wall alone, so the largest picture at the top showed only his head. It was centred in the middle of the pyramid, placed directly opposite the door and exactly at head height, with the same manic precision which had required the filling in of the space to left and right with empty black squares. He seemed, lower down the wall, to be in conversation with another figure, one obscured by the group so that only the back of a head was glimpsed. There was a thin streak of grey that might have been his interlocutor's face, though no feature could be distinguished. Ridinghouse, even blurred, was unmistakable. The blackness that had so shocked me was his beard, counterpoised against the dark sockets of his eyes. He seemed to be looking straight at me. The face was remarkable, life-sized, his mouth slightly twisted into what could have been a smile or even a grimace of discomfort, but I knew better. Standing silently in the heart of my house, I read his black mockery.

4

Ridinghouse was a piece of string that, as I pulled, contorted itself into knots so tight that the convolutions could no longer be followed. Ruffey, ever tenacious, held on, even if the line cut deep. Sometimes I could feel him tugging at the other end, now teasing, now dropping clues, compelling me to continue.

John Eluard Ridinghouse was born on 23 May, 1956 in Oxford and under (most would have thought) a lucky star. He was fortunate in finding himself in one of those middle-class, intellectual families that guarantee a solid cultural and genetic inheritance and, incidentally, turn out the finest of screwballs.

By the time the squalling red bundle of infant was laid in the crib, there were already three children to suck their fingers and gape and poke: a boy, at last. The girls in their shabby smocks saw, contrary to all assurances, that a mere inch of flesh shooting out its pale jet made this baby infinitely superior to them. Even Father, always so busy, made time each day to visit the lordling; the baby, gratifyingly, held his finger tight and opened rheumy eyes to stare up so avidly that a lesser man could have believed himself recognised.

Thomas Ridinghouse was, however, a superior man: the proof of it was that he might have thought, but would never have said such a thing about himself. He was a Fabian and a junior lecturer, active in pamphlet-writing and eloquent in public talks, tireless in promoting a cause that was deeply unfashionable. Worrying about first principles and the second classes, the third world and the fourth estate, he passed his days teaching the children of the élite about the Middle Ages. He would not take, but sometimes borrowed, the family money and his children ran wild in the cabbage patch that used to be a lawn and was meant to feed them all. He had bought a solid red-brick Victorian villa cheaply, just after the war, and the upkeep of it and his brood worried him terribly in the few spare moments he allowed himself when not worrying about more global causes and effects. Such anxieties did not stop him pledging spare cash to the 'real poor'.

Luckily, mother was of a more practical turn of mind. She was the sort of woman who organised jumble sales and always picked through the offerings first herself, paying as guilty recompense a little more than she thought the goods could possibly have fetched. Her girls were dressed in remade, but sometimes still recognisable, cast-offs in good cloth; over these they wore jumpers knitted from wool their mother had unravelled. They sat down to eat at a fine old table she had rescued and restored, consuming the products of her garden and ingenuity. She was unimaginably industrious, thrifty, a gatherer of hedgerow berries and picker of wild mushrooms. Far from appreciating all of this, her children longed for the luxury of Sainsbury's tinned salmon, for Formica cupboards and acrylic dresses, for jeans, make-up and pop records –

objects of desire these parents could not begin to comprehend.

Later, as petulant, cruel adolescents, they blamed their woes upon their mother who continued to embarrass them by producing yet another child and another: the last of the six was another boy. Baby Jim did not yet count; young John belonged wholly to his father's sphere of influence which the female phalanx, while resenting, feared to attack and could not hope to influence. Their father was a distant and revered figure, a celebrated man whom they had been taught to admire. Mother was to blame for the people who would ask them, kindly, if they were Catholics, not seeming to realise that these educated children knew what that implied; it was her fault that they were obliged to say no and to suffer the wondering looks. Such a number of children was worse than eccentric: it was somehow pitiable, laughable, reprehensible. They knew that they were old-fashioned to look at, with their sturdy shoes and hand-me-down dresses, old-fashioned in their manners and in their unusual self-reliance and composure, which did not protect them from the casual malice of the adult world.

These same critics also tended to exempt the absent-minded and unworldly man from blame; his wife, accordingly, had to be both lascivious and a little stupid. Having borne so many children, she committed the worse error of rearing them herself in that odd, self-sufficient way, managing and scraping as though she were too proud to seek help or too poor. Nobody who saw the Georgian family silver and the old Turkey rugs could believe that they were really poor; no, it was another form of affectation, of pride. The children kept up the pretence. They could not afford to go on school trips and so refused, proudly, saying that father did not like them to go and so they were thought stuck-up as well as peculiar and were forced ever more tightly together. Only John, inheriting his father's other-worldly air and with it a certain mantle of dignity, seemed not to notice or care about the small indignities the girls suffered daily. He, within their already private world, created his own enclave. Father and son were alike bookish, clever, turned towards the great world and oblivious to niggling, everyday things. When he became a don, the good man rejoiced in the wealth he would be able to give away.

They should have been an idyllic family with their vast quantities of fresh air and good food, of brains and breeding, books and splendid ideals. But Thomas Ridinghouse's intellectual framework, which supported him so solidly, failed to shelter the rest of the family; it was a perfectly wrought edifice, but it only admitted one.

So, in due course, the Ridinghouse girls entered the awkward years and began to carp and harry at their mother, who had no thought in her head beyond caring for them; that was her reward for sixteen years of drudgery. Perhaps that energy of hers sprang from a melancholy root; perhaps the onset of the menopause brought, alongside the knowledge that there could be no more babies, the realisation that this was where her creativity lay and nothing to come could compensate her for that loss. Whatever the precise cause, she waited until the little boy was out of nappies and then, having done her best, she put her head in the gas oven. She remembered to choose a school day, to send the little boy off on an outing and to ask a neighbour to call by, one who could be relied upon both to turn off the gas and to see to the worst by the time the children came home.

Did this mean, as her husband assumed, that she had not after all loved him? Now it would always be conjecture, every theory unprovable: a torture to the man who lived by interpretation of given facts. It was the only question, in the end, that mattered. Without love, her life became a series of meaningless procreations. Looking at his children, he saw her face and fell in love with her, now that she was beyond his reach.

For a time he was a little mad. He brooded and speculated, passionately. One by one, he would draw his children aside and, adjuring them solemnly to speak only the truth, he would terrorise them. Minutely and repetitively, he questioned them about her. Soon the girls would begin to cry. He would turn away, then, with a blank look, would pat them on the shoulder, tell them to run along, not to worry now, to be good.

Behind the locked face, the brain was active. He saw that he had turned a blind eye, precisely as though he hadn't cared, just as though he had believed in the unprincipled axiom that ignorance was bliss. There must have been symptoms of some kind; he had failed to notice them. It had been expedient so to do. Thinking such things, he wandered in a daze of inattention through the house; he was as incapable, now, of noticing the misery of his children as he was of relinquishing his own.

Perhaps he could never have managed his affairs any better; these circumstances were, intrinsically, unmanageable. Perhaps marriage was always like that. Perhaps there existed a barrier between all men and all women that, perfectly invisible, could never be breached. Our vocabularies might never permit exact translation from m to f or vice versa, any more than an English rendering of Arabic – or a Welsh version of German – could capture the flavour or tone of the original. However literal, the translation could not convey a differing mental set. There were concepts, images, so alien that they could not be paraphrased. When I thought about

Thomas Ridinghouse — and his melancholy figure haunted me for months — I felt the desperate sadness, the loneliness. I said to myself that I — more sensitive altogether, more attuned, surely, to the unspoken nuances of a relationship — this paragon of a Ruffey was behaving precisely as the clever blockhead had done. Daily I talked to Annette about all manner of things, all of them everyday. I sensed — knew, rather, that she held me accountable for Ridinghouse. It was irrational and unreasonable, it was because I had been rude — no, unwelcoming — my slight prejudice had led me too far. I had abandoned him without a proper search: mea culpa, come what may.

But Annette never accused me. In the absence of the victim, the nature of the crime remained uncertain: it was an unnatural state of affairs. Then I saw that she had left the photographs in the darkroom deliberately: the impulsive side of her had acted, had got as near as she could to an accusation. She hoped, of course, that I would find him for her. And I wished that I had pushed him into the volcano and thought that I could have managed it, if I had only run a little faster.

I had taken those pictures of Borobodur. At first it was uncanny to find him there; then I saw that, no less frightening, it was rather her insistence on finding him, where I had failed. Of course he had always been there, somewhere in the mass, just as he had always been hidden in the fabric of her life. The day I found the pictures, I found oblivion too, using the time-honoured method of applying alcohol, liberally, to an empty stomach. When a few hours later, Annette's key turned in the lock, the lame husband now was legless.

So it went on: she did not accuse, I did not broach the taboo topic. We thought about him and never mentioned his name. I thought that she would voice blame at the moment of leaving me — and clearly she did not want that; so we hung in the void. I was most passionately, tremblingly jealous. It was a wave, blood-red, a pounding, itching fever. It took the form of a meticulous, insatiable curiosity and each new scrap of information served, not to satisfy, but to engorge it. I wanted to know things about Ridinghouse that he might barely suspect himself; things he would never know.

The search became a cause, an occupation in itself. How many men have known such a need in their lives? It was a pain, as sharp as a wound. I woke each morning conscious of it, lay down to sleep each night with the same need still throbbingly unsatisfied. I hugged it to myself. Once I found myself thinking that I would not tell Annette when I found him – no, I would keep the precious secret for myself. So the original purpose blurred; the search was the thing – and if it took me away from my wife emotionally and physically, I had not the discernment to see it. It seems astonishing, now, to write down these things, so fogged are they with retrospective amazement, with stupid, useless hindsight.

And so I do not think that I can criticise Thomas Ridinghouse for evading his responsibilities. He was not the man to face them. After an attack of grief which seemed likely to leave him permanently disordered, he withdrew to his study and his work. Each child took upon itself its ration of guilt, according to its nature. Jane, the eldest girl, changed overnight, becoming first fanatically religious and then, as that ardour cooled, a substitute mother. She devoted herself to the little ones, her inadequacies making them ever more aware of what they had lost. For afterwards, of course, they realised how much they had loved and depended upon her and missed her constant caring kindness, that had shown itself in a thousand loving gestures, in hundreds of suppers and made-up beds. The gloss and light of the house was gone, it dimmed as the table and silver did. Everthing became tarnished, dusty and neglected. A profound unease set in, for they had been robbed of the future as well as of the past. What sickness had she possessed, so deeply hidden that it had never thrown up a symptom? Could it not attack any – all – of them, at any moment? Examining themselves and each other for signs of her madness, they grew more strained, more odd, more suspicious than ever.

John was eleven, a self-contained, exact little boy, good at school and very quiet. He took to playing truant, first using a series of forged notes, later not troubling to make that effort. This was not known at home for some weeks, where there was no one in authority, and the eventual revelation came as a salutary shock. The superior man realised that he was not the only one to suffer. He remembered, now, that John had played truant before. At the age of six he had run away from home and asked for a ticket for London, receiving instead a telling-off from the station master who had then taken him home. He had not been punished then, for Father did not believe in it. Father had known, instead, how to take the thrill out of the adventure by remarking how deeply the child had grieved his mother and by adding, with heavy, jocular whimsy, that it would have been more intelligent, albeit slower, to go by bus, for no one would have recognised him at the depot; he must plan his escape better next time.

There was no mother's name to evoke this time; a moment's pause, a silent look, did the work as well, if not better. Father spoke (or was silent) to John with good effect, though the girls could not drag from the culprit what promises had been made or threats evoked. And he did plan his escape better; he waited until he was eighteen and when he left to go abroad and then to university, it was for good. There was no family occasion that could bring the runaway back after that. I would like to know what he did with his long days of truancy when he was eleven, but there is no finding that out.

My source, authoritative though it was, could not know everything. It was Jane Ridinghouse who remembered so well, who had been given her father's rambling memories to augment her own. The Bristol University computer had obligingly thrown up Ridinghouse's home address. When the telephone rang in that dim Oxford hallway, it was Jane who ran to pick it up quickly, before the bell disturbed Father. She, the eldest sister, who would utter a first timid confidence and then a second, bolder one.

After John's escapade, the don had roused himself. Father had brought home a housekeeper, an arch enemy to usurp Jane's place and to be humoured with smiles, for Father said they could not do without her. But Jane won in the end. She hung on and holds, at last, a complete dominion over the house and over her housebound father.

Without having met her, I knew her well. She would speak softly for fear of missing the plaintive bleat from upstairs, the pounding of the stick against the bedroom floor. A genteel, nervous voice, the voice of a woman who worried about burglars and the cost of things and how to replace the guttering; a voice that went with small, neat collars and long, woolly cardigans. Yet she could be thirty-five at the most. She was thrifty, worried about the cost of my calls and yet woman enough to be flattered by them. I imagined the unlined face of those who lead blameless lives, the hands roughened by housework and gardening. I imagined a small, hopeless tendresse for the bank manager, perhaps, or the local solicitor, sustained over a number of not-quite-necessary calls, despite the bright photographs of a smiling wife and two grinning children on the desk. I could see her cutting flowers for the church and drawing the vicar aside to discuss arcane theological issues, thus furthering her reputation as the most learned of his visitors.

At night, once Father was settled for his sleep and the tray cleared away, she would listen to the radio and write letters to her siblings, dotting them with observations about things she had heard, plays she might have seen, but hadn't, for he could not be left. She would have her own pride in being up-to-date; how fiercely she would resent the pity of the escapees, who sent her the occasional postcard as though she were a child and preferred the bright picture to words.

Jane Ridinghouse, however adult, would always be defined as a child: as her father's daughter. Because she was intelligent and refused to pity herself and drew considerable, quiet satisfaction from the consciousness of being loved and needed by that helpless man and of never having failed him, she was content. There would be small treats: a day's shopping in London, perhaps twice a year, when somebody could be persuaded to take her place. Every couple of years there would be a proper holiday, abroad, with a school friend. She had cruised through the Greek islands with a lecturer on antiquities; she had seen Delphi and Corinth and swum from the black volcanic sand of Ios. These riches were stored up and, squirrel-like, made to last for several winters. Such escapes depended upon the goodwill of her next sister, who had married a wealthy man; while she would not nurse her father herself, she was delighted to pay for a professional who would and thought herself thus absolved from further duties.

The only time malice entered Jane's voice was when she spoke of her brothers and sisters.

'Of course they have their own lives,' she said, briskly, and, 'They find they manage to get down occasionally if there's a good play on and baby-sitting thrown in. Extra-ordinary, isn't it, how people think the childless must love children, as though the reverse weren't obvious. I can't abide them, I've had enough of children for a lifetime. I had to bring them all up, you know. Ann's three are wild and rough, I don't imagine they'll be much of a comfort to her in her old age.'

She laughed abruptly, a hoarse bark which was a real sound quite unlike her usual, fluttering giggle. I glimpsed, as through a closing door, a tougher, less genteel woman underneath. I liked her best when she slipped out of her role as daughter/sacrifice, but she would always revert to her vicarage manner and become more prim than before.

When she told me about her mother's death, she cried freely.

'I'm not ashamed of loving and having loved,' she said, with the noises of slight snuffling, of nose-wiping. 'People seem to think that it's a weakness, to care for parents so, it's unfashionable, but it's my strength. I've become my mother, and Father is my child now, that's as much family as I need or want. You know, Mr Ruffey, there's always something wrong with people who deny their parents, who think themselves better or different. People always said that John was Father to the life and he liked to believe it but he's Mother too. He has a dark streak in him. Of course part of that is denying the resemblance. There's something I've never told anyone, but John knew that Mother was dead – knew before he was told, I mean. He left school early and came home because he knew something was wrong and he saw the stretcher with her body being taken away. We weren't allowed to see her afterwards; people didn't let children in. Too gruesome. But John saw and he simply nodded, as though he'd known that that was it – that it was going to happen. Our neighbour told me that, it worried her, as you can imagine. Oh, I've tormented myself thousands of times with the idea that he knew what she planned, that he could have told someone ... but it's futile to think those thoughts, I know. I don't believe individuals have the right to take life, not even their own.' She drew a deep, shuddering breath and paused. I found myself listening, when she did, for the tap of the stick. 'John was extremely close to Mother, you see. It's a curious thing, but our parents were very good to us – we each believed ourselves to be the favourite child, and that's rare. But John evidently had some special rapport. But he never cried, not even at the funeral. Don't you find that peculiar for a little boy? And he seemed acutely interested, alert, he watched and took it all in as though he didn't feel it himself, as though he knew something we didn't. He came up to me once and touched my tears and tasted them, as though he couldn't have produced any of his own.

'I never worried about the others, except in a normal way. Jim was too young to understand and Ann had discovered boys and pop and in a horrible, callous sort of way the tragedy made her interesting and she used that, and Beatrix was unhappy but quite normal and Rosie was still a baby and could be comforted. But John had this terrifying calm. I wanted to comfort him, but he wouldn't have it. He kept willing me away. He spent all his time with father, who never talked about it either. Father used to tell him he was a little man and men didn't give in to things – and all sorts of things he regretted much later, that talking about it made it worse and we had to be stoical. So we all just carried on. Underneath we were miserable, but we maintained a pretence of calm, especially John. The funny thing is that Father hardly talks of anything else now, he returns all the time to stories of Mother and what she was like when young – oh, all sorts of intimate things. I think he forgets that I'm his daughter at times. But he should have said more then, when we needed it, but he couldn't poor man, he was too upset himself.' She paused and her nervous laugh echoed down the line.

'Goodness me, you don't really want to know all this, do you Mr Ruffey? I'm getting quite carried away. I can't think why I'm boring you with all this ancient history,' and she said there was someone at the door though I could hear the thick silence that lay in the hallway. Our conversations generally ended thus with her apologising. But it was I who should rather have sought to excuse my avid curiosity, my prompting. She was lonely and I sympathetic and faceless, my anonymity safely coupled to possession of a name. She granted herself licence to speak from the heart and give the 'artist' truths she would have denied her friends.

I became her confidant, her sympathetic ear. Each time I announced myself I heard the same little scraping noise as she pulled out a chair and made herself comfortable and prepared to talk. I prolonged these conversations, even though I had a sense of unease at having induced such confessions. She knew that I was looking for her brother, knew without my having told her that there was an account to settle. She allied herself implicitly on my side and against him.

I am a good listener, would rather listen than talk, and my few utterances come in a good telephone voice, a rich one. I sound like the family doctor, who does not have the time to listen. I know my effect; had I not, long ago, practised declaiming love poems, repeating each sonorous phrase with an ear to the effect it must have, later, upon the victim of the moment? It was a talent to acquire and I believe in industriousness, I wanted to earn my conquests. I need not be too sensitive about such callowness, such self-gratifying posturings, for that is how I learnt to love poetry. I have had my small punishment for that artifice, if only in the early, reckless squandering of Donne, whom I should have treasured up for these, my declining years. And if I can write of decline with composure, it is because throughout this whole bizarre business I felt quite the reverse – felt an upsurge of vigour.

Something of that energy must have made its way down the telephone wires to the dim Oxford hallway. Once Jane Ridinghouse told me I was, for her, a way of confessing; that is a healing force, she said. She told me things I am sure she had never uttered to another person – said, for instance, that mother had been childless for eight years before conceiving Jane and had viewed that conception as a miraculous gift. The five succeeding pregnancies had not weakened her belief in divine intervention. Mother had never used any form of birth control, abhorring the very words, and her quarrels on this subject with her husband had been bitter.

Thomas Ridinghouse subscribed in part to the views of Malthus; that population would always outstrip the growth of sustenance available was an evident truth in his house. (But Malthus' views on the consequent ill-advisedness of lifting the poor from their misery struck right across the grain of his theoretical socialism.) He had tried, unavailingly, to remain celibate, succeeding only in abstaining during pregnancy, for fecundity revolted him. This man had told his daughter all this and more, thoughts which no father should ever utter to a child. He had said that he regretted his three girls, but never her, John or Jim. A curious man, who saw no difficulty in campaigning for the masses without a thought for the individuals in his care; who did not extend his heartfelt notion of equality to the opposite sex. The girls might be nurses or secretaries, if they insisted, but the boys must go to university to fulfil their potential. He had preserved his complex inner equilibrium through many years only to break down at the end. At night, she said, he cried out for his wife as a child whimpers for its mother.

We cannot separate ourselves from our parents nor from our pasts; there I concurred with Jane. She never spoke disparagingly of her father, rather commenting on his idiosyncracies in a tone which, admitting the possibility of others' blame, sought to excuse and explain away his peccadilloes in advance. I felt that I owed her reciprocal confidences, but mine were too complicated to offer.

When my mother first entered the home many years ago I used to visit her and we would relive the vivid near-decade of my childhood. In her pleasure at shared recollections I found my own value. She, who has annulled so much with her selective memory, was the guardian of my memories and I know that when she dies my childhood will vanish with her. I am already old enough to experience advance nostalgia for that day. How these women held my life between them; I treasured up the present for my wife and with my mother I possessed the past too, could listen to her sigh and exclaim over that sad figure of romance, my father, and, measuring my exploits against his, always found myself lacking. After his death I thought that I was a man, not realising that for my mother I remained monochrome to his dazzling, unattainable Technicolour. Each year I came to resemble him more and more, ten years ago, shockingly, overtaking him in age. He is fixed in his prime. There was a time when, visiting my mother unexpectedly, I would enter as his ghost and observe her delight fade with belated recognition.

Now, however, I have journeyed forward in time, have overtaken her and become the old man of the family. She is not quite sure who I am and takes me for a forgotten uncle. Sharp in her ageless trance, she remarks how old I have become, how worn and bald, measuring each merciless inch along the milestones of decay. We are both so altered that we could easily be different people; there is no feature left under her overflowing, Buddha's bulk of the slender woman in her thirties who blew kisses in the air and batted them to me with her fan.

Jane Ridinghouse unlocked the fascinating, alien world of families. I found myself hoping, for her sake, that her father would live for ever. Her life was strange, but I could see how it was familiar and manageable, the summons of the stick preferable to none. Was I not also pursuing the insistent tattoo of my wounded heart? I would telephone her from the quiet of my room, blessing my peculiar working habits that had always guaranteed seclusion and a separate line, listening, as she did, for a footfall, a voice. I remained true to my first impulse, to behave as though nothing had happened, and meanwhile my senses grew sharp. Not a shadow passed across my wife's face without my registering its precise contours; not a thought was half-murmured that I did not strain to hear.

It was easier to travel back in time than to comprehend the present: simple to find Jane, impossible to trace Ridinghouse. 'He travels,' she said. 'Perhaps a postcard twice a year, if that. Oh, he's lost himself very effectively. We never see him.'

Eyebrows were raised at the Indonesian Embassy, shoulders shrugged. 'One among so many – it is looking for a needle in a haystack,' and the official could not repress an involuntary smile at his idiomatic fluency. 'We cannot follow what every tourist is doing. He is visiting another temple – there are so many – and wondering what became of you.' There was no employer or landlady, no wife or mother to report him missing; he was, accordingly, not missing at all.

Common sense insisted that the man must have one friend, one lover, one acquaintance (no doubt) of my wife (whom I could not ask), who heard from him, who kept up a desultory correspondence. I telephoned John Pie. It was the university computer which had so effortlessly recovered Ridinghouse's home address.

'You're becoming a bore,' he said. 'Come if you must. You can buy me lunch.' He rang off with a lack of curiosity that seemed excessive even for Pie, for whom people counted primarily as whetstones for his malicious wit. Pie, I thought, must remember Ridinghouse who had been in his department, who had met Annette in Bristol where, presumably, over-lapping student mores had introduced the aspirant philospher to the art school student. I wished, now, that I had questioned her more about that time which, being pre-Ruffey, had seemed a mere preamble to the real business of life.

On the train down I remembered her claim that we had really met in Bristol, at the Arnolfini which had given me a show in her final year. I had no recollection of it; our memories diverged on this delightful, sensitive point. As a newly estab-lished couple we had indulged ourselves in recalling the first tentative looks, the onset of desire, in post mortems made all the more enjoyable for such discrepancies. It was flattery, indeed, that she had liked me enough to pursue the acquaint-ance in London when chance, and my luck, had thrown us together. I, pretending eventually that I had some dim recall of that first meeting, remembered rather Pie, stomping around and gazing at exhibits with the close scrutiny of one set upon finding nothing to admire. He had not introduced us; the presence of students had been an irritant and he had done his best to remove us both from the pollution as rapidly as possible.

Pie perched, like an old black crow, atop the Wills Building, that arch neo-Gothic monument to carcinoma. Years of prox-imity to the follies of youth had deepened an already profound distaste for juvenilia. The professor awed those young minds of a lofty enough nature to contemplate a subject so contradictory, combined as it was with the dizzying ascent to the Department. Eight floors and no lift: it was a deterrent.

Pie had worked too hard to obtain this sinecure, suffered too many conferences, given too many papers, and the result was twofold: he had an absolute scorn for people who didn't work and simultaneously felt personally absolved from further efforts. He was, at last, secure enough to give ever more of his time to his hobbies and the less Department work he did, the more that little irked him.

There were perhaps half a dozen people in the world whose intelligence he respected and a further dozen worth speaking to. Regrettably, nobody in his department or its vicinity qualified for either category. He would describe the students as an annual disappointment, being either irredeemably stupid or pretentiously mediocre, below contempt for indolence or ridiculous for diligent, second-rate cribbing. He would say, with a sneer, that he found them remarkably unappealing and doubted even their qualifications for the usual student pastimes of drinking and fornicating. Lowly as they were, he still took pains to catch them out, delighting in setting traps for the unwary, in humiliating them in tutorials which had become a byword both for rigour and sardonic entertainment. Few dared to be amused, however, for this was not a ringside sport — all were susceptible to a sudden body-blow.

I found Pie clearing a giant accumulation of papers from his rat's nest of a desk. He was mulling over a heap of applications when I arrived, tutting and shaking his head, his disapprobation expressing itself in a restless shuffling of the mass.

'Come in, have a whisky,' he said as I poked my head

around the door. 'Sit down and keep quiet.'

He bent his head to the work and I looked about the room which was large and pleasantly sunny, bright with scattered papers. The pigeons on the window sill jumped away in fright as I approached, to regain their perches seconds later, gazing insolently in through the glass. Far below a small cluster of heads darkened the broad steps leading to the building.

'Janine Pilling,' he burst out, 'what business has a Janine Pilling with philosophy?' and he scrawled a 'NO' across the paper. Invigorated, as always, by an audience, he worked swiftly through the pile, muttering to himself, cracking his knuckles thoroughly as he read. I remembered how, at school, Pie had won respect by the insouciant repellence of his personal habits.

'I don't ask for much,' he said, 'just a little intellect, however undeveloped, and they send me clots who've seen a film on Bertrand Russell and think they can "make a contribution".' The sticking out of his thick underlip, at those three words, gave him the look of a predatory perch.

'Let them in and educate them,' I said mildly.

'Good God Ruffey, this isn't a benevolent institution. What d'you think this is? Centre of learning, research, excellence. And we get earnest, bespectacled little sods wet behind the ears. Fistfuls of 'A's, parrot brains, and one capacity –'

'I know, to reduce everything to the mediocre.'

'You've got a memory at least Ruffey.'

'Too much of one. I remember this speech. Next you say that Nietzsche had the good sense to abandon the university early on. You have that option.'

'Indeed.' This hardy perennial bloomed, on cue, cheering him up. He shoved away the papers, dislodging and toppling the heap at the corner, poured us each a glass of Bell's.

'Still,' he said, ruminatively, 'paid to talk. Paid to read books. Got lectures ready for a decade. Cheers, to institutions of learning.'

'Past and present.'

'Now if it's the past you want, I've got some stuff here. Have a look at my cupboard. Keep it locked up. There's some nice little bits in there, copies, West African, can't afford the real stuff. One day I'll go and get some for myself. Have a look. Most of the lady philosophers haven't seen a phallus, though they prattle on about sexual symbolism without a blush.'

His choleric face was split with rare smile of pleasure; he dangled the key from one fat finger with a brothel-keeper's leer.

'Thank you, no. And don't think I want to hear your lecture on the bowdlerisation of art by science and the loss of the primitive and all that stuff. All that pagan lust is ridiculous on you, it's the thin veneer on a civilised core. No, I've come for some recent history. Mr John Ridinghouse. Now you must remember him, Pie, class of '78, student of yours.'

'Why should I remember them? Knew you'd be boring. Ask Gimbal your questions, he's joining us, bother him. I'll want a reciprocal favour, mind.'

'Who's Gimbal?'

'Lecturer in the Department. Personal tutor to your chap. Probably left to avoid him. One of our failures, Ridinghouse, one of Gimbal's, rather. You're like a dog, Ruffey, always sniffing at arses. Why don't you spend your time on something aesthetic and beautiful? Isn't that what you're supposed to do? No — don't tell me, don't want to know, that's a condition of the introduction, not bothering me.'

In a minute he'd swung from good humour to irritation, the effect anything personal always had on him, anything that promised to be messy. He would never ask, for example, how my wife was, for fear of being told. Relationships or any talk of emotions both bored and terrified him. Pie held as axiomatic the principle that men should marry for money. He, naturally, would never marry. His scorn of woman was, I thought, equalled only by his ignorance. Occasionally I have suspected him of plagiarising the works of Henry Miller for his more lubricious comments. I suspected, too, that any woman stupid enough to make an advance to Pie (for it could never happen in reverse) would crucify him with embarrassment, but there was little fear of that. Pie smells rather strongly of old badger.

He slurped at his whisky, tapped his watch, stared around angrily without succeeding in disconcerting me.

'Can I look at the old students' files?'

'Don't take mature students.'

'Don't be obtuse.'

'Gimbal will take you down later. Basement stuffed with them.'

We drank without speaking: silence never worried Pie, he could keep it up for hours until the next thought occurred for which he needed an audience. I did wonder occasionally why I perpetuated a friendship with the old sod. Neither of us worked at it, it just carried on somehow, too ancient a bond to disappear. I was probably his only friend and certainly he'd never introduced me to another. Ours was a select brotherhood of two. Nobody new could meet his exacting criteria, nor would any person of sense put up with him. Pie was born an ancient monument and has spent his life deteriorating as fast as he could.

A timid knock at the door heralded the entrance of a young-looking forty-year-old in a dapper suit, whom Pie introduced with a graveyard face. 'Edward Ruffey the painter,

Albert Gimbal, the ornament of our Department. Gimbal's an orientalist but he overcomes himself and teaches the British philosophers. Buddhists don't drink, so let's be off,' and he ushered us out, disappearing immediately down the corridor in the opposite direction to the stairs.

Gimbal, who looked like a man who could have done with a drink, caught my eye with a look that needed only the slightest encouragement to lift itself into a smile. In the few minutes before Pie caught up with us (still fumbling with his flies, a process prolonged by the inordinate time it took to lever his balls back into position) I told Gimbal what I wanted to know.

'I don't really know what I can add to the Professor's information,' he said politely.

'Can't know less than me,' boomed Pie, now cheerful. 'Make a point of not knowing their names.'

This silenced Gimbal for the descent, but he warmed up during the fifteen minutes it took before the old Rover jerked into sight and halted, wheels biting the curb on the double yellow lines.

'Ridinghouse was set for a First,' he said chattily. 'That is quite exceptional in the Department. We haven't had one for three years now,' and 'I was sorry to lose him. We rather thought he'd join the faculty.' He launched into a helpful explanation of how rare and special that would be.

Pie gnarled and beckoned from across the road with one massive arm, flinging open his door so the passing bicyclist swerved and just got by, receiving a look to scorch the tarmac for his pains. We got in and off the Rover went, screeching around the wedge-shaped block.

'Normally go to the Sumatra,' Pie said, pointing. 'Something better today.' We glimpsed the yellow and red sign as we hurtled by.

'Oh, that's rather nice,' said Gimbal sadly, thrown forwards then against the front seat as Pie made a last-minute decision to stop, after all, at the red lights outside the furnishing shop. Change of lights, change of gear, wild revving, car strains forward, removal of handbrake, car slips back, further extensive pedal action, car creeps forward in third gear, stuttering change to first and then off – I was used to all of this. We seemed to be aiming for a large greeny-grey statue of a portly fellow with a fine symbolic tassel dangling in front of his genitals.

'Vic Rooms,' said Pie and at the last minute followed the road. Gimbal was clutching the leather strap. Pie always drove with sudden swerves and bursts of speed, as though the car would keep pointing itself at other vehicles with monomaniacal intent, and it took all his cunning skill to subdue it. Such concentration was to be encouraged at all costs.

'Whiteladies Road,' he said, 'Blackboys Hill,' making of the names something altogether salacious: the intensity of Gimbal's silent prayers rendered any conversation impossible.

Lunch was in a pub with a dining room attached as an afterthought, a place once surrounded by fields, now eaten up by a housing estate which made its perfectly genuine timbers appear fake. Two couples sat quietly crumbling their bread. I tried, again, to pump Gimbal. He had a way of harrumphing modestly before each utterance, as though in disclaimer of his presumption; he also swallowed continually, the Adam's apple pressing like a steam hammer on the starchy white collar. Such manifestations were exacerbated by Pie's unnatural periods of quiet, during which his eyes, enlarged through his goggle lenses, stared at his junior in open contempt.

'I really don't think I know who John's friends were,'

Gimbal offered. 'It was one of those years when students seemed to want to get their exams, so they didn't have the energy or time for any really good personal problems,' and he smiled at this little sally in his melancholy way. Pie belched extremely loudly. A very long pause ensued. 'Pardon,' he said.

'I do remember one funny little incident,' Gimbal said, leaning forwards confidingly. 'A kind of party trick. He hypnotised a girl in somebody's seminar once, without saying a word, and woke her up to read her paper. People talked about it. Seven-day wonder, I suppose. He was a very good student. I suppose it's a bit of a self-condemnation, isn't it, saying one can't remember any more, but he was never what I'd call the chatty type.' He paused for a sly glance round. 'It wasn't in your group, was it Professor? I did seem to think . . .' and his voice trailed away.

'Got some pictures that'd interest you,' said Pie briskly, ignoring him. 'Early lithographs. Figures from the burial ground at Yamoto, Iwaibe style, very sophisticated for the time. Have a cup of tea and I'll show you. And just one little African fellow you have to see. Lovely little thing, black as hell, smooth as silk. Got an erection up to his bald black head, lucky little sod.'

The couple opposite gave each other a meaningful look.

'The professor is an authority, I believe,' interjected Gimbal, anxious to steer us away from the incipient rapids. 'We have a celebrated rock climber in the Department, Mr Ruffey, regularly out up and down the Gorge. You mustn't think philosophers are all dreamers.'

Pie ignored this, standing up suddenly and then lumbering off for a pee, taking his napkin with him and using it, like a whisk, to flick crumbs off his chest in a perfectly unself-conscious way.

'Oh dear,' said Gimbal, pouring himself a glass of wine and draining it in one gulp. 'It's quite beneath the Professor's notice to talk of personalities, I fear.' (And yet his own would be shredded, an hour or two later, with the finest attention to detail.)

'I'm a little bit of an amateur psychologist, Mr Ruffey, and there's no shortage of material in the university. I have a bit of a theory about John,' (and his temerity induced, here, a bobbling series of large swallows). 'Very much a lone wolf, that young man, one who had some original thoughts, as I recall. But he didn't take things seriously, you see, the proof of that is not taking a degree which was guaranteed. Well we all expected a First, as I said. I think he was a bit of a practical joker. The hypnotism story, now, it was set up of course with the young lady but everyone took it seriously. That would appeal to him. He was very earnest, but not quite sound, if you see what I mean. There was something of that in his essays. Well composed, clever, but a little bit tongue in cheek all the same; it was as if everything was a private joke. Oh, I had doubts about him – I have a bit of a nose for things like that – and when he vanished it confirmed my hypothesis. He was set up to do an MA and then a doctorate most probably. Nobody would throw that up and vanish if they were quite normal, would they? Quite a peculiar young man. Just the thing for the Department in fact,' and he laughed lightly in appreciation of his humour, composing his face as Pie reappeared.

('Gimbal – unworldly?' Pie would snort. 'He may look like a late Victorian curate but he's tough. Relentless marker, reason I keep him. Fails them right, left and centre while he pats their backs consolingly. Queer, doesn't dare do much about it, can't stand that sort myself. He loves violence, shudders at the thought of it. Ridinghouse was strong and silent, just his type. Mesmerised him. One day somebody will ram his Zen Buddhism up Gimbal's backside and that will be the end of that.')

The drive back was accomplished without the accident it deserved. Gimbal led me to the area in the chilly basement where the old files on students were kept, stacked in cardboard boxes. The first prize I pocketed was the black and white photograph, booth style, of the aspiring undergraduate, pinned to his notes. Smooth-cheeked with the overlong collar points of the year, he wore the bored and innocent expression of one fulfilling his duty. His head was tilted back and he stared down that perfectly straight nose, acquiring something of the air of a second-rate Greek statue. A touch supercilious, the very facsimile of his father.

I have, for purposes of comparison, the frontispiece to Thomas Ridinghouse's book on *Rodrigo de Bivar — Symbol of the Reconquista* published, ironically enough, in 1937 when Spain was being devoured by the latter-day equivalents of the warring crescent and cross. The young man in that portrait, only twenty-six, has an equal air of satisfaction. It was no surprise that his son might have pursued the academic path; his first year report and Part One exam results all attested his cleverness and his originality.

'An outstanding student,' Gimbal had written. 'Punctual, never misses a seminar, an inquiring mind ranging beyond the syllabus. Thoughtful, well-argued essays with the scholar's gift of turning up something new in well-ploughed fields. Excellent reading command of German. In all, most promising.'

This file, thin by comparison with those of other students, who had requested innumerable references, was composed mostly of tributes along the same line. Written at the bottom of the last report was: 'Left before taking Final Examinations — JP.'

What kind of institution would permit a scholar such as this to vanish in such an offhand manner? No benevolent one, indeed.

I found, then, Annette's letter. It was tucked away at the back in an innocent white envelope, hand-written, her slapdash feminine script instantly recognisable, her eccentrically crossed t's small barbs to scratch at me.

131A Hotwells Road, Bristol

Dear Sir,

I am writing, as you suggest, to ask for John Ridinghouse's forwarding address, should he supply you with one. I can't help you with your inquiries. If I knew why he'd left, then perhaps I wouldn't need to ask you where he'd gone.
Yours, Annette Huntley.

PS You can reach me care of Bristol Polytechnic Faculty of Art and Design also.

I stuffed this into my pocket. I wanted a portrait of him and in she crept, the aggrieved tone suggestive of much more than mere friendship. Hadn't I known it? I could not paint him; I was a collage-maker, a putter-together of disparate elements and now I was obliged to put my wife in the centre. The soubrette painted by an old man. We were aligned next to the solemn student, beyond him was the bare-legged man on the volcano. Alongside was the winsome child at the ticket office (a Rockwell, this) with the rosy-cheeked ticket master scratching his head under a tip-tilted cap and, glimpsed through the red-brick arch, Father jumping out of his Baby Austin and coming to the rescue.

I needed one of Pie's savage little caricatures, but he would not be drawn on my subject, for all his loquaciousness on every other one.

'There must have been an inquest,' I said. 'A post-mortem. Whatever you do for dead degrees. Something to satisfy the local authority who paid his grant, some explanation for the Senate. Where is it?'

'Why should it exist? He failed deliberately, wilfully. Chose to leave. Perhaps he was right. Escaped — all of this,' and he waved a hand contemptuously around, as though we were sitting in a sweat-shop. 'You're wasting your time and mine. Go and do some work. You working Ruffey? Anything new?' He goggled accusingly across the desk. Pie was always peremptory, exacting of other people's work, their efforts as subject to scrutiny as his, naturally, were exempt.

'Perhaps. Perhaps I'd do better if I got a little help from my friends when I needed it.'

'Wasting time, Ruffey, commodity in short supply. You're too easily distracted. A painter has to chose positive experiences. Distil the essence. Concentrate. Not get waylaid. You've gone soft.'

'I know you'll find something,' I said, ignoring this diatribe. 'I'm counting on you. Consider it your contribution to my concentration. You can see everything from up here.'

'Don't start getting metaphorical, it's just a perspective. Something you lack.'

I examined the tower from the bottom. The Wills Building, which dominated the town in a very satisfactory way, boasted Gothic pointy arches, sooty yellow stone, figures crouched or standing. All of that culminated in slivers of blue at the top where it was pierced through, a bell tower. Inside it harboured a good supply of elderly buffoons to swing on tasselled ropes and knell their mad lurchings. It struck me as pleasing and appropriate that the tower of academia should be empty, up top. Pie, who sat just below that empty grandeur, would help me. I could be confident of that, second, supposition, just as I was certain of my first, that the report — some report, must exist. He valued our relationship sufficiently to exert himself, if pushed. That exertion, however grudging, could be relied upon. Equally I could rely upon him to expose me to some unpleasantness, if he should happen to decide that that was good for me. Character-forming.

There had been many such occasions. On the train I had leisure to recall them. Characters were formed by adversity, as far as Pie was concerned. Where that might be in short supply, he had always been ready to offer his helpful mite; had offered it, what was more, even when there was a good supply of adverse factors ready to hand. That was his phrase: character-forming. It was forever in his mouth when we were young. We were young in years, but never carefree, never unrestrained. War-time austerity could scarcely impose any greater rigours upon our school than those it already boasted: it was a feature of second-rate establishments at that time that they guaranteed degrees of Spartan 'manliness' while hoping for the altogether chancier eventual academic ones. We dug for victory where previous generations had done so for health, the cabbages and potatoes no less wormy for the change. Money, hitherto collected for missionaries, now went towards a Spitfire. The major change — apart from a flash of war fever in the upper part of the school — was that all the young staff vanished, leaving the infirm, the elderly and naturally authoritarian: masters whose inflexibility was often paralleled by an inability to maintain control. Formative years indeed, not because of the learning, which was stuffed into our heads in the most haphazard and old-fashioned way, but for the lessons in survival.

For I did survive it, thanks to John Pie, and what was more

I survived him. Pie in those days was universally disliked. His large shambling figure stumbled about the place and could occasionally be observed walking absent-mindedly into walls. Never a child, he would not kick a ball about or do anything that could be described as playful. Drawing upon himself the double opprobrium of fat boy and swot, he disconcerted would-be tormentors by failing to notice their existence. In class, he ignored master and pupils alike with an oblivion so profound that — short of laying hands upon him — it was impossible to elicit any response.

Once our elderly science master, goaded by his silence, began to shake him, whereupon Pie became inert, a sagging mass of doughy substance, the only sign of life the gleam in his large eyes. He was too heavy to lift. The failure to rouse him rebounded, as teachers' failures always do, upon the master, who succeeded only in humiliating himself. It could not happen again; Pie had become untouchable. Any other boy would have been applauded by his classmates for this flouting of authority — there would have been cheers, or at the least sniggers — but we watched in silence as the experiment proceeded, watched the unfortunate Mr Lewis return, red-eared, to his dais; we observed his shaking hands and said nothing when, soon afterwards, he made an excuse to leave the room.

Nobody wanted to be associated with Pie. The small club of unruly individuals celebrated for their lawlessness did not want him either. With hindsight, I suppose the school suffered him in order to benefit from the valuable list of scholarships we all knew would be appended to his name one day. At the time, however, their tolerance seemed remarkable, inscrutable; not so much a reflection of their weakness, but tribute to his special powers.

It was my glory, mixed with shame, to be his only friend.

As he grew older a kind of formula evolved which saved face for the school. He kept out of people's way, avoiding confrontation, his challenges confined to the written word. By the time he was fifteen, all his essays began by saying that he had ignored the question as its triteness insulted the most mediocre of intelligences – or its incitement to a parade of useless knowledge was more vulgarly phrased than usual – and the more interesting issue was such-and-such. Off he would gallop on his own track. These essays were miniature masterpieces, animated by an intelligent, acerbic wit which he kept locked up for the rest of the time. He did not speak. He literally would not say good morning or pass the salt – not a word, save to Ruffey.

My prestigious position owed much to the school's collusion, its acceptance of the cuckoo. Messages would be sent to Pie and I would respond in his place, concocting acceptable replies. This was so much easier than a confrontation that they never taxed me about them and so I grew ever bolder. The house master would consult with me and I would discuss Pie with him, that betrayal quite cancelled out by the wholly fictional nature of the character I invented for him. It was my first taste of the power of creation. I would devise all kinds of obscure positions for him, culling suitable quotations from his rambling flock of conversational bons mots. My Pie was serious and learned: I did not allow my creation any of the coarse, schoolboy rudeness which characterised the original.

Pie stopped going to school assembly, a dull enough affair, on the grounds of its tedium. Some explanation had to be found 'pour décourager les autres' from following suit. So I drew from the air a chance remark and devised for him a religious stance which I described as 'post-Spinozan rational atheism'. I had no idea what this meant; what I did know was exactly how to present such remarks — with a bland, uncomprehending smirk, a 'don't-ask-me-that's-what-he-said' look of appeal. It was surprising how often it worked. I watched our housemaster scratch ruefully at his scalp and then give the right sort of nod of the head, signal of baffled retreat.

Pie refused to be homogeneous, as my creation was. That didn't matter, neither side could dispute what I told them. My benefit came in being permitted to scrape by where I might have failed, for I was bad at everything but art, which nobody took seriously. This was serious, for the whole educational system boiled down to a scramble to come first in one category or another; I matriculated, therefore, in the subject of John Pie.

He, meanwhile, mastered a great number of subjects, among them the skill of taking Ruffey down a peg or two when necessary. He used to irritate me by taking credit for my special position, which I rather thought I had created for myself. 'You're fortunate that I chose to develop your personality,' he would say, or, 'I raised you from the mediocre, Ruffey.' The small grain of truth in such remarks could make me squirm. (Later he would infuriate me by claiming that he had made me fit for a life in art by teaching me to be an outsider, by stopping me from conforming.) So, whenever I came into his study triumphant from an encounter with authority, he would be sure to make a remark of that nature, as though his silence had not just given me voice, but endowed it with a specific timbre. 'I wonder if I've managed to create any courage in you,' he would say and I would stare at his perfectly unreadable face, eyes hidden behind two smears of glass. If he had 'created' anything in me, it was rather an indifference to embarrassment, which was not at all the same thing.

I was not as different as I thought: he took care to teach me that. On our last day of school, it was traditional for the head to invite all leavers to his study for a small glass of sherry. There, turning a blind eye to the sartorial affectations which the departing seniors inevitably adopted in belated show of independence, he would deliver an improving talk about upholding the manly qualities school had supposedly taught us.

We were clustered around the open window to enjoy the double delectation. The head was pointing to the milling crowd of boys below, a microcosm of the world: his favourite notion. He also believed that he had educated us for life. We were looking rather at the brilliant patches of colour scattered about, a sister's or mother's full-skirted, blue or cherry-ripe dress. The real world offered women, an educational prospect without parallel. So, eyes straying, we nodded, lending his tired ideas some credence. Even the most unrepentantly thick-headed lout saw the advantage of finishing well, however badly he had started.

'Can't touch that. Fit for the kitchen. I've brought my own Jerez. Pre-war of course.'

The voice boomed through the room, the accent and authority that of any Home Counties parent. Recognising it I froze, then swivelled round to look and others, seeing my face or glancing round themselves, followed suit. Bradshaw's little homily tailed away to nothing.

Pie, planted massively in front of the large fireplace, was intent upon levering the cork out of his bottle with one large thumb. From the pocket of his jacket he drew a crystal glass which he held up to the light as he poured a generous measure of the pale liquid. He scrutinised it, then sniffed; tilting back his head, he carefully poured the entire contents of the glass down his throat.

'Fine, very fine indeed.'

Now he retrieved the bottle from its resting place in the other pocket and prepared to repeat the performance. Somebody began to laugh. We all looked at each other, seeking the suitable reaction. Mr Bradshaw stepped forwards, his face re-forming itself from the didactic into a welcoming expression, one eye twitching behind the wire-rimmed glasses. He had taken the job straight after demob and spent a year, mentally, still at war, a further one trying to recreate his previous school and the lost, pre-war world. He could not know the nature of this beast and so he smiled. Benevolence and tolerance were the order of the day.

'Our prize scholar,' he said. 'Congratulations. Have you decided which of the universities you are to favour, John?'

'I have not Harold.' But the thick face was not obviously impertinent, it was amiably creased. Pie leant heavily against the mantelpiece and offered his bottle to Bradshaw's glass.

The head's tic accelerated, but he was still smiling; he shook his head and said, 'Thank you John, I think not.'

'A pity Harold. It is a superior vintage.'

There was a general movement towards them, a shuffling nearer until we were all standing around watching the middle-aged man and the great overgrown boy, whose head swivelled to survey the faces with detached interest. 'Let us all drink to your successes — gentlemen,' Bradshaw raised his glass and looked a little wildly around the room; he was the only adult there. Someone took the sherry bottle and went round putting a thimbleful in each glass and still nobody spoke; Pie's voice, last heard in childish treble, had silenced them all. The circle closed in a pace and I saw Johnstone, a short lad, peeping over shoulders at the rear and finally, recklessly, he climbed onto Bradshaw's desk and knelt there, face agape in breathless expectancy. In the quiet, the hubbub from the quadrangle below intensified in volume.

'Gentlemen! To our scholar, John Pie.' Bradshaw raised his glass, swept it around and held it out towards Pie.

'No tributes.' Pie, with deliberation, put his glass upon the mantelpiece. 'I ask only this.' Two large hands seized Bradshaw by the shoulders, pulled him forwards, held him for a second's agonised suspension and then he kissed him full on the lips. Bradshaw turned a dirty white colour and the sherry from his glass slopped over Pie's sleeve; he tore himself free and as he released himself, there came a roar of amazement, a bellow of laughter which could not be contained. It was a kind of hysteria which affected even Rainham, head boy and model of sobriety. Bradshaw ducked his head, ran blindly pushing his way to the door, followed an instant later by Rainham shouting, 'Shut up, shut up all of you.'

It was too late; we were all galvanised. Pie was swept out of the room in a tussle of boys fighting to get near him, to thump him on the back, in a chaos of shouting and laughter. Parents, witnessing the triumphant mob disgorge into the quadrangle, must have thought him a hero of some kind.

But Pie had planned an appropriate dénouement. He had a taxi waiting outside and he left in it, without another word, with a single, regal wave to the crowd. He was gone before there was time for anyone to recollect that they had, in fact, nothing to say to him. We stood around sheepishly in the uneasy aftermath that followed (and I was angry, for we had planned to leave together) – and it took only five minutes for the mood to change and turn ugly, for the first person to ask me to explain myself. Perjured as his accomplice, I stood dumb, doubly damned, the triumph annulled in a moment. Now that, as he would tell me later, was character-forming.

5

There was no word from Pie in the dog days that followed;
the trail had gone cold. I began to ask Annette questions, to
set tricks and traps. It was scab-picking, a restless fingering
of tissue. Each probe released a small gush of fresh blood to
clot, to form a more enticing protuberance. I might remark,
for example, that we never saw her college friends and led
her on to talk about them with my spurious recollections of
names, anecdotes. She was dismissive; said they had no talent,
that they had wanted things to be easy — and she despised
them for that, she whose ambition was boundless, whose
capacity for work was voracious, whose talent, regrettably,
was minor. She never mentioned Ridinghouse.

I could not form a picture of those days; the one I had I
grew to loathe. Annette at Solo, looking into his face with her
dazzling smile. There was incredible delicacy and sweetness in
the way her lips curved, something bird-like and tender about
the way her head was poised on the long neck. And he,
opposite, sinister as hell, was a black furry edge, a blur which

should have been a man. He hid from me and so did she. I saw that a whole world lay hidden – saw a habit of concealment so strong that it took no effort to sustain. So we carried on; we went out and drank wine and made love and talked, as before, and meanwhile each like a spy in the enemy's camp weighed the other's words and looked, sharp-eyed, for the accidental clue.

An age passed – two weeks or three – and at last Pie telephoned. At once he launched into a discussion of the foibles of mankind, the follies in particular of his nearer colleagues, all neatly dissected and revealed bone-white in the acid bath of his contempt. Again he rang with nothing pertinent to say and then, a third time, he inquired disingenuously if I was busy. I told him that I was perfectly idle and he grunted disdain. 'Come and visit you,' he said. 'Tomorrow all right?'

Up I went to Annette's studio, the large bedroom at the top of the house which she had made her own. She was working. Her productivity ran in inverse ratio to mine and she had, since my portraits were done, set to work like a woman demented; as though she was preparing for something. Through the door I heard her singing. There was silence at my knock. It hurt me, that she could be happy. I suppose it made me want to hurt her.

I announced from the door jamb that Pie was to visit. She gave me a stare.

'What, to stay?'

'I don't know. Perhaps.'

'No, he can't, I mean the man smells, Ruffey, he's bad news.'

She was laughing, she had wrinkled her nose in mock distaste.

'View him as a natural disaster, a hurricane,' I said mildly. 'Unstoppable.'

'You mean you won't say no to him,' she said, all at once angry.

'He's my friend,' I said smoothly. 'Why should I?'

'Because he's such a shit. You know exactly what I mean.'

'No,' I said. 'I don't. You're exaggerating. Friendship's not a competition of virtues. Besides, he's an eminent man, with an international reputation. If you abandon your friends for their failures, you can hardly blame me for hanging on to mine for their successes.'

This succeeded in making her very cross indeed. She came over to where I stood, my refusal to enter her space an ironic reminder that she was not permitted to enter mine, and she stood arms akimbo, her head aggressively tilted forwards, a delectable little dragon.

'You're completely unfair and you know it,' and there was a slight quaver in her voice – not tears, but a kind of angry disbelief. 'Look, he tells people terrible things. You know, mad fascist things, like certain people shouldn't be allowed to breed and all that. He believes it, it's not funny.'

'Those are his jokes. It's just words, quirks. He has a philosophical basis for a lot of it, besides it's his party trick, shocking people. Look on it as a form of camouflage.'

'You really don't see it, do you?' Her tone was incredulous.

'What should I see? You can dislike him, you're perfectly entitled to. But not because of those reasons – that's according his social statements a weight he doesn't attach to them himself. In this case, you simply have to give me credit for knowing a little better.'

It was insufferable; I could not resist the temptation. This argument – for it was more pointed than a discussion – went beyond the desire to ensure that I would conduct my tête-à-tête alone with Pie; I needed in a childish way to score points. To win – to punish her. She was, for a moment, taken aback. Our arguments had tended to the passionate, never to the cold.

'I'm not allowed to have an opinion, is that it? Very tolerant. What are the reasons I'm allowed to have, for disliking him? What's allright by you? The fact that he doesn't much like me either, or how about the way he uses you? He doesn't like you, he's collected you, he doesn't have feelings –'

'An umpire in the game of life? Why not? Emotions are messy things. Look at your acrimony on such small acquaintance and tell me he's wrong.'

She was silent then; I had bludgeoned her into submission with my fluency and I was pleased, I hurried to take advantage of the moment. I remember thinking, as the worst kind of amateur ham might think, now turn to go – stop at the door – turn back, amused note in voice. How easily the question came out.

'By the way, do you remember that fellow John Ridinghouse we lost on Borobodur?'

'Yes,' she said at once. 'Sure.' Perhaps she had been expecting the question all the time, had formulated her answer just as I had rehearsed the question in my head with a thousand minor variants.

'I wondered what could have happened to him. What d'you think?'

'Oh, he'll be all right. People like that always are.'

She was stony-faced, calm.

'Like what?'

'Loners. People who don't have friends or need them. Like your professor. Except he of course has you,' and she gave me an ironic look.

'Weren't you his friend?'

'No, I don't think so, what did you just say? Friendship's not a competition of virtues? Give me your definition and I'll tell you.'

'Touché,' and I looked hard at her mulish little face.

But now, as though she was in the play too, she came up to me, leant against me with her fine hair catching in my shirt buttons, put her arms around me.

'Oh Ruffey, you're hopeless at being tough. It's just not part of you. That's what I like in you.'

There was a long pause.

'Tell me something. You wouldn't be too kind, would you? I mean you'd not try to protect me from something bad. If something had gone wrong there, something serious, on Borobodur, you'd have told me wouldn't you?'

It was utterly disarming, but I didn't want that, I wanted my cold irony, my bad temper. I looked at her parting, the soft hair like a child's.

'Come now,' I said with a bluster. 'You know I would have. You were there – you saw me. I searched the whole bloody place from top to bottom.'

'Of course.' She nodded; disengaged herself. We mirrored each other in our doubts, our mistrust.

'Thanks for telling me,' she said calmly – and whether she referred to Ridinghouse or to Pie's visit, I could not tell. I went downstairs and felt all the dissatisfaction and annoyance that was my due.

It was a restless day, one to fill with errands; I spent it in Bloomsbury. I had a drink at the Hotel Russell's bar, for which I have a certain affection. It could generally guarantee a seat – no small matter for me – and its décor always amused, featuring as it did moulded plaster cherubs high on the walls which a trick of the light had equipped with hair nets. A drink did little to calm me — I was too impatient for Pie, too conscious of my shortcomings. I was missing something obvious. I got up, wandered around. Two corners away huge plastic flaps were gobbling up post vans, others were spewed out. I stood and watched the omnivorous monster for a while. Finding myself a short distance from the Oasis, I roused sufficient impetus for a swim.

Here was genuine sixties tawdriness, unchanged, the same assortment of bicycles and old chairs, the same grizzled homunculus lurking in the corridors. Years of water therapy had given me a taste for the sport and some ability. Afterwards, examining myself, I thought that decay was not, after all, so far advanced. The hair around my head was no thinner, the naked dome free at any rate of ignominious liver spots. Both exercises cheered me more than I might have hoped. I bared my teeth (not bad) at the mirror, told myself action was the cure, went home in a better mood.

After Annette had gone to bed I sat up. Having suffered of late from a whirring of the brain that prevented sleep, I had formed a new, bad habit. I would sit in the study with a bottle of brandy and contemplate the object of my fascination until the alcoholic fog paralleled the mental one.

Deep in the armchair, I shut my eyes. All day an elusive idea had danced through the back of my head and now I sat still, as a child might, to catch it.

The post vans delivered it to me: an idea so simple that I marvelled at my stupidity. Letters. There must have been a correspondence of some sort if a relationship had existed between Annette and Ridinghouse. Proof, if I could find it, though a failure so to do would not guarantee innocence. I was too jealous of my suspicions to give them up easily.

Now I rewarded myself with a drink, put my feet up and considered. My wife threw nothing away. She, who had kept her childhood books, who had arranged our books in alphabetical order and in sections by subject, would never discard such a piece of her past; indeed she clung to it with a tenacity as great as her previous repudiation. As though, flawed as it might be, the past had a quality her present lacked. I stared at the books: here was the place to start. It was to be an armchair exercise in detection, for I was already too drunk to go blundering about the house.

Her books or mine? Hers. She was not enough of a casuist for the double-bluff. Art books, novels, a duplication of dictionaries: it was a dainty conundrum. What would she choose as being of no possible interest to me? I drank a little more. I scanned the shelves, one by one.

Past the biographies I went, discarding mentally, no single one too obscure for a rainy afternoon read. I seldom looked at the art books, but she could not be sure of that. It should be simultaneously unusual and obvious.

Travel? No, we had looked through the whole shelf-ful only that May. There remained the ephemera, the novels, the random texts, the touching attempts at self-improvement. I conducted an internal monologue across the fiction: Le Carré I like, Cheever I look at, Clarke's mine, Conrad ditto – congratulating myself on the catholicism of my tastes, spine by spine. Twenty minutes passed in this way. My eye lit upon the Bible, modestly positioned at the end of a row. What household does not possess one – and who ever looks at it? With perfect conviction I got up and plucked it from the shelves.

It was a handy little blasphemy. The pages were stuck together and cut out in the shape of a flat whisky bottle. A little package tied up with string lay inside. I unknotted it carefully, unfolded the brown paper, saw that there were two postcards and two letters. The first postcard was a picture of mine, made for Arnolfini show five years ago and I thought for an instant that these, then were my keepsakes – an idiot drink-inspired second of hope – and then, flipping the card over I read: 'Interesting man. Will you come with me – Thursday at 7 ? John.'

The second postcard was dated April 1976, two years earlier. It was a cheap, unlaminated black and white picture of sand dunes and a rolling sea with the legend Sables d'Olonne on the reverse. 'A philosopher's sea, cold and grey with a treacherous undertow. Nothing from here to Newfoundland. I'd jump ship and sail away but for you, petite taquineuse.'

The fatter of the two letters was postmarked 14 June, 1977 and was typed, much folded and worn.

'Dear Annette, Now, if I didn't care why would I be writing in the middle of the night? I seldom take trouble to write letters and now I must, because you listen but fail to hear. I think you merit the compliment of a letter and it's a rare one. Take that at its stated value, no more or less. Nothing is hidden between the lines, I am going to be as plain as possible.

'I am a simple type and I enjoy my privacy. There is nothing solitary and romantic about me at all. Because you're complex and devious, as women are, you will insist upon discovering a mystery, making an emotional upheaval. They are your emotions, not mine, enjoy them if you must but don't confuse the two.

'Now you're going to accuse me of being cold and incapable of emotions. What a lot of accusations come under the name of love. I don't like threats and abuse and they will have to stop if we are to be friends. There's a threat for you – do you like it? No amount of pushing will make me do what I dislike and hard words have no effect on me. I don't intend to offer you a set of expedient lies. I have no interest in romantic love or any kind of love and I prefer sex with women who enjoy it, as a physical act, as I do.

'You aren't going to like any of that, I know, try to understand it properly. I'm not trying to reject you or have you "on my terms". I would enjoy making love to you, but there seems little point in it when your pleasure rests on expectations beyond the act. It's very pernicious, your idea of love, it takes away pleasure so neatly. What do you mean when you say you love me? That you want to abandon yourself to me, that I am to take charge of you, give you a false security? This whole notion of subsuming self is a very curious one. Why can't people exist on their own? Why are they unhappy until they have someone to love, a cause to suffer for? It's a way of finding justification for a small life. It is all weakness, self-deceit, a kind of sickness. You want to infect me with it, but I'm not susceptible. I'm not trying to be vain or clever when I say that, please don't consider me a challenge. I've never had the sensations you feel and I am curious about them. I can imagine that I would enjoy the experience and certainly nothing would cure you as quickly as believing those feelings of yours are reciprocated – but I don't have them in me. I shall tell you why. I don't believe that we can love anybody outside ourselves. We love ourselves and we say that we 'love' other people because they produce feelings of pleasure in us – as music does, as a sunny day does – it is as simple as that. Imagine a perfect state of happiness: possessing those feelings for themselves, without an object or excuse.

'Now the reason for this letter is simple, it is – how to cure you? For it is a disease you have, all uncontrolled passions are. Do you want to spend the rest of your life being miserable? You're so energetic, so alive. You were made for pleasure, to be independent and free. I believe you when you say that you're unhappy, but it's not an unalterable state. You are within your own power – who else's could it be? You seem to think I shall take pity on you. Pity is self-imposed suffering, don't expect it of me. That's what love boils down to – suffering in the name of pleasure, first self-imposed, then thrust upon others. It's not so very altruistic after all, is it? Don't expect your object to be grateful.

'You have a vitality and exuberance that is very precious – don't let it drain away in unnecessary battles. You can have all the love affairs you want, if that is your taste, but keep a clear head, don't lose control. Now you are trapped, you have trapped yourself and you think you love your cage, but you're wrong. What you make, you can master.

'Start by pretending to be something else, to be free. Copy what is effective and you will find that the mask you adopt becomes natural in time, that you become what you pretend to be. It is as simple as that. It must be positive. Call it freedom or happiness, or whatever you like, but choose freely, choose for pleasure, for adventure – not what you think will please me, but what pleases you. And if you don't like it, choose again, choose the opposite. It doesn't matter – you will be free. That is power: to create yourself. It is such a simple idea, isn't it, and yet terrifying to the weak, but I know that you're not weak. Test your powers and you'll see how strong you are. I shall applaud you, I know that you can do it. I wouldn't write you a letter as long as this if I didn't have that confidence. John.'

The last piece of paper had an address: 36 Little Russell Street, WC2. It wasn't much of a letter.

'Dear Annette, I leave England tomorrow. Can you come tonight? J.' And this gave me as hard a knock as the other letter, for I recognised the date, the chief in our calendar of trysts: the night she had seduced me.

I didn't go to bed until nearly five. Plenty of time to learn the letters off by heart, to wrap them up, put them away, then unwrap them for a last, masochistic perusal. Annette wrapped herself around me and I did not push her away. I stroked her hair a little. It was comforting, even though I felt as though I was caressing the noose around my neck. I got up very early and told the bleary face in the mirror that it was an advantage, to be sure, to need so little sleep. A benefit of age. It grimaced back at me with savage teeth as I scraped at the stubble, cutting my chin twice.

At eight-thirty I stood in Bloomsbury, indeed had dawdled on the pavement for half an hour already. The street boasted an electrical shop and a hairdresser's: the rest was residential, tall flat-fronted houses in varying states of repair, each separated from the pavement by a deep well and iron railings. Number 36 was a boarding house with aspirations to better things. Hotel Little Russell was written on the glass above the front door in gold letters that squashed into the side. Having failed to take account of the width of the S's, the painter had compressed the two L's into a single column, giving the whole an illiterate flamboyance. The multiple rows of bells gave away the true character of the place. I pressed Manageress's Flat and heard a faint buzz. A little time passed and then a blonde head stuck itself out of the basement window.

'What is it?'

'A room, I've come about a room.'

She peered up and then beckoned and I saw that a steep stone staircase led into the pit. I hobbled down it while she waited in the doorway, arms crossed.

'You married? Any children, dogs? We don't let animals in.'

I crossed this first Rubicon and now she smiled.

'Come in then. It's protection for all my guests, me being careful,' she said, and, 'You never know nowadays, do you?'

Indeed. In Mrs Kiriakou's language that amounted to an apology, accompanied as always by a self-bestowed encomium. She was a woman with two certainties: her virtues and those of her establishment were unassailable, one fed upon the other. Neither was susceptible to abuse. I fixed her with a sincere look.

'I'm so glad you're in, Mrs Kiriakou.' (We had already exchanged cards, like Japanese businessmen.)

'I was recommended here by John Ridinghouse. He told me his landlady was a treasure.' I smirked ingratiatingly. This was a proposition too self-evident to draw forth a smile, but there was definite softening around the jaw. Ruffey's smirk was a terrible sight, more of a leer, but this did me no disservice in the eyes of the landlady. It was obvious that the establishment was hers. The room we stood in was hideous, but expensively furnished and she had spoken of 'my guests'. The clincher, however, was the bank book on the table next to a ledger and a pile of correspondence, all outside a caretaker's orbit.

'I'll show you round first,' she said. 'Then we can have a cup of tea down here.' With this unalluring prospect in view, I was obliged to follow.

I am thoroughly familiar, now, with every inch of worn linoleum, but at first glance the curious layout of the place defied all architectural rules. The boarding house hoped, in better times, to metamorphose itself into an hotel of splendour; it guaranteed future appreciation of space and elegance by an interim policy of exploiting every last inch. An extension had eaten up the garden and created a succession of half-landings. There were steps everywhere, up and down into rooms, everything a different height where the ingenuity of the absent Mr Kiriakou had seen the possibility of inserting another bolt-hole. Corridor edges had been snatched away behind plasterboard partitions, balconies glassed in and made into rooms, sliding doors inserted to admit a sidling entrance.

There were notices everywhere saying 'Respect your Neighbour' and 'Silence Please'. These pieces of paper sought to stop up the structural lacunae to no avail, for the house resounded with a hundred whispered conversations, snatches of music and the whistling of distant kettles. Each numbered door exposed the cupidity of the landlord. 3A, B, C revealed the fission of one room into three remunerative cells; else-where were to be found 8D, 11E and 12F. He had economised with one alphabetical set of stickers, saved yet further at the top of the house by judicious use of a felt-tip pen.

Mrs Kiriakou trotted up before me, showing off her shapely legs in seamed nylons. She was a small, thin woman, surprisingly buxom, got up in some kind of party dress with a frilly hem. She was nimble and quick in all her movements, though I could have given her a couple of years. She waited for me at the top of each staircase with a patient look. Then she would tip-tap away, flicking at spiders as she went, kicking detached morsels of lino back into place.

She understood perfectly the value of contrast, showing me first a room which boasted a wall inserted next to the door, cutting the window in half at the other end. A single bed and wardrobe jostled for space. I walked to the window, where there was a small gap and, peering around it, met an eye looking back; it withdrew with a gasp. A creak from next door indicated that the frightened occupant had sunk upon the counterpart of this horribly stained mattress. The landlady nodded, as though satisfied.

Up we went again, my heavy footfall resounding down the well behind her clicking heels. The next door was opened with a flourish: here was magnificence indeed. It was the very best room in the house, that eminence achieved solely by virtue of its having been neither bi- nor trifurcated. It retained two windows and the appropriate measure of wall to match — it was some twenty feet long and about thirteen wide and, befitting its handsome proportions, was kitted out with a bed-divan, a leather-topped desk that had not yet lost all pretensions to gentility and a mahogany wardrobe with matching chest of drawers. Mrs K, drawing a loving finger across these treasures, forbore to notice the trail she left.

'A proper gentleman's room,' she said and cocked her head, awaiting the correct response.

'Very nice indeed.'

It was about half the size of my studio. She was not satisfied. 'It's lovely and quiet up here,' she said. 'And there's a private bathroom, just down the corridor. I keep this for long-term residents. I don't want people in and out, spoiling it.'

'I'd take good care of it, I promise you,' I said and she nodded several times.

Back in the bowels of the house we arranged ourselves cosily on her two-seater sofa and she gave me a bitter brew in a dainty china cup.

'Nice cuppa,' she said appreciatively, leaning back and crossing her legs, her skirt too tight for that elegant gesture. The top limb cantilevered alarmingly into the void; along its bony ridge, she gazed admiringly at her tight, black patent leather shoes.

'Some places ask for references, but I know people. You learn, in the hotel trade. I can tell everything from a person's face. Of course I have to take a deposit, to protect myself, two months rent in advance. The lovely big room I showed you is fifty a week, linen changed once a week, breakfast all in. It takes a week to clear a cheque so if you want to move in straight away it'll have to be cash.'

She said all of this quite rapidly, watching me closely, and I gave her a fatuous smile.

'It's a bargain, you know. That room will be snapped up if you don't take it, I can't hold it for you. Mr Ridinghouse will tell you I don't give it to anyone.'

She saw nothing contradictory in all this.

'It was Ridinghouse's room was it?'

'Oh yes, I keep it for him, but he'll not be back for a long time now so I can give it away; I can't just leave it empty, can I?'

I nodded agreement with all or either of her assertions.

'Tell me Mrs Kiriakou, do you have a forwarding address for him? I was rather expecting that he'd be here – we've lost touch recently. He's a distant relative of mine.'

The knees realigned themselves and she straightened up, becoming businesslike. 'Now do you want the room Mr Ruffey? You see I couldn't think of giving out information like that, that's confidential, unless it was to somebody I knew. I can't just give out a person's personal details. My guests trust me, anyone will tell you, I'm the soul of discretion.'

'Of course I'll take it,' I said, drawing out my cheque book and making calculations which were rapidly corrected: two months stretched to ten weeks at Mrs Kiriakou's. I could afford it, I thought, and the idea of spending a few hours in his room was strangely enticing. I wrote out the cheque and handed it over and she folded it up at once and concealed it in the pile of papers on the table.

'If you could just give me the address I'll make a note of it on my cheque book,' I said firmly. Fair was fair. My new landlady jumped up at once and fetched the black book.

'Such a pity you've missed him,' she said. 'He was here just a short time ago. Oh well, let's see. Not everyone leaves a forwarding address' – she well knew how to be provocative. Daintily, she ran her lacquered nail down one page after another.

'Come and look, dear, I don't have my reading glasses,' and she patted the seat next to her, giving me an enticing smile, obliging me to shift into near-adulterous proximity.

Four months ago, he had written in that crabbed hand 'From June 30 Hotel Manchuria, Palang, Java, Indonesia.' In May, when he met us, that must still have been his destination. I thought with savage pleasure that a man who knew his movements that far in advance was no vague hippie wanderer. No absent-minded gipsy he, to throw himself down a volcano or from a temple upon a whim.

'Let me see, dear,' and Mrs Kiriakou now held out the book at arm's length, squinting balefully. 'Go on read it out.' She nodded without listening. 'What did you say your job was, dear?'

'Civil service. But I travel a lot.' I cast around for an explanation, decided to inspect historic buildings if necessary, but she asked no more. She smiled at me with a little pout. She thought we were enjoying an agreeable flirtation, though whether that privilege was due to my assumed status or to the need, having betrayed a confidence, to enter at once into another one, the devil alone knew.

'What a piece of luck finding that,' she said mendaciously. 'Today's your lucky day, Mr Ruffey,' and she sucked in her cheeks in an alluring fashion and leant an inch nearer. Her palm lay open, nearly touching my thigh. I wondered if I could bring myself to pat it, with a touch of old-world gallantry. My hand refused, it lay limp on my knee and disobeyed me and as I formulated the first of my impertinent questions in my head I saw her looking at me with tears in her eyes, as though she'd inadvertently bitten her tongue. It took me a moment to understand that this was her melting expression.

No amount of buttering-up would extract any more information on my subject from my new landlady, who was ready enough on every other. She inferred, delicately, that we should know each other better and then proceeded to tell me her life story. Mrs Kiriakou was at heart a romantic and clearly thought the tale of one adventure might precipitate a second. She had married to spite her family and the proof of it was a wedding picture of a young and almost pretty girl in an olive grove, squinting into the sun alongside a handsome chap, short and heavily muscled; upon close examination it could be seen that he was standing on a large stone. He had put her through many harrowing experiences, but her etiolated face was so unmarked that she couldn't quite believe in her right to draw the pension, though she queued up for it all the same. Her weakness for bachelors manifested itself as a tendency to tell them exactly what she owned and simultaneously to warn them that no one took advantage of her. Few addressed thus seemed inclined to try their luck. Nevertheless, each favoured lodger imputed to the next black designs and unfair advantages deriving, supposedly, from a greater place in her affections. A day would surely come when Mrs K would undertake the promised repairs, would gratify each individual with the lavish furnishings she assured them they deserved. She would describe them so exactly, her hands measuring their magnificence in the air, just as though they really did exist outside the storehouse of her head. Mrs Kiriakou complained bitterly of the restrictions imposed upon her by the authorities — the Health Executive or the Fire Brigade who ruined everything. She would say, with great heat, that they had made her put in doors that weren't in character with the building. If it were not for them, the Little Russell Hotel would, she implied, have been a palace of polished mahogany and glittering chandeliers.

It was possible to grow fond of Mrs Kiriakou; possible upon certain feast days to dare to plant a dry kiss on her powdered cheek and to be offered by way of return a glass of the retsina which she drank to remind her of her days of glory. As a property owner she had a particularly soft spot for those who had also had possessions, once, and who understood the exorbitant expenses privilege brought with it – for gentlemen. That word created awe in Mrs Kiriakou and brought out her best glasses and her ceremonial lace cloth.

I could not hope for any credit as a painter, for not only was she quite ignorant of the visual arts, treating such fancifulness with the lower-middle-class acerbity it deserved, but she positively opposed a practice which was so messy, which would stink the place out and leave ineradicable stains in the carpet. My credit rested on a cash basis: that, an educated voice and an opportunistic adoption of the free and easy kiss-me-quick ways of the gentry were the quickest route to securing the position of favourite without which life in her establishment could deteriorate to sniping exchanges, if not heavy artillery, in a matter of days.

I went directly to my travel agent's to book a seat for Jakarta, proceeding undeviatingly along my line, as though it were chalked onto the pavement. It was an all-too-imminent departure. The fabrication of a story for my wife now took over my thinking and so I forgot completely the small matter of Mrs Kiriakou's cheque. I had meant, naturally, to cancel it. I had seen at once that I would not go there again – that idea as ridiculous as the notion that my simple failure to cancel a cheque might have consequences of any kind.

A greater matter which I had equally forgotten was John Pie. It was disconcerting to see his portly figure at the door. He had made himself thoroughly at home with bottles and ice; leading me into the drawing room, he offered a drink.

'Your wife regrets her absence — said you knew,' he said. 'Thought we might eat out tonight if the little woman permits. Unless there's grouse on the menu here.'

He gazed innocently around and swallowed half a glassful; he considered my precious malt his preserve. Thoughtfully, he would adulterate my drink, but never his. His toe artfully pushed a black suitcase an inch or two further behind the sofa.

'Forgotten what a big house it was,' he said. 'Lots of room. Cleaning woman wouldn't let me look, said to wait here.'

My opinion of Mrs Derwent at once leapt to the topmost possible notch. 'Dinner at my club then? You not a member of anything decent, are you?'

These ingratiating manners soon achieved their desired effect: the establishment of the suitcase in a more appropriate place. 'Few things to do in town,' he said vaguely, to explain this novelty. 'Not in the way, am I?'

We sat in his club, our substance reflected in the brilliant polish of glasses and the deferential air of the waiters who gently placed the menus in our hands with the solemnity befitting a ritual occasion. The place gained further in lustre from the diners, most of whom had a handle to their name which the staff used as carefully as their silver chafing dishes.

'Good evening, Professor.'

'Good evening, Partridge.'

Both parties smiled at their own feat of memory, rather than at the other's compliment of recognition.

Pie in his rusty black suit was perfectly at home; my lighter, smarter, version was not. Money wore faceless grey, it glinted ancestral cufflinks. It might indulge in a pin-striped suit, but never forget a tie: my borrowed one hung incongruously dark. I was a different type: the arty leaven imported to amuse, to rise to the occasion. Lovers of real art traded it here. They bought and sold, discussed their grants and levies. This gerontocracy was England, its heart of oak polished over centuries of candle-lit suppers.

I could play the part with a degree of conviction, but these actors lived their roles. My spiritual eating house was the Star of India, where I felt sympathy when I saw the empty seats and kinship that could never be expressed for the waiters who hung around the unused bar and heaved crates of bottles up and down the back stairs. Privilege roused my egalitarian instincts; I was ready to be disobliging.

'If you've got something to tell me,' I said, 'spit it out.'

'Coarse, Ruffey,' said the gourmet, gobbling down foie gras on toast and licking his fingers. 'Thought you'd want to tell me something.'

'Such as?'

'How you're getting on. Work, life,' he said vaguely. 'Things.' He could not quite meet my eye. The attempt at guile was so blatant and the confidant role so absurd on his great shoulders that I began to laugh. The thick face wore by turns a look of surprise, faint annoyance, then a smile of sorts.

'Don't want to get involved, interfere,' he said lugubriously. 'Never did want to know about your private messes. A friend's a friend though. Don't like to see time-wasting. Not at your age. No time left. Your abiding sin, being distracted. Take my advice. Work, leave the rest, plough your own furrow.'

'But that's precisely what I am doing,' I said in a reasonable tone. This was the second time that he had warned me off; that he should consider that errand worth a journey to town was remarkable. 'Your advice is always valuable, despite the appalling frequency of its delivery, but it's quite redundant,' I said. 'You don't know what I'm up to.'

'Your motives are your own terrain. Hope you've charted it to your own satisfaction,' he said, dismissively, but he was leaning forwards and anxious to know more.

'Indeed.'

'Artists have to cull experience,' he said, grandly. 'Discard the trivial.'

'And who can say what's trivial?' I said lightly. 'So you've got nothing to tell me about my quarry?'

He shook his head.

'Quite right. Never betray a confidence. Some things better left unsaid, Pie, I quite agree with you,' and achieving, thus, a mutually infuriating opacity, we settled to eat. And if I, gazing at that jowly face, was left to conjecture a hundred different and unlikely things, he was seemingly unaffected, a placid, chomping ruminant already beckoning to the wine waiter. Up the fellow trotted, all but rubbing his hands in a Heepish show of deference. Pie instituted a long discussion which involved the sampling of this and that vintage, neither of which could hope to equal the perfect Platonian nectar he held in his mental palate. Admirable, insouciant Pie. How expeditiously he hopped into the saddle of one of his hobby horses; with such a variety stabled, there was always one trotting nearby. I was silent. A lesser man might have tried to rouse me into companionable small talk. Pie, uncaring, ate and drank.

'Hunger and thirst,' he remarked after a long interval. 'Pathways in the brain. Columns of nerve cells firing. Ping!

Little sign lights up. Burgundy, gin and tonic. Brain's like a computer.'

Quite distinctly, I heard the whinnyings of another beast.

'New study of yours is it, the workings of the brain?'

'Always looking for illumination,' he said, contemplating his glass as though that were to be found there. 'The nature of perception's always interesting for philosophers. Scientists know a lot, relatively, about the brain. Nothing about most of it, mind you, but they've located certain cells. The ones that deal with vision. Interest you, Ruffey. Columns of nerve cells which collect information, colours, differences in the edges of things, it's fed into the computer. So we calculate distance, stereoscopic vision. Neurotransmitters. The cells communicate. Some of them can reduce pain, increase pleasure, natural opiates. They try to link that physical behaviour to consciousness, moods, not enough information. They don't have the words for it. Consciousness is a job for philosophers. Same old mind–body dichotomy. They theorise that mind and body are one, now, nice notion, cells for everything, but you can't stimulate consciousness with an electrode. You can stimulate certain cells that do specific jobs. Brain mechanisms, wiring. You might get a rational response, but it won't tell you what rationality is. No behaviour in a nerve cell.'

'So do the philosophers define it any better, consciousness that is?'

'Thousand and one theories but no. Not really.' He smiled; he had talked himself into a genial mood. He listened when I said anything; for Pie, that amounted to charm.

'Doesn't matter in a sense. Matters for philosophers, it's their job, it matters for me. Not for you. Do you need certainties, proofs? No. You need a little bit of experience, some white meat some dark, a few convenient beliefs and a nice developed set of artist's neurotransmitters. So you see something and ping! Make a connection, there's a stimulus, a subject for you. The information has gone in. You've got all the tools to work on it. Style, training, experience. Out comes a picture, you've added a piece of truth to the world. Personal, universal, manifest, it's lovely art. Rounded. You've not had to run up a thousand dark alleyways for some bit of interpretation almost too difficult to explain. In some back-room at the Jesus Reborn University of Lower Wichita there's a bearded little sod waiting who's going to take twenty thousand words to argue it down.'

'You make my job sound easy,' I said with some bitterness.

'Not easy. Easy for you. Isn't it?'

'Yes, I suppose it is. I have temporarily misfiring circuits.'

'Your glass is empty,' he said, craning forwards, and he waved to the wine waiter, ordered another bottle. 'Distractions. Told you so. Too much easy living. You've gone soft, need a shake-up.'

I smiled at that. His prescriptions for me were never sweetened. We changed the subject and talked about physiology again, or rather he talked and I did the listening. I thought about the nerve cells collecting information, the post vans shuttling in and out. I let myself drift upon his flow.

By the end of the night the kinship of spirits was ours. In Piccadilly he insisted in orienting himself by the stars, a manner of proceeding which delayed our return considerably. It was gone one o'clock when a taxi dropped us at the door. Since my wife had unaccountably failed to make up a bed for Pie, I performed that task while he completed his preparations for the night. These consisted merely of removing his outer layer of garments. Sitting in baggy underpants and string vest deformed by a vast belly, he drank a nightcap, puffing voluptuously on a large cigar. Behind its aromatic cloud, he looked remarkably like Old Nick.

'More claret,' he said, holding out the glass. I went downstairs and behind me a large befuddled shadow stumbled on the stairs. In the kitchen we laughed stupidly at some mishap with the corkscrew, or perhaps it was merely the hilarious way the wine gurgled out of the bottle, its astonishing redness. It wasn't until Pie ostentatiously dug me in the ribs with one elbow with a jerk of the head towards the doorway that I realised Annette was standing there, watching us.

I remember that I took exception to her critical stare. Perhaps I said, 'You hop on up to bed, there's a good girl,' or some such thing. She was angry and that seemed funny too, rib-ticklingly so, that she should stand thus on her dignity. Perhaps I said as much; that she had no great claim to represent sobriety or propriety, though these are long words. Worse things can befall a person than being laughed at a little; this does not seem to me to be an unforgivable crime.

At any rate she decided to be cross, she took herself off and in due course we followed, in our own way. Entwined, we lurched very slowly up the stairs. I helped Pie into his room, divesting myself of my jacket in the process. It was in the way. I was in no very admirable state, but filled with a certain sottish pleasure at being marginally more able. I got his shoes off, an unappealing task which took a long time and was accomplished with gruntings from both parties. Slowly, I carried them away. Carefully, I returned and aligned them very neatly in the centre of the room. They weren't quite right. I examined them closely for a long minute, nudged them a millimetre into position with my toe. For a second, it was touch and go with my balance. Making, then, a splendid recovery, I turned to see Pie rifling unselfconsciously through my pockets.

'Jakarta,' he said, my plane ticket in one stubby hand.

'Give it to me.'

'Dieng plateau,' he intoned. 'Prambanan. Cetah. Sukuh. Cdeung Songo. High plains. Warm black nights. Come with you.'

He began to copy out the number of the flight onto the back of an old envelope. It took a long time and we both laughed a lot.

'You won't get a seat.'

My voice sounded feeble and lack-lustre. I wondered what I meant by it. Perhaps this was what I wanted; that seemed an interesting idea. I listened to myself and waited for my firm, confident 'NO'. I seemed to be silent. Swaying, I looked at Pie, who seemed to be exhibiting no doubts. I thought, all at once, that he wanted to keep an eye on me – and that it would be expedient for me to do the reverse. The proof of that was that he did not even ask me why I was going, or what my ultimate destination might be. Instead, he gave me an accomplice's wink. 'Acts have many,' he said, 'colours. All equivocal.'

A moment later he had fallen back upon his clothes, eyes closed, mouth open. I took my ticket, put it back in my pocket and went up to bed where I fell at once into a deep, dreamless sleep.

6

In Jakarta we stepped into a liquid wall of heat. Sweat prickled, crotch, armpits, toes degenerated into a damp, pre-fungal state. Indonesia did not merely assault the senses; this was a hi-jack.

The cab was upholstered in shrill, pink nylon fur — a thoughtful touch, this — to cushion the knocks of progress. A pink plastic globe wiggled and bobbed as we went, releasing a sickly sweet excretion through its circle of perforations. The driver swerved through the pancake flat city along the freeway, seats tilting and jumping with each daring manoeuvre. Proceeding with enormous caution, as though to take the enemy by surprise, Pie eased off his jacket and liberated his arms. Great, damp blotches came into view and straight away swamped the globe with a tidal wave of pungent odour.

Pie wedged his bum into the corner and I anchored myself as best I could, easing my leg into the only possible position, inches above the irradiating transmission. Through the haze and glitter of headlights, I tried in vain to find landmarks from the great Dutch port, remains of the orderly residential streets, the green-gardened villas. It was all office blocks and expressways. I had not taken in, that summer, how vast the city now was. It had crept out in all directions, a sprawl of concrete and tin, the posters in homage to Sanyo and Sony and Toshiba proliferating as we neared the centre. There, giant paintings of vaguely recognisable, smiling faces – was that Bob Hawke? – signalled more international aspirations.

All at once the machine swerved and joltingly coughed down a heavily rutted road. The hotel was a minute's drive from the wide boulevard and decades back. A dozen old bangers were parked in the dusty forecourt around a large blinking neon sign. The drivers in their standard garb of epauletted, short-sleeved shirts stood around in clusters, smoking and gossiping, waiting for someone to emerge from the shabby fifties building. The whole concrete façade was a lattice-work of thick brise-soleils, creating little squares of shade, each with the unsightly protrusion of an air-conditioner. There was just room above the box for a small and necessarily deep-set window, to afford a small, blinkered view. Someone had had the happy idea of painting these boxes blood-red inside, pink outside, giving the effect of row upon row of baggy, drooping eyes. We went in under their sleepy baleful stare.

It was Pie's choice; the lobby evoked his West Mall flat so uncannily that I realised that the flotsam I had taken for his landlady's bounty might actually be his by choice. This small revelation did not augur well. It took a few minutes for the receptionist to appear. Above her trademark batik dress, she wore a lime cardigan; her hair was pomaded and scraped back into some sort of gold mesh snood and every couple of minutes a long fingernail shot out to pat or tuck in some straying tendril. She smiled vaguely at me past the contorted figure of the professor. He searched through various inner recesses of his clothing for the document which revealed the full extent of his iniquity. He found it, a pink form.

'There,' he said, jabbing at it. 'Pie. One twin, one night, booked by telex. From England.'

The girl picked it up fastidiously by one corner, examined it closely. 'For Christ's sake,' I said. 'Look, we need two rooms.'

'For one night? It's a perfectly reasonable economy. Not a pleasure for me to share either.'

The girl stared blankly past while we debated the point, waiting until I had argued him down to say that ours was the last room. Nothing in that empty place made this very likely, but then she had no cause to turn down the sale. I had plenty of time to absorb the mournful interior while Pie slowly filled in the form. There was no incentive to linger under the faded travel posters, nothing anyone could want in the glass cabinets lined with dusty sea-green paper and piled high with grubby reproductions of ethnic artifacts.

We took the key and went past a green, stagnant pool, slouched through the empty restaurant tables that fringed its irregular contours, took a small detour around the trio of gamelan players who increased both volume and tempo in a hopeful manner as we passed, diminishing Doppler-like as we went. The only evidence of guests – but that plentiful enough – was in a corridor lined with dirty food trays and in the loud discordance of a dozen television sets through thin doors, many of them ajar. Small creatures, who I hoped were children, eyed us slyly through these slits.

The room smelt of Flit, mustiness and filth. The walls were marked with the dry red smears of a thousand insect deaths. The twin beds were flanked by tapering-legged tables with pink shaded lamps bolted on; from inside their plastic shells came the unstoppable, constant hum of an excitable radio. Listening to this despite myself, staring up at the fat green arrow which pointed the way for Muslim prayers, assailed by the ancient odours of the pillow and wet with a film of sweat the half-arsed air-conditioning did nothing to dissipate, I cursed my friend. It was not until the whining torment of dive-bombing mosquitoes gave place to the greater agony of the early-morning traffic jam that I fell asleep. Pie had been snoring and snorting for hours, periodically whinnying and shaking in five-minute bouts, and I had had a night to consolidate a great number of fascinating perceptions, chiefly the one that I must have been off my head to let Pie come with me.

Event and consequence went on with their own peculiar logic without any of it being precisely my fault. I could not question our presence here any more than I could tap that fly on the shoulder and ask what on earth possessed it to crash noisily into the window pane, again and again, in its angry, hopeless search for an exit. Tossing in that sweaty pit, I even envied Pie his snores. Certainly I envied him his certainties and freedoms. He had nobody he must inform of his decision to go. He had not had to squirm through a maze of possible excuses, wriggling around for a plausible exit.

I had summoned up the authority of the thirty-plus adult years Annette and I had spent apart: an ignoble trick. I would be away for a week or two in the country, I had said. I needed to retreat occasionally for artistic, recuperative purposes. She was not to try to contact me. I had been grumpy, difficult, unable to work; I implied that I would return a changed man. Don't worry about Pie, I had added generously. I'll get rid of him for you.

It was very thin, yet she had made no demur. She had sat

and watched me pack a bag, stuffing in sweaters that I would retrieve later and hide in cupboards. There was no knowing what she believed. I had seen irony in her crossed legs, her swinging foot, a tolerant disbelief. There had been the implication in her yawn, her way of cocking her head to one side, her half-smile, that this was a piece of eccentricity, a continuation of the other night's episode and she was not going to criticise. I was charged up with anger. Without it, I would never have fuelled the escape.

The bright morning brought me clearer thoughts, a plan. In the hotel lobby a thin tourist map of the most irritating sort, where hotel logos block out major cities, informed me that Palang was not far from Malang.

What was the rush? Pie announced that he was on holiday. From the depths of his case he produced the proof, a much-folded straw fedora which now rose into a leprechaun's peak eighteen inches above his beefy jowls. He had rushed back to Bristol to collect this necessary item, his passport, to fill the black case with books, the mental baggage without which he would not move. There was no hope of prevailing upon him to fly to Yogya or to Surabaya — that expense was not to be borne, nor would he consider the cost of a driver. He consulted a table of fares and I, knowing that what he earned in a week would surpass most Indonesians' annual aspirations, fulminated in the rear. He would save us some £4 or £5, he announced, not because that mattered in the least, but because it was always better to travel as the people did. Was I in a hurry? He folded his face into a portentous frown.

I had voiced stupidities of this nature too often myself to make a convincing case; besides, when had I ever been permitted to win an argument against John Pie? I would not squander my little pitcher of rhetoric upon this occasion when every precious drop would be needed later and besides, this was altogether a question of degree, his economies being sordid where mine were picturesque.

So we found ourselves waiting at the station for the guichet to open with no conviction that we had picked the correct one. A friendly crowd surrounded us, giggling and pointing. Pie leant upon the wooden barrier, deep in his book. We could all stare at him for as long as we chose without his noticing or, if he noticed, caring. I wondered how much nurture had contributed to nature in his case and whether he had ever had to overcome some softness, some gentle tendency, a longing for affection and esteem. The battles, if they had ever taken place, had been secret. It struck me as odd that he had never undergone periods of flux and change, as I so memorably had, never said 'Ah, I was young then, but now I am mature,' only to rediscover that exact state of mind a decade on. Pie had glided smoothly from being a young-old professor into his accomplished old-old version. After a time, I lowered myself onto his case, which thus acquired its only claim to usefulness.

Eventually the wooden window slammed open, galvanising the crowd. A young fellow startlingly attired in a dark brown fedora and hugely flared jeans with a T-shirt bearing the legend 'The US Army Wants YOU' leant over to help me up. 'American?' he said, sticking close. As Pie attempted to explain to the ticket-seller, who spoke no English, that we wanted tickets to Yogyakarta, he peered over my shoulder, smiling. We were to travel, not, as the seller naturally assumed rich tourists must, on the Bima express, but on the slow train which, for a quarter of the price, offered perhaps one eighth of the comfort. All of this went on with a good deal of noise, Pie's booming baritone raised in the erroneous assumption that volume assisted clarity against the high contrapuntal chorus of voices raised in assistance and explanation, the odd English word said with smiling display of gap teeth, laughter from the children, the flare of another kretek being lit somewhere and, a second later, the powerful aroma of cloves drifting by.

I began to enjoy myself. This sensation survived my weariness and even the wooden bench seat. On the slow journey we overtook only the even slower coal-fired loco-motives. Eventually we escaped the shanty towns and chugged on to Bandung, past distant volcanoes and start-lingly bright green patches of highly cultivated terraces, silver flooded padis and dolls' house towns painted white. Pie was far too intent upon annotating his book in wavering pencil to look. He liked nothing better than to review his fellows' output and the volume, stained with dried mosquito corpses and fat, black fingermarks, acquired a patina which cor-responded admirably with his opinion of it.

At last, in darkness, we reached Yogyakarta. I shook Pie awake. His volleys of shuddering snores had for five miles fascinated a troop of small children who swayed in a huddle at the doorway, brown eyes fixed unblinkingly upon us. At the station, surrounded by becak drivers, our short, spirited discussion on where to go was resolved by Pie lyingly insisting that he had booked rooms for us at an hotel. He sat with his case on his knees, thigh wedged against mine, issuing instructions in a clipped bark. These were naturally incomprehensible to the small pedaller, whose bulging calves pumped up and down with surprising force for one so burdened. Down the main street we went though flocks of scooters, the drivers' girls perched elegantly side-saddle on the back, a right swerve that ignored the traffic lights, a sharp left between concrete pillars and into a darkened driveway. We pulled up alongside a great pile of earth and rubble: it was a building site.

'Hotel Garuda,' the driver enunciated and now he smiled.

'You thinking of camping?' I said to Pie, who grunted. I made out a three-storey building with a central part and two outstretched wings; we stood in what must once have been a courtyard. A stained glass canopy on which the name Hotel Garuda could just be seen hung over the firmly padlocked door. The building looked fresh in the dim light of the street lamps, the green—grey dado along the sides not even dusty, but assault was presaged by a giant crane which hung over the hotel from the rear.

Pie, muttering to himself, began to walk along close to the building with the air of someone determined to force his way in; our driver trotted alongside him, pulling at his sleeve, talking at him. The lights along the far path were still connected, the mosaic glass flashing colour over their faces, glinting on the man's two silver teeth. They disappeared to the rear and I waited in the becak. At last Pie returned and stomped up to me, shaking his head and still peering angrily around.

'Shut for rebuilding. But I booked it this morning. From the hotel.' The driver stood patiently at his side. 'Bloody receptionist must have cocked it up. Can't have understood. Her mistake,' and still rooted to the spot he mumbled on to himself in dying fall.

'Puri Artha Cottages,' I told the driver, enunciating clearly. We waited.

At last, accepting the inevitable, Pie climbed in. As we jerked over the bumpy ground, the driver making his way round big lumps of concrete and tangled undergrowth, my friend said, 'I brought a woman here once.'

'What?'

'You're not the only one who makes sentimental journeys.'

Now we were back on the main street, turning off, then, on to the familiar route, past the rubbish dump, over the bridge. The school, a white-washed Colonial building. I spotted the fan-shaped palm which adorned the green lawn of a perfect little Dutch villa, bordered by a low garden wall along which a chain looped itself in proud, ceremonial redundancy. The road ran downhill and our driver picked up speed. The night was warm, the small breeze of our motion deliciously refreshing. We were on the long, straight road that led out of town, passing under the wooden painted arch which, more than anything else, resembled a Red Indian totem pole. Here the bushes were filled with pale splashes of blossom.

'Who was she?'

Pie was staring ahead, jowls wobbling inches away, and I thought with a surge of amusement that perhaps – who could tell? – he was musing on his lost love. It was as romantic a conveyance as anyone could hope for, as starry a sky. We could both be visualising a very different thigh from each other's to press against.

'Well?'

'Eh? A whore. Most expensive one for miles around,' he said with simple pride. 'Memorable for drinking only beer. Made her belch like a German.'

We turned down the little lane and into the Puri Artha's flower-filled courtyard. The becak driver looked completely done in; I paid him with two handfuls of the light 100 Rupiah coins which had already accumulated to click in my trouser pockets. The receptionist nodded at me in friendly recognition; forestalling any manoeuvre on Pie's part I asked for two rooms. He never stayed in establishments such as this. I had a fine view of his face as he took in that the room rate was $56 a night and that he would be bearing that cost alone.

The place was built intelligently along three sides of a

square, the traditional way of giving each room natural light and ventilation. The first floor rooms opened on to a verandah, those below straight on to the garden, a little paradise of flowers, shrubs, ponds. From the outside they all looked the same; walking into my room I saw the interiors were identical too. Recognising the red, quilted bedspread, the intricate wooden wall carving, all at once I could not stay in it.

I inquired about getting to Prambanan, went then to find Pie. He sat in the open-air restaurant over a gin and lime, contemplating the menu.

'Not bad,' he said, generously, adding with a kind of gloomy approbation, 'You always were self-indulgent, Ruffey.' He had already ordered a surprising number of dishes which started, now, to arrive and continued to do so as fast as he could demolish them.

'You can get a car to Prambanan,' I offered.

'Seen it,' he said between mouthfuls.

'Borobodur then.'

'Why? Seen it. So've you.'

I stared at his all-too familiar features for a long moment while he chewed on and the repercussions of this remark bounced around in my brain, as though it were a hollow chamber, echoing alarms that had been rung before. It was a measure of the esteem I felt for him – no, call it rather the most cautious respect for his intellect – that I did not believe him capable of making a mistake.

'What makes you think I've seen Borobodur?'

'Haven't you?' He stopped chewing, raised his face. 'Won't ask, then, what you did on honeymoon. Go, if you've not been.'

He reared up suddenly, dropping his fork with a clatter and clapped his hands together.

'Got it.' He showed me the smear on his palms, picked up the fork again.

'Don't you want to see the temples? Aren't you here to dig for bits?'

'Amateurs are not allowed to play. Not even distinguished ones. Your stupidity is astounding. Years of research, Ruffey, painstaking reassembly going on. International experts. I'm on holiday. With you.'

I was appalled at my own naïveté. It had never occurred to me that I would not be able to shake him off at the appropriate moment.

'There are a couple of things I must do,' I said, tonelessly. 'Nothing to trouble you with, but I'll have to go off tomorrow for a couple of days.'

'I'll help,' he said. 'Come along. Think I should.'

We glared at each other.

'No,' I said, bluntly.

'But I insist. Friend in need and so on.'

'Look,' I said, and I was enraged, both at my own stupidity and at his damnable tenacity, 'you can't. You're not necessary, or wanted.'

He shook his head in a mockery of concern.

'Not yourself, Ruffey. You need looking after.'

'Pie,' and I forced myself into a reasonable tone, 'why did you come in the first place? I have to understand. Is it a game of some sort?'

'Don't know. You tell me. You're the sportsman, taker of risks, not me. I like my grandstand seat, no time to waste on participation. But I like to watch the combatants.'

'And I'm one?'

He studied his glass, gazed around – the old bugger was enjoying himself.

'Perhaps. Didn't say that.'

'Deviousness is written all over your ugly mug. Come on, what's the game? You're not here upon a whim, you've got a purpose,' and I said this as lightly as I could, for while I would never plead, equally I could not hope to threaten him. There was no appealing to the better instincts of a man who gloried in not possessing any; he was a philosophical terrorist. There was no bludgeoning that creased, monstrous, Buddha's bulk, that sat unmoved and unmovable in obdurate calm. He swivelled chomping jaws to look upon me in faint, scientific interest.

'Couldn't plan to come, could I? Didn't know you were going.' It was the tone of a man being reasonable in the face of idiocy. 'You know me, I don't lie, Ruffey. Truth is very subjective. I don't know what yours is. I'm answering your questions all right. Perhaps they're the wrong ones. Here as your friend, nothing enigmatic in that. The game's life, Ruffey, trite enough. Don't know if you're a combatant, come to that. Why're you here?'

I wasn't going to answer that; I had a better question ready.

'Have you communicated in any way with John Ridinghouse since he left the University?'

'No.' The jaws continued to rotate; the question didn't surprise him at all.

'Don't you want to know why I'm asking?'

'Obvious. Got some notion about him. Going to tell me?'

'No.'

He gave his head one of those infuriating, ruminative shakes.

'You're the victim of your vices. Curiosity's one of them. And of your virtues mind you. Ridinghouse was a failure, he's of no interest. You are, though you're touchy, stubborn, vain, sentimental. But you have gifts. Wasting time here, Ruffey. Go and make pictures, it's what you're good at. You're too soft, too kind to other people. You squander your time.'

'And you're the ungrateful beneficiary.'

'Didn t say I was ungrateful. I can even praise what happens to benefit me. Praise from the self-interested, such as myself, is what keeps worthy impulses alive in other people. Besides, you don't waste your time with me.'

By this time we had left the table and Pie had thrown himself heavily onto a flowery rattan sofa, sprawling with his head near a little bush of blossoms which seemed, in this light, perfectly artificial. I had now succeeded in destroying my Indonesia altogether. I said to myself sourly that when I came with high expectations, it fell short of them; when I came with none, why, that was what I got. Even the thick tastes of peanut sauce and coconut were false and metallic, the brilliant night marred by the bugs and mosquitoes. I had grown too old. I preferred the flawlessness of memory to the real thing.

Pie called for a bottle of whisky. Alcohol, that necessary lubricant, did its work. It warmed him to loquaciousness, relaxed me to the happy state where I could simultaneously absorb and reject his words. Scarcely one of our adult encounters had managed to do without an infusion of spirits, to raise mine and counter his. And yet I cannot drink as much as I used to, practice in this case making imperfect. There is a measure on my desk here, an antidote to the chill, for the wind gusts in in little draughts which eddy over to my corner. The shuddering of the sash is in competition with my gut, once made of cast iron and lately a prima donna, a rumbling wind bag. An instrument of noisy retribution, the latter an office which my pen performs more adequately and in silence.

Sometimes I think I hear my heart beating. A ridiculous notion, as though it too were executing its own fierce drum-beat of disapproval. No, I cannot at all believe that this is to be the new state of affairs. I think of what I possess that never fails me. It is memory, of course; not so much an instrument of justice, but one of desire.

'You cultivate moods,' Pie said after a while. 'Experience, peaks and troughs. Need it for your work. The myth of artistic passions gets great credibility, but people with great passions aren't artists. Mutually exclusive. Artists try hard, do their best, but it's always contrived. A means to an end. You've got to be clever about it, prune the excess, grow the positive feelings. But you're too helpless. Falling in and out of moods and desires as though they controlled you. Women the prime example. Remember that lazy set you were in after school? So-called Bohemians, corrupted by self-indulgence, that great lanky girl?'

'No,' I said. That didn't stop him; no touch was needed to keep this wheel in perpetual motion. 'Nor,' I added, 'do I want to.'

'Sullen red-head, no dress sense, just an example, Ruffey.'

I knew exactly who he meant. Her name was Gina and she was an elegant giraffe, everything about her elongated and freckly-dappled. Her long narrow feet stuck out of the bed at night and they were icy in the morning. She had bright auburn hair, an exquisite profile; she had been astonishingly good at the rubbery, athletic dances of the time, which she performed perfectly unselfconsciously.

'Pea-brained girl. Thought you were something special. You believed her. She battened on you, you condescended, then you apprehended.' He liked this phrase enough to repeat it. Gina was never sullen, though celebrated for her silences. These sprang, not from stupidity or morbidity, but from the great and literal importance she attached to the meaning of words.

'You did no work until you smashed your leg up. Made you think about something outside yourself. Pain makes good pictures, it's character-forming. Always said so.'

'Bunkum,' I said. 'Besides, what's it got to do with you? Why must you sit in judgment? You're always pushing me to repudiate something I've enjoyed, you're not happy until I denigrate it. You can choose to be solitary, why should I follow suit?'

'Try, Ruffey, to proceed from the particular to the general, and not vice versa.' Far from being offended, Pie grew more affable. 'I've nothing against women. All for sex unmixed with sentiment. Not the point though. You lack a critical faculty. In stating an obvious truth about you, I hardly claim the obverse for myself. Didn't say I was immune to women. My business, that. But for creative people like you it's different. You attract camp followers, hangers-on. You attach too much importance to women to be unselective. Involvement on, work off. Notice that they pick you, not the other way round. But what's your art about? Remaking the past. So you've got to take care with the present. You don't see the woman, you see the idea. A painter's view. Invest them with virtues, moralities, allegories, whatever. Dreams. Makes you vulnerable, that's all.'

'Be precise,' I said. 'What exactly are you trying to say about Annette?'

He drew breath and let it out again in a great exhalation, as people do when dealing with the obtuse. 'Nothing. You decide. Talking about Jean, right? Bad-tempered mechanic's daughter with a head fuddled by turps. Thought you were a genius, more fool her. Admiration's bad for you. Keep telling you it's all too cosy. You've learnt to put up with being half-finished, like most people. But it's not enough. There's more. Cyprus was real, you knew that. You made something of it. I was proud of you. There's pain attached to living well, to doing your own particular best.'

Another drink glugged into the glass and his hand came up and pressed hard against his forehead, as though he had a headache.

'Look, told you this in Dorset. Thirty years ago, remember? What's it all about? The nature of the consciousness that perceives the world. Control. Not truth – that's too much to hope for, but a point of view. What's realism on a canvas – what's truth? Nietzsche knew. The painter paints what he likes and that's going to be the thing he's good at. Ergo, that's what he sees. Style. Did the Impressionists see pink skies and green faces? They saw what they liked, discovered something that looked good on the canvas. When Turner painted fields green, people were shocked. Used to them being brown, right?'

'Constable.'

'Same thing. It's important, that subjective eye that interprets in a new way. Blobs or splashes, colour changes, shapes, all that. When you put that with conviction – no art without faith – that's great art. Each age makes pictures of its philosophical errors, you have the spirit of the age, its values, history, uncertainties, man's subjugation to the notion of what's ideal. Very emotional stuff. But to put all that onto canvas and that piece of innovation – style – takes discipline. Not self-indulgence. The gardener prunes or else the bloody garden chokes. Control, that's what you need. The sharp end of experience, not second-rate admiration.'

He looked at me sharply enough, expectantly. I was yawning.

'Never bloody listen, will you? You could be a great

painter, you bloody fool. Not too late. You always were a stupid sod,' and he rose up abruptly, nearly hitting the table, marched stiffly off through the garden and I heard a splash and a curse.

My final nightcap performed its function too well. I fell asleep on the couch, waking at first light to cramps so intense that my progress to the room was achieved by stumbling hops on dead-wood legs. Then, of course, I couldn't sleep. I remembered that walk in Dorset in drizzling rains punctuated by thunderstorms. Pie even then had lectured me in his philosopher's mumbo-jumbo while claiming that he watered down the deadly intellectual brew for my benefit. He had announced that he would collect pagan art and I had accused him of resembling the cruel, enigmatic Buddhas he had a weakness for and thought that, like Nietzsche, it was a phase that wouldn't last. I grappled, meanwhile, with more serious issues: the forthcoming misery of National Service which Pie, who had been exempted, assured me would offer a kind of Spartan paradise with leisure time for thinking while the body toiled. It was precisely the kind of nasty experience he was always predicting would do me good and which he avoided. There had been, too, the problem of Gina, who, far from being the harpy of his imagination, was troublesome precisely because she was so undemanding. Her expectations were so laughably low that it was a wonder they were so seldom met. If she was on my conscience, it was not because she had ever aspired to that eminent position.

Gina was the sort of girl who was almost proud of her failures. When angry with me, she would shout that her previous boyfriend, one Nigel, had really put her through the mill and I was nothing in comparison with him. Noise, from her, was shocking and occurred only in her extremities of self-abasement for which she would apologise, timidly, later. We had regular discussions during which I told her that I didn't love her, adding for good measure that I couldn't love any girl. It was perfectly true; I loved myself too much to have any spare capacity for a less worthy object. She would nod meekly and agree with me, even prompting more of these painful talks. My problem, then, of the callowest nature, was how to dispose of her while retaining the right to sleep with her when convenient. Her feelings about this were not the issue; I was preoccupied with the unhappy realisation that I would never be a painter, and wanted (and was fit for) nothing else. In the scales of these sorrows, Pie's philosophical mite did not begin to weigh.

And yet, on the train from Dorset back to London, I had suddenly felt the prospect of change, however drastic and undesirable, as exhilarating. I went back to our room and told Gina we shouldn't meet again and that she would have more chance of meeting somebody worthwhile with me out of the way. This nasty little piece of opportunism roused her. She started, at once, to pack, picking out her Susie Cooper bowl, her silver propelling pencil — my meagre gifts — and placing them carefully in the centre of her case. It hadn't occurred to me that she would go at once. In twenty minutes she was ready, pulling on her tam-o'-shanter which hid her beautiful hair, ready to depart precisely as she had arrived nine months before, with the same phlegmatic look of acceptance. I asked her to stay. 'Why?' she said in her expressionless voice. I couldn't say why. I knew she would add it to the litany of appalling misdeeds men had perpetrated against her, that she might boast, later, of me as the worst. I even thought I saw the gleam of some sort of satisfaction in her eye at things having turned out so badly. She shook hands with me and went, with great dignity. I couldn't decide whether she was remarkable or simply stupid.

The time to think came a year later. I was in the military hospital at Akrotiri with a legful of shrapnel courtesy of a group of EOKA guerrillas, kids with weapons, one of whom had a fine seam-bowling technique. Flat on my back in the interminable heat alongside the amputees and the man with half a face gone, I was abrim with self-pity. My leg was puckered and seamed, the calf shrivelled like a walnut. It hurt like hell. Later it would throb painfully all the time; later still came the worst of all, an agonising itch that went on day and night. For no anatomical reason that I could fathom, for the bone was supposedly untouched, it was now an inch shorter than the other. I lurched forwards, pathetically, when I tried to walk. There was physiotherapy. I would swim miles, back in England, when I had been invalided out. They told me I was lucky and I knew, looking at the expanding burial plot, that they were right.

I spent hours at the window. They let me have writing paper and on it grew juxtapositions of trunks and limbs, dark cypresses cutting the sky, the lean man in pyjamas, one redundant leg rolled up and pinned neatly, who leant at the window all day and stared at the recruits sweating in the dust and never spoke. Beneath the serene sky, the island was alive with drama, the conscripts scared to leave the base and with good reason, for the terrorists had penetrated even into that.

The British hadn't realised what kind of man they were dealing with. They took Makarios for a priest, but he was a politician, as the great medieval priests were, every congregation was potentially subversive. Cyprus looked just like Greece; here, too, there were men playing backgammon in little villages, horse-drawn carts, donkeys carrying packs stepping daintily through narrow streets. We didn't understand what Enosis meant for them. They had the passions of martyrs, they were recruited as schoolchildren, ready to die for the cause.

My first experience of death was in one of those narrow streets, where sun and shade were so sharply contrasted and life like that, stilled in a moment. One minute a soldier walking and the next a corpse stretched out on the cobblestones, its back a bloody mess. I wanted to know what his face was like; I didn't know him. We were rushing about, roughly spreadeagling the locals against the walls, shouting and searching, for all the good it did us. If I had been alone, I would have knelt beside him, I would have turned him over gently, both to look and because it wasn't right, to die like that. I would dream of his face, later.

The Cypriots were very brave. A man called Sophocles would strap a bomb to his body and carry it into the governor's residence, calmly placing it under his bed; that was how desperate they were to become. An equally brave man would put the thing on a shovel and carry it out and still it would smash every window in the building. We, raw recruits, knew and cared nothing for courage, for heroism. We hadn't a clue what terrorism was like, before. The attacks were called outrages and we felt them, most literally, as such. A hot, dust-covered kid in army fatigues who earned four bob a day for this would find himself face to face with a mad kid a year or two younger and he would die for that, under that alien sun, he would find his bright blood bubbling up his throat.

Back in England, where they sang, 'Hey, you with the stars in your eyes', conscripts just like us were scrubbing urinals, crying at night, shaving the floors of their quarters with a razor blade to clean them. They were happy, lucky. All of that was safe, simple, desirable. We, in Cyprus, knew that we were abandoned, betrayed. Of course we grew up, we had no choice. I was back in England after ten months of army life which felt like as many years.

Then pictures came churning out with brute force. The loop between my eye and the brush in my hand no longer passed through my stilted self-consciousness; suddenly it had connected to raw nerves. There was nothing contrived or clever about these pictures. Forms surged across the canvas, brilliant with colour, the red of blood, white dust clouds, black skies punctuated by the yellow cones that meant death. They were full of anger and the bizarre truths of the place: the white faces of women taken for questioning seen through the mesh grid around the police station, a blown-off hand in the market in a basket of lemons, a hallful of children flayed mercilessly to teach them that fighting and war were wrong.

I tried to write to Gina, to make amends. The words looked stupid on the page. Intolerable, presumptuous of me to claim, with greenly ripe wisdom, that I had suddenly learnt to appreciate what was good and simple, to like life. I knew that she, so literal-minded, would frown and turn the clumsy phrases over in her mind and look for a different truth in them when I wanted only to say that our time together had not been wasted, after all. Words were not my medium. The O's turned into chains or eyes, caricatures, the L's extended themselves into tiny landscapes, curled into portraits. I write now what cannot be expressed in paint and in a sense what Pie said is true, for paint admits what is vivid and simple and there is no fakery in it, no lies or half-measures. Words are a curious, shifty medium.

Nothing seems real, comprehensible, until I have committed it to canvas. My life is a series of pictures. The picture will come, I feel it forming and yet I resist it with this dam of words, the structure which I feel compelled to build. I shall set everything down, precisely as it occurred, and then when I have written it out of myself, when the house is still, I shall creep to my secret hoard of tubes and brushes, unroll my canvas and let the paint flow.

Morning came at Puri Artha and, abandoning all hope of rest, I went out to the early sweetness of the day. The little stretch of the verandah was the same, the teapot nestled in the same thickly padded basket alongside a neatly quartered lime on a saucer. The frogs croaked in their ornamental pond and the room boys in their brown and blue sarongs padded silently, as before, delicately sweeping frangipani blossoms from the path. I sat for a long time in the early morning sun, sucking in the heat and watching tiny geckos scuttle up the walls, quick motion alternating with endless periods when they, like me, hung absolutely still and let the heat mesmerise them.

I wanted to let myself drift back into this paradise from which I had been so rudely ejected as a child, but I could not rid myself of a tourist's eye. It was no longer my home. I might, once, have chattered in fluent Sundanese with my nursemaid, but now it was as much as I could manage to order a drink. It was always a mistake to return and I had compounded it, doubly perpetrated my error. I listened to the blood throbbing in my veins, let the light build crazy patterns inside my eyelids, my skin scorch and still I would not move. I was a stone, part of the earth, and it was a kind of luxury to know that one small movement would place me in the ease of the shade and that I would not make it. With a mere half hour's exertion I could be packed, on my way back to England, but that half-hour did not exist in this infinity of time.

I could not take possession of Java, own it as I once had, as I owned the past. That at least, however flawed and duplicitous, lay here and was still mine; that and the evidence of my senses the only truth I had. Eyes closed, I remembered the incredibly blue sky, split in two by a palm that from my pram had the height of a skyscraper. I had held onto the colours in the misery of alien England, the purple and ochre and indigo of the markets, my antidote to the grey sago pudding of school, the impossibility of the lessons, the mockery of the other boys. My magic lantern, safe inside my head. It was there still, but when I opened my eyes it was upon a cruel parody. I felt the shade crawl across my face and looked and saw the bulk of Pie, blocking the sun.

'We're going to the market. Got a man outside, come on.'

I followed him.

The market was huge, dim, stuffy, sun-dappled through the gappy straw roof in pointillist spots of bright and shade. We walked past pungent pyramids of small, dried fish, sacks of frazzled black scraps that might have been mushrooms, past a dozen different grades of rice. The smells and the complementary complexity of batik made me dizzy, the little stalls turned into tents with a thousand different patterns were suffocating, they glittered bright with gold thread. Alongside hung rows of little girls' dresses, all nylon, ribbon and stiff net, punishment for the skin of any child unfortunate enough to have parents who could afford such Sunday best. Through it all came the shouts of the boys performing acrobatics at the side, hauling up baskets and boxes onto the roofs of dented buses, building up a wobbly superstructure to the cries of anxious owners below.

I followed Pie, who wove through the elegant forms of the woman shoppers in their carefully wrapped sarongs and tight, short-sleeved blouses. We came into a section full of basketware where the smell of new straw was suffocating, the air whirling with dust motes and chaff, and I, stumbling a little over the small unevennesses of the concrete floor, felt overcome, strangling in that atmosphere, desperate to get into the air. I saw a small stall of brightly coloured bottles and sank gratefully onto the wooden bench, declaring that without refreshment I could not take another step.

'Getting on, Ruffey,' he said and walked towards me, failing to see the high step and tripping against it. He fell headlong, his head smashing against the bench with a most unpleasant crack. I bent down, examined him, saw that he was bleeding and stunned. I took my handkerchief and bound it round his head where it grew large browny-red patches, the same colour as the Coca-Cola which I now hastily gulped down. His head, drained, was white. It took the combined forces of myself, the stall keeper and two young lads to hoist him up and sit him down. His eyes opened, focused, he was all right.

'I'll go now,' I said and I felt my feet pressing hard against the ground as I walked away, out into the sunlight and, not without a certain measure of disbelief, noticed that I continued to walk. With great calm I hailed a becak, asked the driver to take me to the hotel. The whole incident had the sharp clarity and sense of unreality of a dream.

I threw my things into my bag, paid my bill, left and went to find a bus. It was as simple as that. And on the bus, finally, I slept, for all the heat and the impossible state of the roads, falling into that wonderfully refreshing and dreamless state which is so oddly termed the sleep of the just. I slept away the morning, waking with a desperate thirst and the idea that there was something very important I had to remember, something tantalisingly close, to do with sleeping, with discomfort. I closed my eyes, the better to evoke the phenomenon.

It came suddenly. When I first arrived at school, I used to lie awake each night, partly from homesickness and partly from a strange dread of the sleeping noises of the other boys. Each movement they made seemed threatening, their breathing noises as hard to bear as their jibes of the day. I had slept every night of my life with a loving ayah to guard me from the bogeymen both of us feared. She always woke, through some intuitive bond, a second or two before I did and so gave me the security of her watchfulness. The abandonment to unconsciousness seemed impossible without that loving presence. I was what they termed highly strung, though the truth of it was that I was half-mad with loneliness.

For months, then, I barely slept and was heavy-lidded and stupid by day, making more mistakes, drawing upon myself more ridicule. One night, staring around in that delirium of fear that filled the hours of darkness for me, I had seen a strange light at the end of the dorm. I watched for it fearfully, saw it again and finally, when it became unendurable and I saw it even through closed eyes, I got out of bed and padded down after it.

Pie, reading under the bedclothes, suddenly shone the torch — not at me, but under his chin, creating a hideous shining skull in the blackness. It grinned at me for a second and then he shut off the beam.

'Come here Ruffey,' a voice said. The dark was impenetrable, the blackout excluded even the comforting light of the moon. No wonder that I, who had dreamt under bright stars, felt suffocated by it.

With outstretched hands I inched towards him, half knowing that it was only that oddity John Pie, half in terrible fear. I crept, at his bidding, inside the foetid tent and suffered the torchlight in my eyes. That was forbidden. Getting into another boy's bed was the worst of all crimes, though I was too innocent to know why.

He pointed the light down and I saw that he was reading a textbook, where other boys — had they dared — would have been looking at comics. Not understanding, I tried to puzzle it out, to read with him. Suddenly he jabbed a pin in my arm and I would have screamed, had he not had his fat hand ready to cover my mouth.

That was the game. I went to his bed each night and sometimes he would stab me and sometimes not. I never screamed. By day, the fat boy ignored me as he did everyone else; at night he applied this peculiar form of torture, to which I submitted. Fear is character-forming, he said with his funny, little-boy pedantry, and so is pain and you will thank me for this. It is an initiation reserved for the privileged few. If you don't come, he said, I will denounce you to the authorities. Where will you go if they expel you, Ruffey? His owl eyes had examined me closely, hoping for tears.

This had been going on for perhaps a month when he stopped it. You've passed, he said. You may consider yourself a friend. I felt proud and pleased. We never alluded again to the 'trial' and henceforth I was under the protection of his caustic wit and he sheltered by my fists. I was of average size but, when roused, my savage fury and resentment made me unconscious of pain and I would shut my eyes and hammer away until dragged off. In due course provoking Ruffey was not considered worth while. It was some time before I found out why I had been singled out. I was, though it took me yet longer to realise it, his first and last victim.

'You're the sensitive type, Ruffey,' he said. 'The rest are too stupid. Of course it's more difficult for you, but it does make you a more interesting subject for me. You can't hope to be clever, you lack the apparatus, but I think there are prospects for you as an individual.' Individual was his most complimentary word for other people and seldom used.

The bus carried on and I sat wedged between two slender men, each in a check shirt and so close in appearance that they could have been brothers. Both chewed gum, passing the wad deftly from one side of the mouth to the other with a practised flick, cheeks bulging in synchronicity. I could not believe that I had allowed the game to fall out of my mind so completely. The nearer I came to the Hotel Manchuria the further back I cast my mind searching for significant detail and coming, mentally, to rest at last on the felled bulk of the professor.

7

The bus crouched in the middle of the square, the sun sparkling on its bashed tin fenders. I had spent the morning in the café, eyeing first it and then its driver, a man so loth to drum up business that he preferred to keep even the matter of his destination a secret. Daintily, he turned his back while his boy carried out the vulgar work of recruiting passengers.

First the driver circumnavigated his vehicle and carried out a purely ocular inspection, staring for a long time at the bonnet as though he could divine the wonders below. After a while he circled again and kicked pensively at the tyres. Now and then he raised his head to scan the heavens, as though to appeal to a greater power. He hunched his shoulders, half scornfully, and drifted across the square for a Coke. It was delicate, positively tactful, the way he failed to meet my interrogative eye. Later he went and sat where his bus offered shade, man and machine communing. It was the boy who clambered onto the roof, who fixed up boxes of this and baskets of that, who dragged across an over-sized water can.

Recklessly, I had turned my back for the time it took to buy and consume another drink. During these four gulps, it seemed that the moment of departure had arrived. I heard a great roar and turned to see the driver in his seat, heads lining each window, a noxious cloud of black smoke emerging from the exhaust. With a curse I took up my bag and galloped lop-sidedly across the square, seeing which the driver nodded his head, shoulders shaking in delighted recognition. He crunched into first gear, revved up again.

I had a moment to claw myself up into the stuffy and chaotic interior. The boy jumped up behind me. Two men shuffled their bottoms together without looking at me, to make room. We were off and turning away from the glittering highway that came down from Surabaya. This was a cart track. The first sighting of a bicycle caused our beast to rear, to shy, sending the sagging tyres into a deep rut with a violent lurch. The little lad dozed, waking whenever motion ceased; at the first stop I got him to put my bag on top of the bus and thus gained a literal elbow-space. It was his job to strain his sinewy arms and legs with such burdens, his task to find a rock and jam it behind the rear wheel while he fetched the can of water roped on behind. With tentative finger-tips he unscrewed the radiator cap, letting out a great geyser of steam; he would juggle the hot metal, hopping up and down and grinning in mock horror, would make a great business of pouring water in, groaning at the terrible weight and returned each time from these labours of Sisyphus with an air of importance, head cocked to observe the audience reaction. A minute later, he would be asleep.

There were, I thought, certainties. That, for example, the age and condition of the bus would always be in direct proportion to its load and the difficulty of the journey. Ergo, on a rough, scrambly road like this, which laboured up rice fields to mountain passes, down rocky hillsides to makeshift bridges, the bus must be a rusty veteran with an engine all sound and fury, packed high on top and so mightily in a hurry that it was touch and go at every wall, at every bullock cart. That there were only two ways of proceeding. An empty bus would dawdle, soliciting custom. Full, the correct procedure was to hurtle at all possible speed, braking at the last possible moment for stray animals and the like. So we went in dramatic starts and checks, paralleled by my alternate thirsts and pressing needs to pee, the second depending of course on what quantity of fizzy drink I had heedlessly consumed to assuage the first.

The night before I had suffered the losmen in Pare, a lodging-house so tiny, so ill-suited to rest that it was a toss-up which survival was the more remarkable, its own or that of its clientèle. For the first hour of the journey I was body only, each organ and stop complaining in a rantery of bad temper. My arse now, that wind instrument, was sobbing for attention and I raised alternate cheeks by the centimetre available in vain search for relief. Cramps, then, in sudden attacks unfairly pinched both legs at once, the whole syncopated and punctuated by a soft, continual throbbing, the resonating sound of a double bass plucked and re-plucked. My sphincter muscle, first timidly and then more insistently, was pursing itself up in a sour spinster's smile and thus reminding me of its fatal tendency to relax at inappropriate moments. Last night (and sweat beaded at the memory) I had eaten two of those small hot peppers that blast out the inside and roof of the mouth, that manifestation a mere bagatelle – indeed positively a pleasure – compared to the acid burns they inflict upon their exit. There had been some of that already and there was more to come.

Now and then in a sudden spasm of annoyance, I bent

forward, that action pushing out a grunt, wedging my forehead against the dirty plastic of the seat in front. My hand crawled down one leg until my fingers reached the ring of mosquito bites around my ankle, the shackles a legacy from the losmen. With clenched fingers, I attacked them in exquisite paroxysms until they gave up their little trickles of juice, bleeding at last. This pleasure passed, alas, in one orgasmic spurt, the itching starting up again at once.

Discomfort at least stretched out minutes, just as pleasure shortened them. Each minute passed, not in its usual too-rapid flow but purposefully elongated, the pain working as a temporal rubber band. Age blurs and accelerates days into months, years. I saw, in slow motion, the sky repeatedly flashing out between the trees, brilliant as a hypnotist's spinning watch, stared at the threads of silver water against the baby green of young rice and then, in careful detail, fed my eye upon a row of endearingly ill-represented gaping flowers painted in crude, brilliant gloss on the gate of the orchid farm.

The landscape was detailed, varied, bright as a dream one and reminded me of the effects of smoking grass, though I hadn't done so for years. There was a wild, fantastic fall of rock succeeded by a carefully cultivated terrace; a serene figure stood with head bowed. Around the next corner a torrent of water splashed down to the old bridge. I seemed to anticipate what came next and even found myself nodding my head in satisfaction as the film unreeled, frame by window frame. I seemed to measure the passing colours against some internal colorimeter, to compare the shades and sizes with an original. I found myself staring intently, to wrap the whole thing up and carry it away in my head to keep — and simultaneously felt that I had done precisely that before and all of this was a mere echoing of that experience.

This half-dream state lasted all the way to Malang. In five minutes, the bus swayed and creaked and shed its load and then, like a camel, squatted down. I stretched, hearing sharp cracks of joints, the twangings of hitherto unsuspected sinews, and stood, a little stupidly, in the middle of the road looking around me. Unlike the usual High Noon township, Malang was pretty. It meandered along the banks of a river, it ambled and rambled. This riparian paradise had a wonderful Imka, a hotel de luxe and not a YMCA at all, equipped with Western toilets. I spent quite a while in there satisfying my two tyrants, bladder and gut, in the agony and joy of simultaneous evacuation. Since I could not know that the high over-head grille gave, not on to the back alleyway as one would suppose, but on to the main lounge, I made no attempt at all to suppress the natural acoustic accompaniments to such strainings and rushings, but let them echo round the tiles.

I emerged a great deal later, flushed with triumph, to order a beer. I was alone with a pretty Eurasian girl, who looked away and back, who smiled and dimpled, whispering behind her hand in the most charmingly furtive and perfectly redundant way. Did I want to change money? She seemed to offer this convenience as atonement for my solecisms in the other. Saying this, she laughed a lot, as the Chinese do when embarrassed or shocked. I did. The friend she took me to (for it was Sunday and the banks closed) was a stout Chinese jeweller who could have been her father. His dusty glass showcases were filled with gold-plated watches and Chinese good luck symbols, ornaments in green, spotty jade and reddish gold. She walked in front of me, nodded at the shop, waited further along the street, giving the whole transaction an illicit air. The fat man did not smile; he held my American dollars up to the light and looked through them very slowly, one by one. The Rupiah notes he gave me were very dirty and he counted them four times before handing them over. When I had taken them, he nodded several times and then, at last, let his lips curve.

I went back to the Imka, ostensibly for another ice-cold beer, to relish the cold hum of the air-conditioning in the empty space. I was too near my destination to come upon it unprepared. Procrastinating, I sat in thrall to the acoustics to the room, which revealed itself as linked to both kitchen and toilets. A waiter, carefully descending the staircase with a tray of glasses and ice, suddenly saw me looking at him. He wavered, lost his footing and, with a sharp cry and a desperate soft-shoe shuffle, flung the whole trayful up into the air. He fell heavily forwards under a prismatic rain of shards, ice scattered like hailstones; scrambling up, he turned a woe-begone face towards me. I gave him some money, for this had been a perfect thing – poor chap – of its kind. And now, because there was no excuse left, I crunched away and found a little bus to take me to Palang.

From the town centre, where I gazed hopefully at a couple of extravagantly decorated Chinese villas, I was directed along the road. There, beyond the paddy fields, the last dingy, sugar-almond facades gave way to country. The sun would set in an hour and the sky was that clear grey-bluey tint signalling the end of the day, when lengthening shadows give depth and substance to midday's cardboard cut-outs. I trudged past the little houses, saw in the distance the dark cone of Gunung Arjuna, a curving away of the dusty ribbon of the road. The road turned, began to climb, and I entered the deep shade of a banana grove. Screened by this soft web of green, the hotel reared up suddenly in front of me.

Hotel Manchuria was a large house in stone and sickly yellow brick behind a wall set with railings, each sharp spike an outthrust hand holding an iron flame. It was the mansion of a rich man, altogether urban; the kind of house that stands, deep-shuttered and guarding its secrets, behind high walls in the great European cities. It should have rested in the shade of a great mosque or cathedral, the half-open gates should have given on to a boulevard. The riot of vegetation should have been formal, tended by gardeners whose silent labour would be the only indication the house would ever give of life inside.

The building loomed tall, symmetrical, its four storeys stretched up as high as they could. The yellow brick curved in to deep-set ornate windows, curved out into balconies with high doors. Above each door and window a smooth-carved helmeted head thrust itself out of the stone, shadowed eyes staring blindly forth. I looked at the detailing of the window panes, the ivy-fluted pillars winding alongside them, and saw that it was built this century, was early art nouveau. In the centre, a stone arch soared massively to the height of the façade, carrying pane upon pane of dusty glass. At ground level it became a door with massive hinges, the hammered bronze handles two grasping hands.

Long neglect had let the paintwork flake away. The hot, wet air had eaten at the brickwork and rusted metal. The jungle writhed up along the ground-floor windows and crept along them, seeking and finding its sucker holds. Assailed, the house clung obstinately to the alien earth. It plunged its heavy granite into the ground and stood, braced, wrestling elemental forces with an impassive, closed face. The tensions were evident in the cracking of brick ribs, the slipping of a stone spine.

It had spawned a monster child which stood inside the gates, a miniature of itself with long, stone buttresses that trailed against the ground like useless arms. The wooden gates were open. I looked inside and saw a pile of wicker chairs left to rot alongside a black, wheel-less Chevrolet which had been propped up on bricks. In the centre of the path stood an ornamental fountain, its dank pools choked with weeds. Beside the path, which had relinquished half its breadth to undergrowth, lay bags of sand, half-filled paper bags of cement, all mouldering back into the fertile land. There was no sign of life.

The door, twice my height, yielded at last. The chill inside was shocking. I stood in a stairwell built on a monumental scale: thick wooden banisters carved into a design of circles and half-hoops climbed up into the shadows. The same design was repeated in a frieze along the top of wood-panelled walls, sections of the panelling divided by great square uprights which turned out into space at a right angle to the wall and were carved to form smooth, hairless heads, looking down. The sun was at the other side of the house and no ray could penetrate the great wall of glass above the door. All was shadow and stillness.

Ahead, under the second turn of the stairs, were tall double doors, another set lay to my left. The handles of these, an arachnophobe's nightmare, were half a spider's body, each side projecting four black trailing legs which fastened on to the hinges. There was no welcoming gleam of light through their glass, no sound at all. I listened, waited; I felt a negative and repelling force. Each second the darkness gathered. There was a light fitting hanging high, but no switch; I looked back up through the penumbra and all at once recognised the shape of the chandelier, the dull brass globe, the glass shades and now the sense of déjà vu was so strong that I felt almost giddy. I conjured up the thread of a memory, tugged at it; I had it. It was the hall lamp from my maternal grandfather's house in Kuala Lumpur, a house I knew from the cracked sepia prints of my mother's photograph album. This was uncanny, and instinctively I made for the light and half-fell down the marble step. Letting the door bang I heard, behind me, echoes upon echoes in dying fall.

Back I came a minute later and went, without looking up, through the first set of doors, to find myself in an office. It was an improvised affair, with a wide counter across one side and, above it, a thick-meshed wooden frame which looked as though it had been purloined from a bank. There was a small brass bell which I pushed, hearing in the distance the faint buzzing sound of a maddened insect. With some relief, I saw a heavy-duty typewriter with a sheet of paper in it resting on a desk, a standard metal desk with a reassuringly ugly neon strip above it. A perfectly normal, seedy kind of office. Thick velvet curtains were half-closed; I pushed them back and found a window open behind, realised then that the cold, numb atmosphere of the place was endemic. The room did not even boast a fan. Far away I heard the faint tattoo of footsteps. I returned, then, through the doors and waited close to them, heard the sound of skipping.

A young girl, perhaps thirteen or fourteen, pushed through the doors opposite and stopped, gravely, to examine me. She was a Eurasian with beautiful, liquid Javanese eyes and long, mid-brown hair, dressed in what looked like a school uniform of brown skirt and jumper, white blouse.

'Come,' said the little apparition and she laid her little paw upon my sleeve in a friendly manner. She smiled and two dimples appeared. Her skin was a delicate café-au-lait and the gold-flecked eyes, matching her sweater, something between dark amber and Van Dyck brown. I smiled back. I had, I saw, been expecting Lon Chaney or Vincent Price, in full pantomime fang and fig.

'Good evening,' and back came the echo. 'Good evening.'
'Do you have a room?'

'Have a room.'

She giggled. It was a good game. She pointed and together we went into the office, examined a row of enormously heavy keys and saw that all were present. She went over to the desk and fetched a form for me to fill in, hanging over to watch in schoolgirl fashion and chewing an already splintered pencil.

'English,' she said. Her soft round cheek was inches from mine.

'You've got another English guest,' I said, with a great show of confidence as of teeth. 'Mr Ridinghouse. John. A friend of mine.'

She nodded, unsmiling, whether in politeness or assent I could not tell.

'Is he in at the moment?' I said with great care, pronouncing each word with exaggerated emphasis.

'He out,' she said. I could have kissed her. It was as simple as that – for I had not dared to compute the exact odds against his being here, had not wanted to lessen the faint chance by any pre-emptive thought.

She pointed to the sum demanded for a night's stay and I paid, receiving in return a key attached to a piece of wood. Guests at Hotel Manchuria paid in advance. This system had been instituted for good precautionary reasons, for they alone slept on the premises. The melancholy man who owned the place, his delicious little gazelle of a daughter, the woman who cleaned the floors and the old fellow who shambled about – all of them went off to the village at night, returning at first light.

'Come,' said the châtelaine, attaching a bunch of keys to her belt where they jangled importantly. She led me through the spider doors, skipped ahead to pirouette lightly, waving an airy hand. 'Sitting-room.' Her white teeth gleamed against honey-coloured skin.

Four high-backed chairs in a stiff row denoted that obvious function; they and a small table were all the furniture this cavernous space possessed. The floor was teak, the walls part-lined in this heavy, costly material. Carved panels of it curved into the massive window embrasures, another reared up to form a mantelpiece twelve feet high with a pattern of domes and minarets, a whole Byzantine cityscape, cut along the top. The hearth below was framed by one great piece of white marble. Its smooth expanse had two sculptured nude figures emerging from it, male and female, their heads and shoulders growing out of the material and craning towards each other, hands touching at the centre. I imagined flames flickering to light the cold stone, the long thin fingers, grazing, both passionate and surreal. It was a winter room, a fireplace to roast an ox in. Seeing through the window Gunung Arjuna outlined against a tropical sunset, I felt the utter strangeness of it.

I kept close to the little girl, followed her warmth to the adjoining, smaller room, also panelled, empty but for a little shrine. A statue of Buddha was draped in red and orange, incense gave off its musty, aromatic odour beside a vase of fading flowers.

'Come.' She patted my arm. Her grubby little feet in sandals shifted about; she balanced lightly, splaying her toes and then wiggling them bashfully when I spoke. I found my voice.

'Your English is excellent,' I said, politely, and then because she hadn't understood, 'English – very – good,' and she echoed these words with another flash of perfect little teeth. She cast her eyes down; she was thinking hard. What a beauty she was. When, for an instant, she was immobile as now, her face had the most exquisite, delicate curves of mouth, of chin, nose, all sculpted out of one piece of flawless material. I watched her, absorbed this momentary transformation into the woman she would become, the face that would exercise a magnetic appeal. She looked up, threw her arms wide, was a child again.

'English nice,' she said firmly. 'Take big room.'

We went back to the hallway, through a door to the right of the stairs.

'Dining room.'

I peered through and saw my head appear in the great mirror which reflected a plain wooden table, half a dozen of the same chairs.

'No food,' she said disarmingly.

The walls of the house were ridiculously thick, even the internal ones built to withstand a siege. Everything was on a monumental scale: rooms too large, ceilings too high. It was a house for giants. Even the stair risers were too wide, too deep for comfort. I followed the delicate figure of my guide up the staircase, holding on to the wide banister which, once polished to a high gloss, was now dull and slightly clammy. Up and round the great space we went to the second floor and she pointed ahead. In the near darkness above us, I saw that a dome spanned the stairwell. When, at last, she turned on the lights, three dim bulbs which burned with a fuzzy halo in the gloom, I made out faded gold stars painted on to dark, flaking blue high above, recognised the aurora borealis of a distant, Northern sky.

My room, lying to the front of the house, was the size of the dining room two stories below, similarly half-panelled and chilly.

A double bed stood alongside a single one, both with their Dutch wives placed carefully down the centre, the unyielding bolsters stuffed with straw. I sat down on the blue nylon sheets and felt that they were damp. She left me there, having, with a flourish, turned on the single dim lamp which threw long shadows into the corners. I heard myself breathing heavily. There were two hard chairs; a mahogany dressing table with a splotched, circular mirror above, its circumference inlaid with marquetry stars that were now peeling; curtains across two sets of balcony doors on a brass rail, slightly askew.

I stood to survey the perimeter, heard my footsteps echo across. I ran my hand over the wall and felt the dampness of the wood, the tiny bumps and ridges hidden in the grain that, as yet invisible, were the work of worms inching past, of water trickling. The rot and decay lay a fingernail's thickness below the surface. Tiny creatures bored and writhed behind the varnish, pushing through tiny crevices that, growing larger, would admit the burrowings and scurryings of ever larger beasts. The great structure hid a secret honeycomb of teeming life. I thought that at dead of night I would hear rodents gnawing, I visualised the sleek black bodies tunnelling through the wainscotting to erupt forth, a red-eyed flood.

This was no good. I went to look around the door in the corner, found myself approaching it on tiptoe. A bathroom of ancient design, the bath a deep, mottled marble basin which gave off a terrible chill. A jug of cold water stood on the floor. That and the walls seemed to have been hewn in one piece from some dark primeval stone, partnered by a basin in the same material. There were no plugs to stop the central black voids.

'Here's a place to murder a man in,' I said loudly and my voice echoed and did not sound jocular. In the absolute silence, I heard the tiny clicks and buzzings of my head. Blood could gurgle down here, water be thrown after it, and who would notice or care in the morning, if the ground under the foliage was rust-red, where the overflow dripped, if the room smelt of the sour sweat of fear, if it reeked of carnage?

For Christ's sake. I backed away, sat on the chair with my back to the wall. It was not possible to be comfortable in this room. It wasn't that it was squalid — I had slept and eaten and made love in a dozen places far worse than this. The room held a presence which listened, which watched me. I felt as if I had been alone in it for a hundred desolate years These were not thoughts a reasonable man would want to sustain for any time; I needed quite urgently to find another human being.

I went to pick up my bag which, quite irrationally, I would not have left unattended at any price. Passing the mirror, I glanced into it. My father stood there, looking back at me. Paralysed for an instant, I closed my eyes, opened them again and back stared the anxious face of Ruffey, Edward not Jack, though the resemblance was increased by the bloom on the glass which made the dome of my head cloudily hirsute. I walked away, as I had just done, returned with the same sidelong glance. Again I saw myself. I knew that I had seen Jack, my father.

Leaning, heavily, against the wall, I tried to conjure up his image in the flawed surface, to recapture his faintly knowing expression. Of course he had come here, in the last decades of Dutch rule, when Chinese and Javanese trade was at its peak of prosperity, when its masters escaped the heat of Surabaya in the East Javanese highlands. He must have ridden down that tortuous track before there was a daily bus service and it had seemed important to him to absorb every detail, to scrutinise each landmark. Jack Ruffey, the recorder of evanescent moments of glory, had taken it all in and impressed it on to the Ruffey cortex. He had come to this house, the most extraordinary of the mansions built and it had both disturbed and impressed him. Certainly it had affected him;

entering, he had seen the chandelier, just as I had, and it had given him a little shock of recognition, a slightly guilty frisson. I wondered if he had come to trade or as a guest; if he had warmed himself at the great fire in the marble surround and talked knowledgeably of hunting. Perhaps they still rode out to shoot tigers in those days, in the foothills of volcanoes.

I waited, trying to empty my head, waited for his memories to channel themselves down the conduit that had so remarkably opened. I strained for it, but nothing came. I have never been a superstitious man, never had any truck with the supernatural, but I did not doubt the truth of what I had seen, of what I felt in that place.

Downstairs in the office the girl leant easily against the shoulder of the proprietor with an affection so demonstrative, a resemblance so marked, that I guessed that he must be her father. He was perhaps fifty, blue-eyed with close-cropped greying hair that had been blond, the slanting planes of his cheekbones echoed in her elegant, feline ones. His arm was around her and she nuzzled at him. Her colouring, transmuted through amber, came from him as did her thoughtful expression, but her grace was native, as Javanese as her mother. He was of medium height, broad with powerful, sloping shoulders and large, nervous hands which moved to touch her hair, to inch along a piece of paper, to tug at a trouser leg. I said good evening. All the keys bar mine still hung on their hooks.

'Good evening, welcome. My name is Leino, Peter. Come, I will take you to the bar. You will not say no to a drink?'

'I'd like nothing better,' I said, with perfect truth, hearing through his clipped tones the faint singsong of a Dutch or Scandinavian cadence. He folded up a piece of paper and put it in his pocket, beckoned to me to follow. He had a long torso, short slightly bandy legs: the build of a farmer.

In the sitting room he reached up, moved a lever hidden above the panelling, watched my face as two panels swung out to reveal a hidden bar built into the wall. It was a curiosity, a sparkling little hidey-hole in glass and chrome equipped with a small bar top and two high, chrome stools, the brightest lighting I'd seen in the place, which turned itself on automatically as the doors opened.

'Come,' he said, patting a stool. 'You will see, I have something good for you, to remind you of home. You visit Palang? Somebody has told you about the hotel?' While he spoke, the good and worthy man drew a bottle of Johnny Walker Black Label from the corner. Opening this, which had every appearance of being the real thing, he poured us both a generous slug.

'Thank you, wonderful,' I said with genuine gratitude. 'I know a guest of yours, John Ridinghouse. I was passing and knew he was here. He's out, I presume he will return later?'

'Prost, or cheers, Mr Ruffey,' and he smiled wrily at my face. 'It is not so hard for me to learn the names of guests. Yes, he will be back. He goes for his evening meal to Palang. We do not have food here in the evenings but we can make you something. A little snack, it is not a problem.'

'Thank you, that would be kind.' The whisky and the company, both so welcome, warmed me to a little speech.

'The bar is splendid,' I said. 'The whole place is extraordinary. I've never come across anything quite like it. You must get all kinds of people here. Film crews and so on. It's a splendid set. In fact I'm surprised I'd not heard of it sooner.'

'Thank you, yes, of course, the films,' he said, not as though it were true, more in recognition of a kind thought. He smiled, ruefully. He had sad eyes and the smile did not reach them. 'I am not yet thinking of the films you know,' he said. 'Cheers,' and more of the nectar went down sharpish. His cheeks, close up, were not healthily ruddy but full of broken veins. He refilled again; he was a systematic drinker.

'What's the history of the place, Mr Leino? I think my father stayed here, in the thirties or forties. Many years ago. Was it an hotel then?'

'Call me Peter, please. I have a name which is very difficult, for the Indonesians. So I am calling myself Peter, it is easy. I am from Finland,' and he nodded satisfaction at my look of surprise.

'You are thinking, what is a Finn doing in Java? And what is a Hotel Manchuria doing here? That is also a question, yes? We found each other, the two foreigners, a long time ago. It is a big romance for me, this hotel. I fell in love with her and she for me. There is another lady, living near, such jealousy between the ladies is always happening, no? They fight it out, but I won. So I am a lucky man with two wives, one for day and one for night. So there is no reason for me to go back to Europe, and so I stay.'

He refilled the glasses promptly. I knew which wife would get him in the end.

'One wife is enough for me,' I said and we both gave a polite chuckle. As soon as his smile faded, his face took on its habitual worried expression.

'And the little girl is your daughter?'

'Wait, please.' He held up a hand. 'First you are wanting to know the history of the place.' He emptied his glass, fidgeted with it, spinning it around.

'Now it is a special story my hotel,' he said. 'A very romantic story. Also sad.' He didn't hurry, he would not abridge. I was beginning to understand him. Everything was rehearsed and there was no interrupting him; he would answer my questions just as soon as he got through his little set piece. All the time, now, his hand moved, carrying out a continual programme of rummagings and twitchings, the glass refilled with indecent haste, the drink not relaxing him but making him more tense. His voice, emerging at its own leisurely pace, began to take on a disembodied quality. It seemed to come, not from him — for I avoided looking at him, there was something pitiable and slightly crazy in his constant motions — but from the great empty room behind which I saw reflected in the mirrors. The room itself crept away, seemed to expand distantly out and backwards, to grow more cavernous and we humans were tiny in it, clinging to each other for the light and the warmth of the whisky.

'A man from the North built this house for his wife. Not a Finn, no, he was a Russian, a White Russian and a romantic man. It was his dream to bring together the East and the West. He went to Europe before the war as the sons of the rich Russians did, to travel and to learn. But he did not go back. He came to the East and then he fell in love with Java and stayed on, and I think he imagined to go home one day but not yet. We all think this way, not yet. Then he fell in love with a girl, a very beautiful girl from a rich family from the old Mataram dynasty in Yogyakarta. That is, you know, the last real kings of Java. She was a Muslim of course. Her father did not want this marriage and she ran away then and they married. He built this house for her, it was his inheritance and he even became a follower of Mahomet. There was nothing he would not do for this girl. He began the house in 1912, then by the time it was finished it was 1917 and then Russia was finished for him. He could not go back, now he had to be an exile, he would never see his father again, the whole family died in the Revolution. Perhaps he knew something. You see Mr Ruffey, this house is a Russian house in reality, it is his memory of his father's house in Moscow. There was a famous architect, a man called Shekhtel, who built his father a wonderful house all art nouveau. And the young Russian remembered his father's house and designed this the same and he made here his little Russia but with a mosque and with everything to make his wife feel happy, his Muslim wife, even you see the bar is hidden away because he did not drink. You know, it happens often like that, that the adopter of the religion – the convert – is very holy afterwards. But really I think the religion was his wife.

'Well it is difficult because of course the Dutch did not approve a marriage like this and she, the wife, was clever. You know the women in Java are very free, no veil, they run the markets and the land, everything' (and he made, here, a little grimace of the traditional variety and poured himself another great slug). 'The wife was very beautiful. I have a picture of her, light skin colour and lovely, but still a Javanese dressed in European clothes that were looking a little funny. She wanted, I think, to be also European, she wanted the high life. Because, you know Mr Ruffey, in those years there was plenty of money and trade was good and all over the world there were new things, films and cars and music and the dances and the whole new age, and she wanted it. Because she could not be any more the traditional Muslim wife. So he brought here a car for her, he brought in everything, marble from Italy, everything the finest and he invited many many people. You have to imagine the house was full of life of people and parties and music. But then she wanted to go to Europe and he would not go. This was too small for her, but he would not go back, because there was nothing for him that mattered without a Russia to go to, here was his home. It was very sad, the knowing that you cannot ever go home. I think also he knew that even in this new free age, it was still not easy for a Javanese woman married to a white man, because the Dutch would not visit, no, the old Dutch guys they were very stiff. They had no children, that was good. For the children it was very hard, always, they do not belong here, they do not belong there, where should they be? Even today, some things they are always the same. Who wants a fifty-fifty? So things were not good and became a little wild. The people who came here are not always proper, not the wives but the young men and the loose ladies and the travellers and all the funny interesting people, they all flirt and the Russian did not like it but what can he do? Poor man, the wife did not want to be here with him all alone. Then of course come the money problems because they spent and spent and there was no more money coming from Russia, it was all finished.'

He gave a deep sigh. He was folding and refolding the piece of paper from his pocket, opening and then closing it and now wrapping it round his fingers, a continual motion which was automatic, for he did not look at what he did. I saw that the paper was covered with tiny sums.

'So in the end it went bad. The wife left him. She ran away in 1932. She was forty by then, quite old but still beautiful. She ran away with a European man who said he will take her to Europe, but this man left her somewhere and the husband went to take her home and she would not go. Nobody knows what happened next but I think perhaps she was a prostitute. So the Russian came back on his own. He went crazy, I think, he would not let in anybody. All alone here, every day, locked in. Not even the servants. All the people of Palang they work in the great houses, everybody knew all about the stories. In the end he died of a broken heart this man, alone here, quite quickly I think. Some people say he was starving to death. It was very sad and romantic. My wife she tells the stories – her family always was working here, in the house. So some weeks pass and the people were breaking in here and they found him lying in the hallway. He was staring up at the sky up above, the painted sky, quite dead. And then this one owns the house and that one and then one day came another man from the North to see the place. I was in those days thirty-five, not so young, but still travelling. So I came to stay, it was already a hotel.'

'And you decided to buy it?' He frowned.

I had been too quick to fill a purely theatrical pause.

'Yes, but not so quickly, not so simple. At first I was wanting to stay a little and then go home and then I found I do not want to go. It has, you know, a special atmosphere. Then when I met my wife here she did not want it, no. She told me many bad stories, she was making up bad things to make me give it up. But I could not go away. Always I thought about this sad Russian. You know I think sometimes I am like him. I dream about Russia sometimes, it is funny, no? And he never forgot his childhood and all the things lost for always and so it was his dream. I could understand it, the way he made the house so beautiful. I, who do not have a rich father, I had to go away to work and then come back. My wife was not pleased. Wives are all the same, no, Mr Ruffey?'

He was squeezing the piece of paper, the crumpled ball squashed ever tighter. Silently, the little girl materialised in the mirror. She slipped into the space beside him and began, very gently, to stroke his hand.

'All the same,' I said. I watched her and she looked only at her father, the great eyes travelling between his face and the hand with a solemn look, her hand stroking, stroking.

'So,' Peter Leino said, 'perhaps I am also a little bit a romantic, no? I am making my dream. Everybody comes here and says like you that it is a jewel. What do you call, a gem?'

I nodded. Gradually, he was losing his set expression and the knuckles turned from white back to red and still she went on stroking his hand.

'This pretty girl is your daughter?'

'Yes, yes,' impatiently, for I had pre-empted him again. He made an effort; he drained and then refilled the glass of good cheer.

'Please, Mr Ruffey, you will tell me what you think. All the people say don't change it Peter. Of course, why should I want to change? Everything will stay. But I say to them as I say to you, it is very nice but it is also a commerce. I have to make a swimming pool and a good restaurant, I have to repair and make modern the bathrooms. People expect these things. It is a house of fantasy, I will not change the dream, but a pool, why should it spoil it? I say no. But we must have more customers and to change costs a lot of money and I worry that I am losing then the old guests who say, if you change, then we will not come. How can I make debts if the people will not come? So, what do you say, Mr Ruffey?'

Adroitly, the girl drew out the calculations of despair.

His hand lay perfectly still, at last, as though hypnotised. Her face, turned up to his, held an expression of the utmost tenderness and sweetness.

'Well? You are not going to call me a commercialist, I hope?' The tone was jovial, but his look, fixed upon me, was intent.

'Certainly not. Of course you must improve, modernise a little, don't listen to them.'

'Yes, you are right. I will modernise very carefully. With love. Then we will have the buses with the tourists stopping here.'

He sucked down the whisky; he had, in this time, drunk over half the bottle.

'It will be splendid,' I said, and my eyes met those of the

girl, her intelligent, gratified look which thanked me for whatever it was I had said.

'Yes, dancing at the pool. High society. I think it will all be as the good old days, if they will understand I think they will let me.'

'Of course they will let you.' He gave me a curious sharp look and then drew the girl near in an affectionate gesture. She never took her eyes from his face and I noticed, now, how her lips framed some of his words, as though she was learning them by rote.

'Now I will get you a little snack, no?'

'Please, that would be wonderful.'

The pair of them went off. He was still steady. Behind his back she sent me a look of young, grave wisdom. The way they leant upon each other was the saddest thing in the world. And, as they left, so the room darkened, and drew itself out yet further so that I leant, quite involuntarily, further in to the brightness. I saw that the glass shelves were cracked, the chrome chipped, that the lampshades were filled with a tidemark of frazzled insects.

The silence coiled thickly, a spring held by a giant hand. The walls absorbed the jungle noise, the splutter of traffic, they sucked in sound as they did the heat and annulled both. I swallowed and the sound was loud inside my head. It seemed an age, but was perhaps ten minutes, before his footsteps echoed through to me. There was chicken, he said, and rice. I asked if Mr Ridinghouse generally returned late.

'Oh no. There is not yet a night club,' and he gave me his most melancholy smile. Punctiliously, he escorted me to the dining table, leant over it to offer a beer. A leg from the scrawniest of chickens that had ever scratched out a roadside existence lay before me on a small brown cushion of rice. The plate was warm, but it had the air of something that had stood a week. I attacked it without enthusiasm. I was pleased when, returning, he offered his company, sat next to me and opened two beer bottles.

'Food I will improve,' he said apologetically. 'So much to do, sometimes I can do nothing even to begin. An Indonesian now, he would throw all away quick-quick and build up the new. International style,' I nodded; he took full advantage of the unconscionable time it took to subdue and throttle down each mouthful.

'Perhaps I am wrong. Perhaps I do not know what is right for this country. I think Europeans have understanding of these things. You, Mr Ruffey, a man of culture, you can understand. Mr Ridinghouse, an Angelo-Saxon type' (he was proud of that word, pronoucing it with one extra syllable) 'he is a little more of a Finn, underneath. Not a funny Javanese Finn like me but a quiet one, also a romantic. I asked him my question, as I say to everyone that comes, what I shall do. He was surprised that I ask. "How can I tell you what you already know?" he said to me. He was laughing. He said, you know you cannot be an idealist and a hotel keeper also. And I said why not? Then he said dreams are for the night time, not for the day. "But here," he said, "destinies are accomplished. You will see. It is all planned, it is a question of time. History will repeat itself, that is its purpose".' He repeated the last phrase again wonderingly — but I was straining to hear what sounded like footsteps in the hallway.

'Do you understand that, Mr Ruffey?'

I shook my head, temporarily gagged.

'But it is wonderful, the affinities between the peoples. In the language you see it,' and the footsteps became distinct, came nearer. I put down my knife and fork, a gesture he mistook for interest.

'Take, for example, the Finno-Ugrian language. It is used

by nearly thirty million people.' The footsteps began to climb the stairs. I rose. He held up a brown-freckled hand.

'Just a moment please. I do not think —' but I had heard enough and said, 'Excuse me,' hearing a thick, angry note in my voice. At the door I paused, heard the steps ascend the stairs above and so I followed as fast as I could, hearing in echo of my uneven footfalls a purposeful ascent, a man's tread, a storey, more, ahead of me. I hoisted myself, panting, to the second floor. Silence. At the end of the corridor, a door stood ajar. A long triangle of light lay, a dense yellow, upon the floor. I went towards it and it seemed to me that the light, far from issuing from the door, led to it and insinuated itself like a wedge into the crack.

A laugh trilled in the silence: a woman's laugh. Two voices, then, making a silvery reedy sound, the trills and chirrups of a conversation between nightingales and then a high-pitched bubbling squeak, like a woman's false laugh and then, after a short silence, more babbling. It was not language at all. It was the sound a couple of clever birds might have made, imitating humans.

I stood still, cocking my head to hear better and all at once the sound swelled, seemed to echo, sweetly in my head, round and round. The hairs of my entire body stood up, even the hair on my head rose and I could not move. I was fastened in place with icy shackles that stuck to the skin and, running down from my legs, pierced the floor. There was a swirling around me, I smelt a faint, powdery scent and then it was over and everything was normal again and there was Ruffey standing in a gloomy corridor in an odd, frozen posture, so tensed up that at the first step I nearly fell over. My knees had locked; it took a moment for them to obey me.

I went up to the door, knocked, heard nothing. I pushed it open slowly, letting the light spill over me. Slowly, I edged my good foot over the threshold and, not wishing to go any further, examined the room, left to right, up and down, until there was no centimetre I had not scrutinised. A desk with a book upon it, twin beds, three unmemorable chairs, the great height lit by a number of lamps, their weak wattage combining to create the effect of one decent bulb. I edged in. In the wardrobe hung a jacket; in the chest of drawers I found two shirts, two pairs of underpants. The book, a black notebook, empty; the bathroom a replica of mine, empty. I noted all of this as I had been taught, long ago, to remember surface patterns, to notice colour, brush strokes. Detail could obscure the importance of a picture and so I stood back, looked again from the doorway with the idea that I was missing the obvious. And yet there was nothing to see, no trace of personality, no inference to be drawn.

And then I heard the footsteps again and I followed, went up another flight. Here was a kind of sitting room big enough to hold two billiards tables, dim and shadowy with balconies looking to three points of the compass.

Another large, dim room lay to the other side of the stairwell. Nobody there. Now, returning, I saw that from here a narrow staircase wound up the side of the dome and I went up it, slowly and quietly, past little doors which must have been servants' quarters, the size indicative of the status of their former inhabitants, and then I was out in the warm wet air and found myself on a metal balustrade, surveying the roof, standing the height of a man above it.

I gulped in the air, which was delicious with the smell of greenery and soil, the humid oppressiveness that signals the approach of a storm. I had swum up through the musty smell of a place lost in another time and, breaking surface, now filled my lungs with the raw, live night. I went down a little metal staircase. The large flat area was lit by a series of flares around its perimeter. Looking closer I saw that a number of shrines had been set against the parapet, that the flares were little fires lit in front of the painted plaster figures, the flames flickering sooty orange.

The distant sky had cracked open, yellow fissures streaked down between dark clouds, but the sky above me was still clear, the moonlight and flames throwing an almost phosphorescent light. I began to walk around the edge, half looking at the figures, their crudely painted faces grimacing at me, half at the view. Meanwhile, though clearly the place was deserted, I kept an eye open for anybody who might be up here. It was so high up from the ground that I seemed to stand miles up in the air above the mountain. The road below rushed past the toy houses. Ahead, I saw how the land beyond it stretched flat, with nothing to distinguish it for mile upon mile.

Now the cracks in the sky were narrowing, turning a clear violet and fine threads flashed distantly across the sky near Gunung Arjuna. I heard the rumble of thunder and felt the electricity in the air.

Returning to my starting point, I saw that the steps continued up and around the exterior of the little dome, which was covered in a kind of dark bitumen. There was a little platform further along, then the steps curved up to the summit in such a way that they could not be seen from roof level. On the far side, away from the door I had come through, a wooden lean-to stood empty.

It seemed to me that the little shrines were all angled towards this dome; it was becoming hard to tell, for the wind was rising and the wet air tore at the flames, now tangerine-coloured and raggedy, threatening to extinguish them completely. I climbed to the balustrade, tested the first metal rung and found it sound. Holding tight to the handrail in this uncertain near-darkness, a little fearful of losing my footing, I went up. At the platform I paused to view the approaching storm which now rumbled ominously and which, in bright flashes, lit up the whole sky to my left with brilliant streaks which, fading, left red scratches across the retina.

Another careful step and another. A piece of the cupola had been cut away at the summit to make a small shallow dais; in the centre of this, facing the volcano, was a large squat figure sitting cross-legged. A Buddha, the master figure to which the smaller ones paid their obeisance. Peter Leino, like his distant predecessor, had adopted the faith of his wife. I thought it apposite that he, too, had sought to make his mark upon the place. I went nearer to look, for it was curiously hooded. Straining my eyes against the lurid background, it seemed to me that it moved. I stood still, one hand on the railing, the other clenched in readiness. You old fool, I thought, you're past it, you're already breathless and listen to the way your heart is pounding.

The great bulk rose and turned slowly towards me. John Pie gave no start of recognition. He hurried to the steps and I, barring his path, stared at him. He had a blanket over his head; I saw in the next flare a jagged mark on his forehead. It gave me pleasure.

'Can't you see the storm? Let me by Ruffey, you fool,' he roared against the wind.

'Where's Ridinghouse?' I didn't move.

'I don't know. Let me pass,' and he made to push by me but I held firm, braced against the railing, taller than he was and fitter and ready to use force as he, arms holding the shawl like an old woman, was not. He looked, not at me, but over my shoulder at the lights flashing on the volcano, and I remembered that Pie was terrified of lightning and thunder.

'You knew he was here, you bastard. Why didn't you tell me?'

A hollow booming bang rang out then and at once huge drops of rain began to fall, a cascade soaking us both, plastering long strands of hair over his eyes and he pulled the blanket up and worried at my arm like a terrier.

'You shouldn't have come up,' I said viciously and repelled him, pushing hard at his soft, spongy mass; still his face was turned up, it shone livid in the next flash and I saw him recoil as the thunder came almost instantly and he seemed to cringe before it.

'Let me by for Christ's sake,' and I roared back:

'Why did you come here? I won't let you down until you tell.' The noise of the rain was tremendous, deadening all sound.

'Aversion therapy,' he shouted back in wilful misunderstanding and I advanced upon him and he retreated, his face darting round and he saw, as I did, how the lightning split the sky in great sheets. Now he made a dash round for the steps, but was not quick enough. He stumbled, then, loth in his fear to touch the handrail, now holding it and letting go as another clap of thunder sounded. I took hold of his shoulders and shouted in his ear.

'You knew he was here. Set me up. Planned it, now tell me,' and I shook him, hard, and he sagged back against the railings. 'Tell me, hurry, everything.'

'You're wrong, all wrong, let me down and I'll tell you,' he bellowed, and then he looked at me and in a sudden access of strength threw me off, rushed to the other side, heaved one leg over the railing and peered down as though to jump. I caught him and, throwing both hands round his waist hoisted up all his bulk, pulled in one great exertion and he fell, limply, back. I sat on his chest, pinned him down and laughed, like a maniac into the rain. (I had a vision of how, in a Dorset field, he had run in panic-stricken circles, alternately sheltering under a tree and leaving it for the forty minutes' duration of a thunderstorm which had been an infant in comparison to this.)

He opened his mouth but I heard nothing for there was another crash; water fell into the black cavern and I watched it with interest and, moving a little, sat down more firmly, feeling the sack of flesh expand and contract rapidly as he fought for breath. I bent down to hear him.

'Please,' he said, 'Trust me.' He appealed to the better nature he had always so confidently assumed I possessed, and did not find it. Our faces were inches apart and I knew that on mine sat the strength and cruelty of a god.

'You're the only human being I trust.'

'I'll tie you to this bloody thing and leave you here all night,' I said. His face was a mask of despair, a bleak, rain-washed thing, his limbs now twitching in crude spasms of fear and still, somehow, he held on.

'All be all right,' he said, his hot breath against my ear. 'Better not to ask, to know. Mistake. You're so susceptible, didn't know, trust me, better not to ask.'

'What mistake?' I pushed down with all my weight and he struggled, unavailingly, against it.

'All right, knew he was here. Didn't tell. Go home. Nothing for you here, Ruffey, it was a joke. A joke that misfired, harmless. A bet.'

'What bet?' But he was looking, not at me, but at the sky and I thought for an instant that he was going to pass out and started to shake him. 'You don't know when it'll come, do you? It's like the pin, your fucking pin,' and I was bellowing at him as the storm rolled magnificently over us and his eyes stared up so intently past me, with such wide-open fear, that

I could not help craning back myself. I saw it all happen in slow motion, like a dance in the air.

The flash and bang came simultaneously and for that split second I was blinded, deafened, then I felt myself lifted into the air. Pieces of masonry were flying in all directions, pieces of cement, all brilliantly lit and sharp and I saw a smiling Buddha glide by in a graceful parabola which seemed to take forever before it fell, and nevertheless it was all so fast that there was nothing that could be done and I had no way of saving myself. I was falling, then, and saw ten yards away in the strobe flashes of the lightning a magnificent sunburst of pieces of stone exploding out slowly. I had time, even, to wonder what happened to a man – though I could not see him – when the thing he feared most came to pass. I could even console myself with the notion that it must be worse for him than for me and then I connected to something hard and there was no pain, merely another flash of brightness and then nothing.

*   *   *

This was blackness, not as the void is black, not absence, but presence.

Her back was turned, heat streaming out. I felt it from two inches away. I had my eyes closed, but I knew that she was smiling. I could sense the way her cheek curved. I read her mind. Through the dark I felt her thoughts and knew she was happy and so was I. I knew that in another minute she'd turn and touch my face, my hair. Yellow hair, angel's hair, she called it. The whole day I stalked her. I always knew where she was. I tracked her by her spoor, her scent. That was a game we played, my finding her. I found her now, gently I stroked her back and she moved, supple like a snake, wiggling back against me. She knew a thousand ways to pleasure a man, yet every touch was delicate, new. The bloody bed creaked, she tensed up straight away. Neither of us moved for a long minute and then she relaxed again. It was exciting, the danger, the fear of being caught. We increased our pleasure with it and now I touched her with great care, as I'd touch a chick, and she was getting bolder, she moved her legs and stretched out and made the faintest little sound, an almost giggle.

Her skin was fine, very fine and soft. We were different species, she was centuries more evolved than me. It changed texture, softened, when I touched it. My fingers travelled down her spine, which was so fragile, made out of little pieces of china. There was a noise outside; I heard it long before she did and felt her tense, heard her listen as the footsteps came nearer. There was the sound of somebody fumbling at a door and turning the knob. We were suspended, weightless. That was a sensation I knew well, a pleasure, not to touch when in a minute it would be possible to touch again. We prolonged it. Even when I, with my acute ears, heard the cupboard door open in the room two doors away and knew that we were safe, I didn't move. I was breathing in the flower scent she put on her hair. Gardenias.

She was bold, more daring than I'd ever be. Now she reached back with her practised paw, reached down her clever little fingers and I caught her hand. She mustn't touch, no, not yet. I knew how to punish her for that. We were dancers, we knew all the steps, it was a ritual dance of intense and tiny delights. I knew to stretch each moment out to infinity.

It was so sweet, almost unbearably so, the forbidden fruit I stole so quietly in the night. More delicious each time. The last night, the last time. No, I hadn't wanted to think of that, nothing should take away from this moment. It was always there, the feeling that things were ending. Even though I made the night multiply into years, still the morning would come. I always knew, I couldn't forget. There was a whole part of me that was damnably commonplace. And she knew it, she was serious at once.

'Jack?' It was a tiny whisper, hot breath thrilling in my ear. 'Jack?' Gently she brought her hands up, stroked my face. 'Don't be sad, Jack, we have tonight.'

'I'm not sad.' But I was, I couldn't help it. I was doubly damned. I'd have given her the world, if I could. She was so delicate, a woman who bruised easily. Forbidden. I couldn't look at her, greet her in the street, for fear of being seen. I was a betrayer, twice over, when was a man so unlucky? I had all the guilt, all the duties. At the darkest point of the night, the thoughts sprang like wolves to bay at me. The same ones, always. I had a terrible pity for my wife, for her needs, they clutched at me like drowning hands. Nothing was enough for her. Everything I did seemed to test her, to rip at her ragged nerves. And I was cruel, I knew it. Mine was a jovial, uncaring laughing kind of cruelty, I couldn't manage any other way, it was harsher for never being admitted. We went about our life together preserving a silence, it preserved her. She never accused. She never gave me a way out. She was blameless. No man could leave a woman so helpless, not from that silence. It was a subtle trap that she had caught me in. Her love was fierce and unforgiving, cold. Her dead white skin repellent, now, no warmth in her. I had to be drunk to make love to her. Then, when I couldn't perform, she would shrink away in fierce, silent anger. But nevertheless, somehow, a child on the way. She had me fast now, she knew it. She was a child herself, helpless in this angry love. I dared not tell her now. What had I done to deserve this cold love of hers? It was a beast, more savage than any in the jungle, it could not be tamed. She would injure the baby, her eyes said it, her eyes threatened. She would do anything to hurt me.

I ran my hand down slender hips and pushed away the vision of my wife's clumsy walk, her swollen body, the anger and worry in her eyes. Leaving, the silent reproach, that I should be going now, now.

'Come back, Jack.'

I stroked the long rope of silky hair that reached to her buttocks and caressed her face. There were tears in her eyes and mine. There were only three hours left to the dawn. Rolling over quietly, to lose myself in her, I thought with great bitterness that if I must lose this, then I would have lost everything. It wouldn't matter, then, what became of me. When I went away, it would be into blackness, the chasm. I saw it coming. It made each moment vivid, it etched them into my head. This, at least, I would carry with me always, this sweetness and the scent of her hair. We were melting, falling into a dark pool where there was only this sensation, this movement. This ebb and flow. There was nothing else in the world but this. In the deep, velvet darkness of the night, we were surging, plunging, weightless and free, down, down to the deepest depths.

*   *   *

Something was dragging me up and I fought it. I reached back for the darkness, for that swooning fall, reached for warm flesh and touched something hard, a rock. I was being claimed back by a whole raft of noxious sensations, heat and gumminess around the eyes, something sharp in my back, a numbness in my bad leg. There it was, my old man's body, relentlessly demanding, aged decades in an instant by some cruel joke. After the numbness would come something yet more horribly familiar: a terrible attack of pins and needles. I fought it all, I tried to let my mind drift. Impossible. Consciousness was there, as sharp and real as an unpleasant revelation.

There was somebody else here. I knew that even before I opened my eyes, that gesture delayed as long as possible by a number of maudlin procrastinations. Grumpily, at last, I let in a chink of light and saw the glare of day. Ridinghouse sat cross-legged beside me, facing slightly away. I stared at his profile, the thickness of beard, the patrician delicacy of his nose and then I closed my eyes firmly, willing him away. They opened again, to squint around and see where we were. Planks of wood, roughly cut, a garden shed. I raised my head an inch, subsided at once, feigning sleep. We were in the lean-to. I lay on rubble of some kind. On cue, the tingling in my leg started up and I cursed silently. There was only one cure, to stamp and walk on it and so with a grunt I sat up, began to shake and pummel the dead thing into life, to massage the foot, force back the blood. My head was throbbing violently.

He turned. Slowly the head pivoted and for a long moment we studied each other. I made a grid of his face, looked so I would know it forever. In my head I was sketching, shading in the hollows under the eyes that gave their darkness more intensity. The bright light accentuated his pallor; his skin had a chalky tone. I blocked out the shade of the nose; with tiny strokes, I grew the springy, melancholy tangle of a beard. The neck was sinew and gristle; the leanness had been transmuted into an almost elderly frailty of joints. In four months he had aged decades.

I took that straight-backed shape with its spindly arms and legs, its oversized icon's head, and I placed it where it could never be lost.

8

Pain is truth, Pie said. Irrefutable, character-forming. Did he ever waste his breath on sweeter words, did he ever voice the notions of pity, of compassion? He said that I was too soft, too kind to other people. He warned me against the evils of the flesh. He would approve of this monastic life, though not, of course, of its purpose.

I can see a splendid Pie of centuries ago. A cardinal, the massive figure swathed in a scarlet cassock, the stentorian tones schooled to speak softly in private, to crash and boom from the pulpit. A man of immovable faith, granite belief, a man of doctrine. His ingenuity would be used to forge iron traps to catch souls. How admirably it would have suited him, how safe he would have been. He would have relished the pomp and circumstance, the banquets at which he would drink his choleric face into a papal purple, the delicacies to swell the priestly gut. His year would unfold in stately ritual: high feasts and fasts, robes of silk and hair shirts, incense and the smell of burning flesh, the exquisitely sensual contrasts animated by the only thing that mattered, power, which he would have enjoyed more than all the rest.

I miss the old bugger. I drink to him, cheers! The whisky which I smuggle in is my universal panacea, blanket and inspiration, ink for my pen and raiser of spirits. I have been drinking today in celebration. Firstly at having got so far, secondly because it is my birthday. I congratulate myself on my powers of recall, so detailed and crisp, remarkable, surely, for a man of fifty-three. I laugh out loud at my own jokes when they occur, though I fear that is not often enough.

It is surprising how much I find to relish in my clockwork life. All day I scratch away here, staring at the window opposite. When the little mice there appear, I frown at them to frighten them away, as though they had less right than I to look out at the street. Two girls live there, nurses, who are already dressed in their uniforms when they pull the curtains back, appearing, unlike Ruffey, always clean and brisk. Our eyes meet and they pretend not to notice me and I wonder if they can see the bottle on the desk.

I work, and it must be true, for Mrs Kiriakou tells everyone this approvingly, like a man possessed. She speculates. She calls me her poet. In order not to disabuse her, I carry my papers with me everywhere, for she ferrets and snoops and delves. I have a shiny briefcase which bulges mysteriously and tantalises her. I carry whisky in it. Tube by tube, paints and sable brushes creep into it, a knife, a bottle of linseed oil, and I hoard them as a miser his coins. I have smuggled in a canvas under my coat. Soon, when this work is done, I shall begin to paint.

I am turned disciplinarian: Ruffey is a clock-watcher at last. In these weeks, habit has gained an ascendancy to rebuke a lifetime's dilatoriness. My steadfastness amuses me and yet I cherish my routine. There is safety in the familiar, the predictable; it is not to be despised.

Every morning I take my briefcase and go out to walk, to clear my head. I breakfast in a tiny café run by Italians, full of steam and smoke and the smell of eggs frying in a thick, black saucepan. I watch the office workers hurry in, snatch their greasy paper bags, their plastic cups. The girl there smiles at me. Without a word she brings over coffee as I like it.

I have learnt to recognise the Scotch-egg eater, the little man who riffles luncheon vouchers, the girl with ferocious spiked heels who always has mayonnaise on her sausage sandwich. The boss whose tongue, like his hands, is never still, looks over at me and winks when he makes one of his jokes. His daughter has wispy hair dragged up into a knot, deep, sad Italian eyes, those flat sandals old women wear. When she comes to wipe my table she shows me photographs of her little boy, holding the edges carefully with her fingertips. She tells me, with a sigh, that her mother spoils him and that she would raise him differently, if she could. Because she does not want her father to hear, these conversations imply a sotto voce intimacy we do not really possess and occasionally I see him give me a sharp look. I see her sometimes in the evenings, hurrying away, awkward in high heels. Sometimes she is carrying a plastic truck or an unwieldy teddy bear in blue nylon fur with staring eyes, toys from the market. She smiles at me with a touch of awkwardness and won't stop to talk without the protection of her white overall. She is a simple girl, kind, not pretty but with the bloom of youth. Adversity has not soured her; she is still innocent. Over a second cup of coffee I warm myself with a fantasy of a simple life with such a girl, a loyal one, who would repay kindness tenfold. I imagine, even, my tentative approaches to the little boy – his mother's anxious face. I find that I am smiling at her and (what compliment to my five and a half decades) she looks away, blushing, she busies herself shuffling bottles of sauce. It is the plainness, the simplicity of this fantasy woman that attracts.

I grow sick of speculation, only to take up the pen and ferret anew. I am tired of thinking and do nothing but. My gloom at the opacity of events is succeeded by moments of hilarity when I congratulate myself on my lucidity. I tell myself that there need be no pattern, no reason for events — and then in the next instant I think I glimpse a master plan. Certainly, it would be easier to make a new life than to interpret this old one. I am trapped, though, by my subject matter, as surely as that poor girl who will never work in a different café. I cannot do without my past.

And will the end, then, bring relief? The quicker my pen eats up the page — the faster I gallop towards the here and now, the more I flip over the same question. Endlessly, I toss that coin and it twirls and spins and just as it is falling — in the second before it hits — why my hand simply shoots out of its own accord and pockets the thing. I find my indecisiveness, my dithering, appalling. The issue is whether or not I give this to Annette. How it plagues me, nags at me, this issue of choice, this whole fiction of free will. How can I decide, when I cannot gauge the effect?

I resolved at the beginning that I would be frank and dispassionate. What, otherwise, was the point of all these words? They should not multiply our confusions. I would record, not as an eye that perceives and evaluates, but as a camera does, panning and framing in perfect neutrality. At once an opinion sprang in — and another — and then I said to myself that I would at least avoid cheap emotions. There would be no morass of self-justifications, no slough of regrets. Within my natural limitations, this would be as accurate a record as I could devise. But I could not avoid bias. Neither that of style, nor that of selectivity nor (least of all) the constant intrusion of Ruffey into the facts. I could no more oust myself than I could force my eyes to cease to impress upon my memory of shape of things. So be it. I doff my hat to Professor Pie: there is no such thing as true representation.

And yet (and this is vanity and nevertheless I will put it down) I claim one merit: consistency. I have included all that I remember, whether it does me credit or not. Words are powerful things. Out they come from a mass of turbulent, inchoate thoughts and suddenly a vague notion is speared at random, it ceases to struggle and hardens at once into an opinion I scarcely knew I held. I do not dispute these opinions, but some of them surprise me. Pie said thought could not exist without language. His truths were locked into the words of others, hidden between the syllables, clasped tight; what an avalanche of words he threw to pound out each certainty. Once I envied him his semiology. Now I am not sure. I long for the pellucidity of paint, its enviable fluidity.

There are too many delicate, evanescent moments, memories untranslatable into language. Tastes, for instance, and sounds have a quality which is perfectly precise but too refined for clumsy words. What artful synaesthesia can convey the taste of a mango or the silvery reedy tone of a flute? It is a sound I want, a plaintive note that haunts me. I heard it that morning after the storm in the poignant sweetness of a young girl's voice, the high delicate quaver between girl and woman. She sang to herself, warbling in a child-like swift obliviousness that had already turned the catastrophe into a game, a song to the complex harmony of life. She came skipping past with something in her hands, put it down, danced back to collect something else. It looked like a doll but it was a plaster figure, a buddha, split in two. She smiled and showed it to me.

I rose up then in staggering stages, went out and saw the Finn sweeping fragments together at the far parapet. The air was tangy fresh and smelt of pine and sap, crushed green matter. The roof was a chaos of splintered wood and rubble. Next to Leino there was a hole, as though gouged by a giant finger, where the lightning had struck.

I half-hobbled and hopped round the dome, avoiding the debris and pools of water. Laboriously, I climbed up it, picking my way through the concrete fragments on the steps. There was no sign of Pie. Now, descending, I went over to Leino. His face was red and set; he leant on his broom and watched me approach.

'Coffee or tea,' I said. More than anything else in the world, I wanted a cup of proper English tea, with milk. We stared at each other for a moment, a jousting of fierce glares, and his eyes dropped, he gave in. He hated me so much for this assertion of my rights in the face of his greater disaster that he could not bring himself to utter one word.

John Ridinghouse and I had breakfast together. In the dining-room mirror, I inspected the jagged wound over my right eye, the shiny bruise. He sat next to me and I observed his perfect stillness in the mirror. His hands lay on the table, long-fingered and slightly dirty. I could not stop myself from monitoring his image as though it might, vampire-like, disappear. The thought was simultaneously worrying and ridiculous.

The window was open and warm air came in. The storm had cleansed the building. The old man shuffled in with tea that was black and bitter, but marvellously hot. I stirred in sugar, gulped at it too fast and burnt my mouth. This heat, this taste, was something magnificent and it hardly mattered whether it hurt or not; to be alive was a jubilation. How many such mornings come in a life? Once, perhaps twice, I have tasted the crude joy of survival. Everything was sharp, colours heightened, tastes shockingly strong, even the thunder in my head welcome. It seemed to me that I had experienced more than a storm, that I must not only have lived my father's life, but also have died his death, to waken so triumphantly alive.

To recapture that sensation I must evoke the image of John Ridinghouse. I succeeded all too well in fixing it. I stop, close my eyes — and up rises that monochrome face, imbued with a melancholy so profound that it had become substance. The blackness grew out of him and hung above his head, like giant wings folding and beating slowly together in a swirl of icy air. Odd, that I should associate that face with my deliverance. (Here is a cynic's apophthegm worthy of the professor: the misery of others incites to good cheer). And daily I evoke him, daily I try to commit him to paper and daily I shirk the task. I do not want to put down all that I know about him for the most ignoble, the simplest reason — because I do not want Annette to see it. There. Easier to own up to lust, betrayal, envy — anything rather than that miserable little worm of spite. I have mastery over her while I hold my peace. No, I cannot show my wife this, an old man crowing spite, rejoicing at the misfortunes of another. Truth is a relative concept: incompatible with frankness of that order.

And yet to begin with I wrote only for her. It was a fine motive for I alone could make all clear, I alone had that power. And if it was not, as it happened, my story alone, why that did not matter. I would make it my own. But it is not quite as pleasant centre-stage as one might imagine. Events do not always possess the definition my words give them; in my head they are more opaque, diffused.

There is nothing intrinsically virtuous in telling the truth.

Truths can hurt. It was not virtue that opened my mouth. When I came home from Jakarta, I told Annette where I had been; more, I said that I had seen Ridinghouse — that he was alive and well. And then I left, for what I described as a period of solitude and reflection and I even gave her the address, observing her closely (but she betrayed no consciousness of it). The perfection of her artifices has indeed developed mine. And so I came away knowing that I left her a prey to ceaseless speculation — and thought that her state could hardly differ from my own and that there was a kind of justice in it.

I told myself that in passing on this meagre scrap, I had done the correct thing, even while my heartbeat speeded into triumphant, gloating velocity. Jealousy is a wicked, permeating passion, slow to seep away even when washed out with icy facts. With love comes jealousy and with that the desire to punish; later comes the bitter taste of self-reproach.

I dream of her constantly. My wife is remarkable. She is all that she should be and nevertheless false. Her infidelity is a masterpiece of mental mockery, designed for my torment. There is nothing physical in it, no crude coupling to inflame an old man's imagination. There is nothing I can do to stop it; I could as well control the beating of her heart.

She came here last week. It was a chilly morning. She missed Mrs Kiriakou by a minute. My landlady leaves the house twice a week, tearing herself away to wheel a trolley round the supermarket, for that important visit to the bank. She is so loth to go that she dithers on the pavement below — for the crucial event she fears, whatever it might be, will surely occur when she has just turned a back for what she calls a sec. I know the times of her exits. I saw her clutching her straw basket, pivoting in uncertain circles on high heels. I waited for her to look up: we have our little rite de passage.

My kiss is most elegantly fluttered from my fingertips, not at all presumptuously. It is a chaste and respectful salute from on high that sends her away. She and Annette passed two doors away. She would have viewed Annette with the utmost suspicion. My wife – this fiction entirely her own devising and accordingly suiting her so well – is an elderly lady, bed-ridden most probably, somewhere in the country far away.

I felt anger when I saw her; it was six weeks since we had met and she was defying my unspoken edict. I did not want her here. I had reduced our marriage to the humming telephone line, to the grubby, greedy pay telephone in the echoing hallway, to the crazed linoleum I stared at while mumbling something that was not even an excuse. I noticed time only in the most artificial way: that I needed to buy an overcoat, that Mrs Kiriakou had at last signalled the official passing of the season long gone by turning on her heating.

So it was as an invader that I spotted this girl with a red coat that billowed out behind her, a purposeful stride, a face to stab at my heart. Like a thief I rummaged for my stolen treasure and crammed the papers into the drawer of the desk so there would be no trace, no clue for her to take away. I watched from above as she scanned the street numbers, saw a little pause of disbelief as she pushed the bell and then she was lost in the doorway.

She made the room seem shabby and yet she, the brightest thing in it, seemed unreal. I watched pensive fingertips trail across the furniture and wondered savagely how many hours she had already spent here.

'Not much of a place. What do you do here all day?'

'This and that. Nothing much.'

Descriptions do not do her justice; she is bright, lit-up. It is a face that makes you want to smile, to keep on looking and then smile again. I had forgotten what it felt like, to love.

I knew that I loved her, but it was like an old man, in good health, who boasts of his years but does not feel the burden of them. But love, like old age, brought harsh inevitabilities. I did not feel the pain of it until I began to write. Then, remembering the early days, I fell in love with her all over again. Even now, I feel my terrible susceptibility.

She opened her little brown bag and started to rummage in it.

'I got a postcard from John,' she said. 'I thought you'd like to know.'

She held it out.

'Good, fine,' I said and did not take it — for an instant I had had the contemptible idea of saying, 'John who?'

'Yes, exactly. He is fine and that's good.' It was pertly said. 'Look.'

'I am sure you're right,' I said. In perfect perversity I would not look. I might have said (but did not) that it was I who had asked him to send a card to reassure her. I might even have added that she could have trusted my word as well as his — of course I said nothing. I offered her a whisky instead. (Truly, a demon had got into me to make of Ruffey such a miser with words.)

We lay companionably enough on the bed. We talked as strangers might, seeking to impress. I described the desperate flirtation I was carrying on with the landlady and how she would loiter at the top landing in the hope of moments of dalliance.

'I see,' she said gravely. 'An uncontrollable passion. Do you think it will last long?'

Smiling, I spread my hands in a gesture of Levantine inscrutability worthy of the departed Mr Kiriakou.

'You see this place has a special quality,' I said.

'I see all right,' and the corners of her mouth turned up.

'All kinds of people turn up here. You'd be surprised. It's an education.'

'Indeed,' she said, mocking me. 'And education can go on for ever, can't it? What have you learnt so far?'

Nonchalantly she stretched out her arms, folded them behind her head and waited. I propped myself up on one elbow, began to stroke her hair. 'Lots about women,' I said. She wriggled around until she was half-facing me, her tight skirt pulled up to her thighs in an abandoned attitude. Her eyes, half-closed, watched me. Another tiny shift, for comfort, a little stretch: now I saw a stocking top, an inch of velvet thigh. She watched me as my hand started the long, slow journey up from the knee and the eyes did not close until I began, with agonisingly slow tiny movements of one finger, to pleasure her. Could a woman fake that shudder? Was that sigh abandonment, or calculation? I measured against a mental scale of verisimilitude and then, anticipating the questions which would surely come as my penalty – and which I would equally surely not satisfy – I surrendered to pleasure and to power alike. Silence is power, just as words are; I had not properly understood, before.

9

This account I kept from my wife.

Ridinghouse was wasted, brittle. I remember that he paused for a moment against the spider doors and that the shiny metal legs seemed to sprout from his thin shoulders and bony hips. I remember his lack of curiosity. He had entered another realm which had different realities and he wrapped his melancholy around him, he hugged it like a cloak to his thin shoulders. How pale he was. He came and sat down next to me, looking around dispassionately. I have seen that look on the faces of disaster victims. It was the blank stare of those who have moved beyond pain and pleasure, those who are no longer capable of being surprised.

My ruddy health was a crude contrast in the mirror. Beside my bulk, my beak of a nose, he was monochrome in pen and ink. We drank our tea. The old servant returned and put a tray on the table; there were two bowls of something glutinous that looked like a kind of congee. It tasted like savoury wallpaper paste. Ridinghouse barely looked; he dipped in his spoon mechanically. And I, eating mine with the most luxurious of sensations — weighing the delightful balance of the spoon in my hand and feeling the saliva gathering in my mouth — I could not stop staring at him. The waxy flesh of his hand repelled me and yet I wanted to touch it, to feel for a pulse.

'I hoped you would still be here,' I said at last rather carefully, a sentence that might have suited a London cocktail party. The eyes swivelled to watch me; he went on spooning the food into his mouth. He made no sign of having heard; his whole attention was elsewhere, or nowhere.

'Look, are you all right?'

I could hear that my tone, which had aimed at the solicitous, was infused rather with irritation. He wasn't going to reply.

Then I saw from the slight angle of his head that he was listening for something, that he was utterly concentrated. A moment later I heard it: light footsteps moving past in the hallway, the sound of skipping or dancing. Then he turned around. He focused his attention upon me, our eyes met.

Staring back at him I had the sensation of things receding — not objects, but ideas, as though my thoughts were being wound back onto the reel. I felt the strange mental lassitude that can overwhelm a man at the acme of ambition realised. Lives could be lost in that bottomless ennui; empires could totter and fall. I understand that a man might need only to stretch out one finger to save himself and that he might choose not to do so. I was hanging outside myself, outside time, trapped in an indifference so great that it could fill the cosmos. He looked away. Then I saw my hand travelling towards my mouth with the cup; that act begun in another century was accomplished now and the tea was still hot. I was back in my thundering head, back with the delicious contrast of violent sensation, with the hot, sweet tastes of life and the throbbing of the blood-caked wound on my temple, which I would allow myself the luxury of exploring later.

'Of course I'm all right,' he said. That was the strangest thing of all: to hear the normal English baritone, the voice that sounded slightly amused. He went on eating, he blinked. He didn't know what he had done; I don't think he realised the effect he had upon me, upon people; the strong man releases his mangling grip with the same insouciance.

'What are you doing here?'

'Research.' It was an ironic inflection.

'What kind of research?'

'Nothing academic.' He shrugged his shoulders contemptuously.

'Anything. I support my travels, it doesn't take much.'

'But what are you doing *here*?'

He didn't reply at once. I had leisure to wonder what my answer to that same question would be; to wonder why he didn't ask. His eventual answer disconcerted me.

'Haven't you ever felt that you'd found your place?'

I shook my head.

'We all have a place, where we're meant to be. Once you've found it there's no leaving. No wish to leave.'

'Here?' I schooled my unruly eyebrows into a less sardonic expression.

'Here. You know what's here, you can feel it. There are dreams here, destinies, memories. Come on, you know this country, you know the kind of thing I mean. You can feel it too.' Calmly, he contemplated my stubborn face. I had a moment's unease, wondering what he could read in it.

'There are plenty of stories,' he said. 'I even have one that is appropriate for you. Do you know the artist, Walter Spies?'

'The one who lived in Bali?'

'Precisely.' There was an ironic gleam in his eye, a faintly mocking hunch to one shoulder.

'An American journalist wrote something about him in a book that came out in the thirties. There was a whole colony of Europeans there, writers and musicians and artists, trying to document the culture before it dwindled into a tourist attraction. This man, Powell, wrote for the same reason, to record the real stuff. His story about Spies was interesting. He had an encounter with an evil spirit – a leák – in the body of a woman who was pregnant, who died before giving birth. He had a witness with him, you understand. There was a Javanese there who saw it too, an archaeologist. An educated man.'

This piece of corroboration was offered in a manner I found faintly offensive. It went past irony and came closer to malice. It was like hearing a warning shouted out by a stranger, in a language I didn't speak.

'They were near a burial ground and saw a light moving there. It vanished and then reappeared, a violet light moving in circles. They were nervous and went back to their car. They found it covered in rotting meat and clods of earth. You wouldn't expect a Balinese spirit to be a litterbug, would you?' The corners of his mouth turned up in a smile that held no warmth. 'The next morning a pretty young woman was seen near the village. She was laughing silently to herself and rocking backwards and forwards. The villagers knew at once what it was. A leák. An evil spirit – the spirit of the unburied dead.' He paused, with his eyes on mine and as he lingered over this phrase a vision seized me – not of Bali, no, it was prosaic, ugly. I saw with the extreme precision of shock the cracked black and white tiles of a kitchen floor, the body protruding, ridiculously, hideously from the oven, legs twisted, open, vulnerable, the skirt pulled up. The body sagged to one side; I took in the hard, yellow skin that rimmed the heels of stockinged feet, the red-knuckled hand that lay on the floor. She had brought cushions in from the sitting room to prop herself up; I could see her choosing the big one, the one with a badly faded cover, which would mark least. That was the worst thing, that planning, that forethought. It was worse, even, than her face, which a horrid compulsion would force me to see. One single step, which I would regret for ever. I knew her so well, I had to look. I could not have done otherwise, I loved her too much. There was still the hope that she would lift her head and smile — that it was a joke. The beginnings, then, of an appalling grief, welling up.

The vision began to fade, leaving a pain behind the eyes where tears were not being permitted to start. I would not cry out, I would not admit, even, to having seen her there. I would never accept it. I heard Ridinghouse's voice.

'She moved to the grave and they all followed and saw her there, still laughing. They shouted at her, but she took no notice. Finally one or two of the braver ones went near. The leák lifted a corner of the shroud and rolled herself underneath it. When they came nearer to look, they found the body of a woman who had been dead for two weeks. They buried her that same day.'

'I see,' I said, meaninglessly. My mind, performing its own acrobatics, now artfully evoked my mother. Not his but mine, with her trembling hand raised, the big head quivering as she spoke. It was something knowing in his voice, it was that clever malice of his that reminded me of her. He had the intensity of old people. His apathy — his absences punctuated by whims and long-winded lucidities — all of these lay in the repertoire of the nursing home. He had that same sudden manic energy, I heard it crackle through his speech. He was looking for his mother; his were the memories of death, of loss. How had they got inside my head? And then I thought that I was not alone with him after all; that death had also come to meet him here.

'Don't you like the story?'

Why was he looking at me like that? The idea passed through me, as an electric current, that if I could experience his memories, did he then possess mine? Why else would he mention Bali? I was a painter because, all those years ago, a child had sat in the sun-dappled shade of a bamboo house and watched a man work a miracle on a piece of paper. Nobody else in the world knew that. His painter was not my man — but he could have been — they must have known each other. That Ridinghouse might be able to see into the hearts and souls of men appalled me. It was a violation, the most wicked kind of robbery. I stared at him (he had disconnected again, he was looking blankly at the mirror) as though I might see through his eyes. I saw him stiffen as he noticed the blur in it. I saw the tendons of his neck stand out, saw him light up with a fierce intensity. But it had been there for some time. I opened my mouth to say — but it's only the little girl. Something kept me silent. Was it the white blouse that made her look so ethereal? She was looking at us and in that instant she saw that she was observed and at once she pivoted lightly, slipped away, appearing through that cloudy bloom to dematerialise. As she went, he appeared to sag, to shrink a little. When he turned back to me, it was as though a film had rolled up to cover his eyes, as though he was protecting himself from the painful brilliance of the sun.

I could never have liked him, I had come too far for that. But I could still feel pity. That was the emotion that now mixed itself with the complex ferment of repulsion and fear. That was the emotion I would cultivate. Pity is an independent creature, feeding, like guilt, upon contrasts. There need be no fellow feeling in it, no real sympathy. I tried an approach, clumsily.

'Have you been ill? You don't look well – you look as though you've had a fever of some kind.'

It took him a long time to find words. He was listening the whole time. The current wasn't switched off after all, it wasn't apathy. The invisible radar never stopped turning, tracking her through the building.

'Ill? I am never ill. I've never felt better in my whole life than I do here.' He lifted his head to examine himself better and saw nothing amiss. I looked at the sunken sockets of his eyes and followed the curve of bright bone under the dark hair, bone which looked too near the surface of the skin. He offered me another of his mirthless smiles.

'You see, for you the story needs witnesses,' he said. 'For all the western world – the civilised world – nothing exists without proof. Leáks and bogeymen are for children. But the people here know better. The unburied dead can walk. It just requires a particular kind of innocence to see them, the innocence of a child.'

He was still smiling.

'You see a child can walk between the two worlds, there are no boundaries. It's the adults who teach children fear, they are naturally invulnerable to it. The child is our conduit to the other side because it doesn't realise there is a difference. Adults with their inhibitions and repressions are excluded. We may sense, but we can't see. Now Walter Spies saw, he was unique, of course. I have wondered if his artistic talent wasn't a factor.' He looked at me. 'Don't you see or hear anything here?'

I shook my head. There was a secret world and he was excluded from it. It would devour him without permitting one consoling glimpse of that other side. I had walked in his skin and I had seen his mother again, as he never would. He was trapped inside his sack of flesh. I could not tell him what I had seen. He was still staring at me in that penetrating way he had. It had the same unsettling quality as a blind man's stare. Now I found him, everything, oppressive. I wanted to get away, to breathe normal air. To stand in the hot sun and hear voices raised in laughter and discussion, to smell cloves and coconut oil.

'Look,' I said and because I was speaking with too much urgency, I tried to slow myself down, to sound flippant. 'I nearly forgot. Would you do me a favour? It's a little thing, just to send a postcard, to Annette? To tell her that you're all right?'

'Annette,' he said, in a calm but distant voice, as though he was trying to remember who she was.

'She was a little concerned about you. After we met — when we lost you, on Borobodur. You remember. She got into her head the notion that something might have happened to you. Women, you know. You know how it is.' I put on the right sort of deprecatory, oafish smile.

'Annette,' he repeated, musingly. 'How persistent she is. You must be flattered. She must be the most determined person I know.'

'You know my wife well,' I said and grinned, trying to make that remark appear less savage. 'Of course she's determined, what woman isn't?

I waited to hear what he would find to say next; I was itching (so much for pity) to lay into him, to redesign his molars with a knuckle sandwich. But invisible bells were ringing. He was alert, pricked up. Without making the slightest noise, he sped to the door and opened it. I heard, then, the sound of footsteps coming down the stairs.

Leino and his daughter descended from the high, dark dome. The hotelier was covered with a fine white dust which gave him the chalky finish of one of his plaster statues. He looked slightly ridiculous; it was the comic patina of the pastrycook. When she saw us, the girl paused and then made as though to run back up the stairs. Her father said something. Proudly, she lifted her head. She began to walk down with tremendous grace, with a kind of fluid, exaggerated glide to carry her slender body over the wide, deep steps. Her eyes were averted. It was a piece of defiant obedience. Neither of us moved. I saw Ridinghouse looking, willing her to look at him and she, silently, refused. It was not the way a man looks at a child.

A moment later she and her father passed through the set of swing doors which led to the main entrance. Ridinghouse continued to watch the two silhouettes through the glass. The father bent over; he was whispering, his mouth an inch from her ear. Now with a swirling motion she was gone, out through the main doors which let in a flash of white sunlight as they swung open. In my mind's eye, I saw her running up the road, the brown knees twinkling under the school skirt.

We could hear Peter Leino muttering to himself in some glottal language which must have been Finnish. As he came back through the main hallway, we heard the lugubrious throat-clearings of a defeated man. He looked at us still standing there. A half-shrug of the shoulders; he seemed almost embarrassed. 'A bad day, no? Girls. What is a father to do? And yet I love her, more than anything else, everything.' A sweeping gesture indicated the relatively minor volume of his attachment to the hotel. There was nothing to say to this. He looked at us.

'Well? Are you going up to see your friend?' This remark

was addressed to Ridinghouse, but it had a galvanic effect upon me.

'Pie. Where is he?' It was a statement of fact — an accusation — I whirled around to look at Ridinghouse and saw that he was blinking, stretching, a little dazed as one is, upon waking. He gestured with one thumb.

'Upstairs. I dragged him down from the roof. I could barely manage the weight, he'll be bruised.'

I imagined a spider trailing a burden three times its size. Roughly, I touched his shoulder and half-pushed him towards the stairs.

'Come on — come up with me, now,' and I pushed again. He made no resistance, indeed he started to climb in an almost lively way. We reached the second floor; here he paused, to gesture down the corridor at the door opposite mine. He was different, more alert and I, too, felt that something had changed, as though a gust of warm air was eddying through the building. He was released, that was it. Her absence had released him; when she left the building nothing more could happen. Ridinghouse was right, she was the conduit through which everything flowed.

I think that I was smiling that involuntary grimace of realisation as I knocked on the door, for I remember him looking at me oddly, and I thought bugger me, he's actually going to ask a question. But when there was no answer, I did not hesitate to push the door open. The room was empty. There was a reddish-brown streak on the bolster and more drops of the same colour in the indentation of the pillow where his head had lain. I sagged upon the bed.

The harsh, jerky noise startled me. Ridinghouse was sitting neatly, cross-legged on the armchair; he threw his head back with an exaggerated movement. I watched him sourly.

'I told you that things happened here,' and he rocked

forwards, as if helpless with laughter. 'Do you know something? I said that to Annette. On Borobodur. She asked – she asked me what it was for. The monument. That's what I said then, that it was like that. That kind of place. Where extraordinary things happened.'

It took a long time for him to calm himself down, to overcome the hiccuppy bursts of laughter.

'You can see the great illusionist has gone,' he said, gesturing at the empty room with an air of satisfaction. 'Run away, fled.'

'From you do you mean? Why should he do that?'

'Because I know his secret.'

I watched Ridinghouse join his fingertips together so that the long, thin hands obscured his mouth and half his face. The curious notion came to me that he might know things, with his head, but he could not feel them. He lacked some essential component. Perhaps that was why he, alone, was immune to the emanations of that place. Or was I alone in picking them up so clearly?

'Of course you don't know, can't know. I shall have to explain.' He was enjoying himself. I was sure that, though I couldn't see it, there was a smile in that beard.

'The professor is a confidence trickster. A con-man. He is an expert in a special kind of fraud. He steals ideas and calls them his own. It's very cleverly done, a little bit from here, a little bit from there, but because he's greedy he's never been able to resist taking more and then more. He can swallow a whole person, regurgitate the essence, spit out the bones. And still it doesn't fill him up. He is a hollow man. It's all bluff and bluster, under that hard shell of dogma. I broke it, you see, by accident. That is why he's afraid of me. Now, I wonder why he brought you here? He would I think have taken some trouble to keep us apart.'

'But he didn't bring me here,' I said.

My reply pleased him.

'No, of course not. Poor professor, you had to know.'

Then, because for a long moment he said nothing, I fumbled for a suitable spur.

'Yes,' I said, 'I would have found out. I would have seen through the illusion.'

Now that word – chosen almost at random, chosen because he had termed Pie an illusionist – had a very particular effect. Ridinghouse held up one hand, as though to request silence, and then he stood up and started to pace backwards and forwards with a heavy stride. It was as though he inhabited a body of far greater mass, of double the weight. He began to speak very deliberately and in a loud voice.

'You see before you a man floating in the water.' An imaginary stick jabbed at an imaginary wall.

'Is he floating? Not swimming, not floating. Unnatural, the posture. The colours. Heightened realism? Illusion? Anti-realism? What is it? Aspects of this picture are not true. You –' and he pointed the stick at me – 'do you look like this when you float? Can you swim? Never mind, it's impossible.' He paced heavily across to the far wall and back again and again the stick hovered in the air. I understood that we were in a lecture hall; I knew whose lecture it was.

'The picture, then, is deliberately wrong. Contrived, untrue, artificial. Why? Because that is what is intended. He does not float. He does not swim. He is in another state. Dead or alive? Something else; a state of abandonment, of knowledge. Something new. That's the point. The painter creates the truth. You can see, here, the artist creating the world.'

A pause, magnificently done, for effect. And the artist was Ruffey, the picture that of my father. Wheels within wheels.

'Got it, you in the front row?'

There was a sly smile on the Pie face.

'Got it.'

'You didn't know?'

I shook my head; it was not at all clear, in which persona he spoke.

The lecturer settled himself upon the arm of the chair and stared angrily round at his audience.

'We have discussed Nietzsche's assertion that truth must be created, not discovered. It's difficult. What is meant by that, is that there is no absolute truth. It cannot be defined upon a single scale. A shifting perspective is required, just as the painter shifts perspective for each new picture. Now people have deduced from that absence of a universal standard a nihilistic stance; that any standard will do. So they say Nietzsche's a nihilist, a wrecker. No. Not what the man meant. Not what the painter means, when he moves his viewpoint. In art — here — look at it — you see exactly what he means. For Nietzsche, the truth is an act of creation. Precisely as the painter creates, ever anew, ever different. No picture more "true" than the next. Simple.' The booming voice had quietened down, was almost gentle. 'Understand this. At the heart of his thinking is this act of creation. Not the void. A sense of aesthetic value. Look at it.'

Now he turned away and in a characteristic gesture mopped at his face with an imaginary handkerchief. When it came from the face, Ridinghouse was smiling.

'What did you think the professor was doing messing about with tribal totems?' he asked with a rhetorical flourish. 'Why the pagan culture? He needed it, to get a sense of the world — that aesthetic value. The lecture merely extended that. And then he went a step further. He had to involve himself with the creative process personally. How could it ever be sufficient for the intellect — the genius — to write commentaries? No, he had to be the creator. So he created you.'

'What do you mean?'

It was a Puckish smile, incongruous against the tired texture of his skin.

'Don't you see it? Artists are very important, but the people who create them even more so. The professor played God. For him the person who creates something new ranks highest so he created a new category, the creator of the artist. That's what he told me, that he had created you — not biologically, naturally, but the artist in you. He said you would never have been a painter if it wasn't for him. Rubbish, naturally. Gods don't need to boast about their achievements. That is what did for him, the itch to proclaim his divinity. A very human failing.'

He had said his piece; he made a small bow to signify the end of the performance. With great care, he folded up his long arms and legs, like a praying mantis, to sit. His pleasure in his bon mot could not be concealed; there was a smirk on his face.

'Pie said — in a lecture — that he'd created me?'

'Oh no,' and the don manqué began to elucidate. 'He told *me* that.'

He had just the right tone of patient zeal, the air of there being nice points to be made if I would just bide my time.

'He was giving me a tutorial and I dared to question his point about the artist creating truth. I said it was arbitrary, erratic, that great painters chanced upon discoveries. He hated that idea. Truth, you see, couldn't depend upon the whims of chance. It couldn't be random or in the hands of fools. The idea mattered too much to him, he'd made an emotional base out of it, so he couldn't relinquish it. He made the mistake of boasting. He said that he knew better. He understood the process of creation – through you. It was all to do with selection – choices, tastes, and so on. "Things that could be taught – nurtured," said I. "Precisely," he said and then he said that he had made you what you were. He was serious. So I called his bluff, I said that if he could create a Ruffey, then so could I, I'd take a wager on it.

'"You a betting man?" he said, oh, he loved that idea. "Got anything of value have you?" He was greedy to prove himself. I offered my degree. It was worthless, of course, but he jumped at it. You can imagine how the idea of my failure appealed to him. But I knew that I was going to leave anyway. So I said my stipulation was that if I won, he had to leave the university at once. He accepted it. There only remained the precise formulation of the bet. He thought it up. That each of us should try to influence the conditions of your life in such a way as to create a masterpiece. Intellectually, emotionally, it didn't matter how, but it had to be demonstrably the result of the particular influence. He believed it could be done, he leapt at the idea. Proof, do you see, of his omnipotence. That was why it was easy to frighten him. It only took a few cryptic postcards. One when I left Bristol, to remind him that the bet was still on. Another when you married Annette. That was a coup for me, or at any rate the professor could be made to think so – he knew that I knew her, you see, I made sure he did. He's an unworldly man, that was why it worked. He had to believe in my powers, because he needed his to exist. He craved the proof of it. Without you his life is second-rate, derivative – but with you, he had his place in history. That is why he admires the pictures, all that gratuitous emotion. They collect up the emotions of a lifetime, everything he's missed. I don't imagine the professor owns a Ruffey. He doesn't need to, they are all his.'

I said nothing, I was absorbing what he had told me.

'Do you see?' he said, and then, more intently, 'Well, do you see? Of course he's fled. He can't bear to be found out, it would ruin his life. Here you are — and he didn't bring you, it's rich. I have no powers to compel him to do anything, nor anyone, of course not, but he doesn't know that. He'd never accept it, either. His Ruffey — he loves the idea even more than he fears losing the bet. I need do nothing further, you see. He'll carry it on all on his own.'

I cannot begin to describe the look of extraordinary satisfaction that spread across that pallid face, the wide and malicious grin. I was half-lying, half-sitting on the bed and now I felt myself sink back, as though body and brain could not work simultaneously and the spinning turmoil of the latter needs must negate the strength of the former. If the drowning man sees his life pass before his eyes, then I was drowning there. I saw, in vivid jumbled panorama, a succession of tableaux vivants — saw myself as a child timorous and sharp with fear, a wild creature feigning obedience at school and Pie my saviour and tormentor. I heard, in horrible cacophony, echoes of the thousand-and-one statements he had made, his bombast and bile, a hundred haranguings. Admiration's bad for you, he had said, and pain is good. I made you. Had he said that? I was no longer sure. I raised you from the mediocre. Pain was truth, he had said, and fear; they formed characters and he was right. I thought of Cyprus, which he had urged upon me, and of my women, whom he had always despised. He had always warned me against unnecessary involvements, against going soft. I remembered Dorset and the holiday in France, the fortnight in Tuscany, the gorging and swilling which had never ceased, through which he had lectured and hectored me. That was the nature of the man. Nobody else would ever take such trouble with me, he had said, and he was right; he had taken trouble, just as he had caused it. I thought of our last day of school. He had betrayed me, but it had not mattered, in the end. His only friend. I had always known that. Why had that not mattered more? Because his attention was flattery, to me.

And I thought that he had always urged me to work, to live and work harder, to spurn the derivative and second-rate and I had always relied on his good will, just as I had always had to reckon with his bile. Always, he had believed in me. The discoveries he had urged upon me were mental, intellectual, solitary – as onanistic as his pleasures were; I was too hedonistic, too gregarious for them. And yet I had to reckon with over forty years' worth of incidents, of meetings, of words – his, not mine. His influence. The force was so familiar, so often spurned, incalculably great or small. Pie had followed me to Indonesia for reasons he could not explain; he had tried so hard to deflect me. He had spoken of a bet and said, in the same breath, trust me.

I lay on that bed where he had rested and it all whirled around me. I felt the cold sweat on my face. A betrayal so great that it could not be discussed; my mother, on the boat, was nothing to this. The noise of my breathing was magnified in the quiet, so loud that I thought it must come from Ridinghouse. Raising my head with a tremendous effort, I saw him still sitting in the same place. He was inert, his eyes were closed. I saw the skull shining through the skin.

Here was the man who had started it all (for Pie had done nothing out of the usual – had not sought to meet me, had not even spoken to me for months before Ridinghouse thrust himself into my life). It was Ridinghouse who had cast his spell on Mount Bromo, who had hung in the sky, an omen. He was the one who had followed us to Solo knowing, all the time, what effect he was having upon Annette. He had engineered these meetings. He had planned the disappearance: crude, but effective, just as the postcards to Pie must have been. He had forced me to take notice of him. He had forced himself into my life and it was shocking to say to myself — but it is true, I have thought of nothing else since. By these means, he had come to dominate my life.

Of course Ridinghouse would deny that he had even tried, for he wanted to win. There was no weapon, emotional, intellectual, physical they would not use, to win. I had been raped, violated. I was hollow. Two hollow men had emptied me out.

For a long time I lay there. The pictures jumped about, reformed their crazy kaleidoscope. Do you see? Ridinghouse had said. I saw, had always seen, far too well, far too much. Faces advanced and receded. Annette, the bright dress in the alleyway, the beaming look of pleasure which I knew had been absent before: my wife in the labyrinth at Solo. Her complicity, which I could not gauge. The other face was Pie's: an open-pored, fleshy tuber of a nose stuck in a book, heat-sheened under an absurdity of a straw hat. These two faces, which would not go away: the only people I had loved in all my adult life. I knew that I had loved the man, now that he was lost to me.

At three o'clock I looked at my watch, at Ridinghouse. He stirred; he leant forwards, the blank stare fastened upon my face, but whatever he saw, it wasn't me. What had roused us? I did not know, I had heard nothing. I did not have the power to move him. A greater force was required for that. He was looking through me, and I saw that I did not exist for him, that I was part of a distant past which no longer counted.

I saw all that and more; a couple dancing in the great hall; slowly they circled under the stars, his hand on a bare back, her white satin dress clinging to a slender body, the dark hair hanging loose. The man turns and looks towards me; they both look at the mirror. Not Ridinghouse after all, but a melancholy dark face, clean-shaven with blue eyes that examine the face of the woman – no girl this, her eyes are full of knowledge, her lips expertly outlined in red. A flawless, dark-skinned beauty; he sees only her and she, licking a voluptuous upper lip, looks at me. An imperceptible nod of the head: an assignation. I do not know if it was Ruffey she saw or his father; if the head in the mirror was blond or not – our eyes met, but I cannot tell who was looking out of mine. The sad Russian danced by with his lady love and bent his head to examine her face, to read the message in her unfathomable eyes.

The little girl had re-entered the house. I knew it and so did Ridinghouse, looking hopelessly through the air (how cold it was now, I was shivering). His head turned from side to side, slowly. I had to go, I knew that I had to be gone before the night came.

I left the room; I don't think Ridinghouse noticed. I went down to the office to collect my bag. Leino was there, flicking slowly through the big ledger open on the desk.

'Have a good journey,' he said, politely. He looked up for an instant as I went and I saw that his blue eyes were red-rimmed, as though he had been crying, or drinking, or both, so that they matched the venules on his face.

The heat beat up from the road, the afternoon sun was dazzling. Each foot followed its fellow along the dusty highway in stumbling haste, each piece of ground a little advance gained.

I was thinking that history repeated itself. I was thinking about loss, and what I had lost; about my father. He had been an unsatisfactory hero – no hero at all. His bravery had been flawed by the wastefulness of his death, a life slipping away in the water to no purpose. It was unforgivable. But, after all, everything was open to interpretation. There was the difference of a hair's breadth between stupidity and courage, between beauty and ugliness. It was entirely a matter of perspective. A story: the man who loves a famous courtesan. She is a beauty with a small black beauty spot on her white, pointed chin. It is a charming little circle which accentuates her flawlessness and he adores it. One day, however, he sees a tiny hair growing out of it. He is disgusted. He cannot bring himself to look at her.

A matter, then, of perspective. Late in life I had been given that rare thing: a new perspective. It changed everything, everything was turned upon its head. I considered my father, that tender and disappointed man. It was a different life, seen through his eyes. Not, after all, a wasted life; he had made his choices. He had done what he thought was best. In a little while, I heard the sound of a bus rumbling up behind and I turned to flag it down.

10

The clockwork wound down. I had written myself out. I examined each corner of my room a hundred times; I stood aimlessly at the window and wondered at the frenetic movements of the people below. For weeks I had scribbled on, undisturbed by the gurglings of pipes, the tappings of Mrs Kiriakou's heels, the humming murmurs. The house was never silent. The sounds of life went on all day, all night, in snatches of music and conversation, the creakings of beds, the groans and sighs of their occupants, their quarrels and reconciliations. All was channelled up through the twisting funnel of the stairway. Now I found that I was listening to it. I was almost preternaturally aware of each footfall, each door opening or closing. I found myself listening as though my very life depended upon it.

I was waiting for that refined, artificial vacancy of mind I must achieve before an image begins to form. I stole like a thief to finger my paints, to stroke the brushes. There was no point in getting them out. Why could I not work?

My head was too full; like a kaleidoscope, bright fragments of my life whirred through it, were shaken to be shaken again, images forming and re-forming so fast that they made me giddy. And all the time I was listening, waiting for something, I was restless, dissatisfied. I began to watch time passing on the second hand; I could stare at it for ten, twelve, fifteen minutes at a time and, counting up the wasted minutes, I felt pleased. It was an adolescent's stupid pleasure in waste, an adolescent's infinite boredom and twitchy, irritated list-lessness, born of the consciousness of an infinity of time ahead.

Mixed with this idleness, this futility, was a deep pessi-mism. The shadows on the wall seemed sinister; like dust, gloom gathered in the corners. The djinn of the whisky bottle had lost his magic. I began to feel that I was not meant to work at Mrs Kiriakou's, that an unquiet spirit inhabited my room. His room. For the mischief came from him, through him. That sense of doom was all his. Was he then thinking of me? Did his radar extend so far?

I decided to go home. Nothing could force me against my inclination; I would have returned to my wife in due course, anyway. But Ridinghouse provided the acceleration; it seemed a perfect little irony, of its kind. I remember thinking that perhaps I needed to get on with my life in order to work, for my life is my work and vice versa, the one propels the other along and always has done. I avoided thinking about Annette.

She did not even seem surprised; both of us had mislaid that capacity. Other capacities were not as they should have been. What did I expect? First came the sound of her key in the lock, the cheerful voice in the hallway. 'Mr Beech, a new coat, and dead smart,' and then her footsteps in the hallway, on the creaky board at the bottom of the stairs. The window-cleaner had affectations both sartorial and social which she loved to mock, just as he loved to hear her. They teased each other, the Cockney and the Sarf London girl. 'Nice bit of cloth, Mr B. But it is Savile Row?' She stuck a jolly face around the doorway and, seeing me, stopped, stared, recovered in an instant. 'Yours?' she said in comic horror, 'Good God.'

She made me put it on for her, so that she could say I looked like a bookie in it, no, worse, a crooked politician – and, recovering her sangfroid, could assert, even, that I shouldn't be let out on my own.

No, I said, I shouldn't, and would Mr Beech accept it? He did not disdain that season's cast-offs, providing the label was a good one. That was how I re-entered the domestic sphere; the coat was fuel for conversation, everything was, anything, bar my long absence. We would not discuss, either, the inexplicable reappearance. We got through the days on a succession of small topics. Soon I began to work, but nothing would come right there either, and so I sketched and threw away and was uncomfortable in myself.

At night, keeping to my side of the bed, I began to pretend to be asleep and despised myself both for the sham and its necessity. At night I had a demon on each shoulder to plague me: Pie and Ridinghouse to watch and exclaim and swish their horny tails and prod me with their cartoon forks.

It was in a dream that I saw Ridinghouse for the last time.

I was floating in an ominous darkness, one that was not blank, but occupied. I heard a laboured gasping for breath, for air that was foetid and hot. I sensed the warmth of a body close to me. A scrabbling noise started up, inches away, and I thought that it must be animal, not human. It was too loud, too near; the blackness contracted and, shrinking away, I understood that the space was tiny, a couple of feet across. I touched a corner, and another, in rough brick or stone.

Then through the darkness shot a tiny shaft of light that was piercingly bright, that widened, that became a hole, white-glowing, an inch or two across. The breath was held for an instant then expelled in a shudder. It was a human being. In that brightness, something moved, a blur, too fast. And then, close to me and next to that spy-hole, I made out an edge that had to be a nose and an eye. Ridinghouse's black eye, which rose up and then was gone for a hand came up to the light and began to poke at it and another hand was thudding, beating against damp stone in hopeless effort and the breathing was hugely magnified and laboured in the small space we occupied. His arm, his shoulder, the whole body strained against the wall, against the place where the light came in, the weak spot. In another moment, the frail body slumped back and I saw the light again. I felt, without seeing, how the trapped man half-lay, the eyes fixed upon the brightness, unaware of my presence, of anything in the world bar that. In that brilliant sunlight which came from the other side, from another world, I saw a blur approach that could have been a face. Closer and closer, taking the light away, but enough, still, for me to see a cold blue eye rimmed with angry red. Then that too was a blur, a blackness, and the whole world was blackness and heat and the agonising noise of another rasping, painful breath.

Two weeks later, or three, I came home one day and saw a woman sitting on the steps of the house. She was tall, neatly dressed, respectable looking. I took her for one of those crazy spinsters who, self-appointed scourges, roam the High Street proclaiming the second coming or denouncing the evils of the flesh in their quavering, genteel voices. Then, from ten yards away, I recognised the way the thick dark hair sprang vertically from the forehead. She wore a black suit so old-fashioned as to be nearly avant-garde and one of those penitential grey raincoats that nuns affect.

'You're Jane Ridinghouse,' I said.

She rose, turned her serious face to me.

'Edward Ruffey,' she said, 'I imagined you differently,' and she blushed at her temerity, the turkey-red tide rushing up her neck to stop just underneath her chin. The unspoken meaning was precise. That was the sort of woman she was; one compelled to voice the truth, as she saw it. I forebore to reciprocate in kind. Of the many pointless comments that could be made in such circumstances, that seemed the least fruitful.

We shook hands; hers was encased in stout leather. Inside, she drank down a whisky like a man. She was bony, un-womanly, very like her brother with eyebrows that nearly met. It was a very fierce face, at variance with the gentle voice.

'You were looking for my brother, weren't you Mr Ruffey? That's why I came.' When I nodded, she did too, dis-concertingly.

'Well I knew that, and I thought you might have spoken to John, I wondered about it. After we did. I mean, did you speak to him later?' She stopped, took a breath, made an effort to compose herself.

'Let me get to the point. He is missing, he's been reported missing in Java. It's all very confusing because he went missing another time, in a different place, so at first, you can't take it seriously. But this does seem to have some truth in it. A European reported it to the consulate. A Mr Liner — it sounds German, doesn't it? But perhaps he was English, to take an interest. This time, I believe it, I think he really is gone. Oh, I've expected it for years, I'm not surprised. But naturally I wondered if you'd found him, spoken to him, you see.'

'The recipient of a final message? My dear Miss Ridinghouse, what an idea,' but this, which was supposed to sound jocular, came out as patronising, flat. I strove to inject a little genuine warmth into my voice.

'I really don't think you should worry about him,' I said. 'These things always sound very dramatic. My wife and I reported him missing, you know, last summer, and then he turned up after all,' and I told her of our meeting and of his subsequent disappearance and of our concern to find him and I suppose I made out our part in the affair to be rather more altruistic than was the case, and if Annette and I sounded a most united couple – well, she was not at home to contradict me.

'So you mustn't worry,' I concluded and she turned upon me his bright, perspicacious look, one which made me feel uncomfortably aware of various inaccuracies.

'But you didn't think he would turn up,' she said in her soft voice. 'That's why you contacted me.'

'But he did. I saw him quite recently, you know, nearly three months ago, so I really don't think there's any cause for alarm,' and I got this part out quickly, because it's easier, when telling a lie, to get it out fast. She sighed a gentle exhalation.

'I don't need a cause,' she said. 'There are things one simply knows. Won't you tell me about it, about your meeting?'

So I described the place – a quaint old corner of Eastern Java, I think I called it, and to compensate for a lack of detail on our conversation, I said that there was a girl there Ridinghouse had fallen for, and that that was undoubtedly his motive for choosing the hotel and that he might have left unexpectedly because they had fallen out. I am not proud of this explanation, but it seemed to me that it might do.

Jane Ridinghouse raised her eyebrows. 'Not a girl,' she said. 'You were doing quite well, but that won't wash. John's emotionally illiterate, you see.'

She settled back in her chair; held out her glass for another drink.

'Do you know how the illiterate get around? It's a triumph of interpretation and bluff. To ride on the Tube and get off at the right stop if you can't read the signs takes bravado and learning by heart. You have to eavesdrop and interpret — well, you see, it's a lot easier to learn to read. That was John. He pretended to have feelings, but he didn't. Or at any rate those he had were buried so deep that they didn't ever surface. But he was good at pretending, he'd get involved with people to experience their emotions vicariously. He was curious, you see, almost obsessionally so. He knew he was missing something that mattered. In a way he was quite open about that, he would sniff out strong emotions like a dog, after a bone. He'd look and listen, but he couldn't feel it for himself. It existed — but not for him, like colours to the blind. Of course he'd never admit that he was flawed, but he knew it. So whatever he was doing there, it can't have been a romance — I mean it's very kind of you to think up something like that, but it doesn't ring true.'

'Then I'm wrong. But I can assure you that I didn't make it up about the girl, there was a girl. She was the attraction.' I was as little anxious to gain credit for that piece of supposed altruism as Ridinghouse himself might have been. She smiled; she shook her head very gently. I liked Jane Ridinghouse. I wished there was a way of sounding more sincere — I could see that while she might give me credit for all manner of things, the truth was not among them. I didn't know what I could give her, what might improve her state of mind; whether just thinking I might have that power wasn't insufferably pretentious of me. I could not relay the conversation I had had with her brother, could not explain my wife's weakness for him; that little piece of truth was best left in its bleak hiding place. If I could say nothing good, better to shut up.

I remembered that I could show her the postcard and did. It was easy to locate, it lay openly in a pile of letters in Annette's workroom. I read the laconic message in that recognisable script: 'Hope all is well, yours, John.' It had a date, clearly marked. She thanked me for that poor proof of past existence and then for my time.

'I must hurry away,' she said. 'A neighbour's keeping watch over Father.' She said that as though she'd set a fox to guard her chicks. I accompanied her to the door.

'You mustn't lose hope,' I said, feebly. 'John told me he'd never felt better. Those were his precise words, he was so certain about it.'

Her smile, all sweetness, was her brother at his best.

'Don't worry about me, Mr Ruffey. If I lost hope, that happened long ago. Perhaps I never had any. I know he's not there any more. I suppose I'd like to be reassured that it wasn't all futile, or that he at least thought that, at the end. It's selfishness, to make me feel better, because otherwise it's the saddest life, isn't it? But I'm used to uncertainties, you get used to not knowing things. Life is all uncertainties, you know. It's just that most people manage better when they can forget that. Goodbye. Thank you for the whisky.'

I liked her straight-backed march, I admired her strength. I sat on my own and had another drink, a big one, which was neither a celebration nor a wake but something in between. A libation to the god of lost souls, to the unquiet spirits of the unburied dead. I sat quietly for a long time.

I was free, released. The gaolers had gone away and the prisoner, venturing to the door, saw that it had never been locked. Beyond, where he had been told the high walls lay, there was nothing but the blue sky and the green grass and the misty hills. It was all gone; the prison had existed only in his mind.

Truth, as my old friend Pie used to say, is altogether a subjective affair. I gathered up my set of experiences, my life, and began to form a pattern in my mind, to create order, to create a new work.

The painting is a large one. It shows a vast, dark-panelled room which glows gold at the centre where the fire irradiates the marble hearth. The flames cast their warmth over the stone figures and the human ones. They shine brilliant upon the ultramarine blue of a whirling dress, upon the crimson carapace in the corner — colours which are naturally trans-lucent, which draw the eye.

It is a dance; there to observe and record it is the large figure which dominates the foreground: the man with an ironic face, middle-aged, balding, the man with the crooked leg. There is the camera on its spindly legs, just in view is the white sheet pinned up, the lights that will fix them all in that moment for ever. Soon he will start his work, but now he watches two couples who have ventured onto the floor.

Jack Ruffey clasps a beautiful Javanese girl in his arms and they turn, slowly, in personal enchantment. His blond hair is bright against the dark sheen of hers. Their moment is nearly over; already my mother, slender in her Chinese print dress, reaches up to tap him on the shoulder, to claim her partner for the dance.

Jane Ridinghouse is there, dancing with her father in more solemn tread. They are both tall and dark, very alike, faces strongly marked and they sway in melancholy motion. He, dreaming, looks over her shoulder into the spaces beyond.

There, too, is Annette, dancing on her own, the blond hair whirling, her face half hidden. Not a beautiful face but strong and expressive, unreadable now. Her dress is the brilliant blue of a Javanese sky and she pirouettes; there is something frenzied in her motion, something both brave and sad. Through the window to the left, the bright stars execute their own dance in a tropical sky lit by flashes and split by the dark cone of the volcano. The storm rages outside but the little people dance on, uncaring, intent upon their own orbits.

Because it is always so, part of the complexity of things, there are those who dance and those who watch; those who see the shadows gathering in the corners of the room. Against the dark walls, the little bar is lit up and Peter Leino leans on it. Loosely, he clasps his daughter in one arm; the other, resting on the counter, fidgets with a glass. The girl is looking at him lovingly. He is in conversation with Mrs Kiriakou, her barmaid's dress all flounces, her hands busy polishing glasses as she leans forward, sharp-nosed, intent. Like all innkeepers they plot, they plan the palaces of their dreams.

In the corner to the left, apart from the rest, is the splash of crimson: the figure of the cardinal. His robe is a flame. The massive head is inclined slightly as Gimbal kneels, in slight mockery, to kiss the ring upon one heavy hand, that gesture acknowledged by a slight spreading of the fingers. Pie's eyes look over the kneeling man to the scene beyond with the faraway gaze of one whom his cloth has set apart: a non-combatant. There, on the opposite side of the room, is his counterbalance, the slight figure with his back to the room who, looking into the mirror, observes all things through the glass. Ridinghouse is impassive, his hands hang loosely at his sides. The bright motion and colours of the scene cannot attract his attention, not even the dancing girl. The mirror is tarnished, but still he stares into it. His eyes meet those of the viewer of the picture and it is the viewer who will always be the first to look away.

The picture is signed with my bold, black scrawl. The title is *The Dance*. Some people like it, others say it is bizarre. A critics' consensus has babbled of an apogee, of a late and mature work. 'A concatenation of all that makes up a life,' one of them said, thereby blowing his own trumpet for, like parrots, they love their clever phrases. Another made reference to my Indonesian childhood. I do not begrudge them the small modicum of skill in happening to see the obvious. If this picture were to be my epitaph, I would not be too sad. I leave at least this behind me, to dance down all the days.

It has been shown, but it will not be sold. It is Annette's favourite picture. I often find her staring at it. I know not to ask what it is that draws her to it. Often, recently, I have observed that it seems to comfort her.

We live with our uncertainties, Annette and I, and it is true that in time they cease to irk and rub. I saw no reason to tell her about Jane Ridinghouse's visit; the truth can be cruel. Mine was an expedient lie – no, a sin of omission. Why take away hope? Who can live without it? Perhaps she still expects to hear from Ridinghouse, though I can hardly think so.

My wife is an extraordinary woman. She has the great calm that comes from having weathered a storm, from having passed through elation or despair. Either, both, it doesn't matter. Her face has been smoothed over and made beatific by these emotions, her whole manner calmer and more purposeful, more collected. It is dignity that she has acquired, a splendid kind of dignity, not unrelated to the transition from girl to woman. I admire it immensely, a sensation all the stronger for remaining unexpressed.

It is obvious that we shall remain a couple. We need each other. Another man – and men still look at her, all too often –

could not begin to understand. Her serenity is remarkable. Whatever, beneath that calm, hurts or is wounded, she has learnt to conceal it. It is an artificiality which I prize, which I cherish, as I cherish her. It is a fragile veneer which we both handle with care.

Time passes in this pretence and slowly it becomes real. The artifice in our pleasantries will be rubbed away by their great age and I believe that we shall achieve, at last, a peace which is as real as this curious truce is false, and as lasting. She is an heroic fiction, infinitely sustainable. I admire her tremendously for that and she is aware of my admiration. Who could appreciate her, as Ruffey does? There is no witness more admirably qualified, no audience which could render up such heartfelt, silent applause.

A postscript

It is over a year since I jolted my way to the summit of Mount Bromo. I received, last week, a letter from John Pie. It was unexpected, for after Java he had simply vanished. The university would not, or could not, say where he was. His flat was closed up, my few letters returned unopened. I was perfectly resigned to his absence. I had learnt to think as little about him as I used to when he was present.

'We were friends,' it said, 'and have grown distant from one another. But it is right that should be so; let us not dissemble and obscure it, as if it were something to be ashamed of. We are two ships, each of which has its destination and its course; our paths can cross and we can celebrate a feast together, as we did — and then the brave ships lay so peacefully in *one* harbour and under *one* sun that it might seem they had already reached their destination and both had *one* destination. But then the almighty power of our task again drove us apart, to different seas and different climes, and perhaps we shall never see one another again —

or perhaps if we do we shall not recognise one another; different seas and sun have changed us! That we had to grow distant from one another is the law *over* us.... There is probably a tremendous invisible curve and star orbit within which our so different paths and destinations may be *included* as tiny stretches of the way — let us raise ourselves to this thought! But our life is too short and our power of vision too weak for us to be more than friends in the sense of that exalted possibility — and so let us *believe* in our friendship in the stars, even if we did have to be enemies on earth.'*

We met in his club. We sat side by side as we had done before. We have a comical resemblance, Pie and I, both marked men. Each of us bears on the right temple jagged scars which are almost identical. We eyed each other. He was thinner. Some of his vast bulk had melted away under an African sun which had also tanned him dark. The metamorphosis into rude health was startling, but it was only an effect. The colour lay on him like varnish; it would crack and peel away.

We drank a great deal and he talked at great speed about the dig, his occupation of the past year. He described the painstaking labour (none of it his), the small pieces of pottery and wood that had been found and those that should have been, were it not for the blindness and stupidity of his colleagues.

'Bloody amateurs, dirt-scrapers, rag-pickers,' he called them. 'Not one methodical mind. One token woman you expect. We had three, all prune-faced.'

He ate hugely. We floated on a sea of words, archaeological, on his descriptions of little objects, anthropomorphic, on a wave of claret, anaesthetic.

*The Gay Science, Friedrich Nietzsche.

'Poor Africa, if you retire there,' I said mildly.

'Retire?' He snorted derision. 'Wool-gathering, Ruffey. They'll carry me out with my toes cocked up. What, give the department to those fools? They need me, poor little sods. That was a sabbatical Seventh year. Did me good. You going to retire, give up? We're at the height of our powers.' He leant over and goggled at me accusingly.

'I never give up,' I said. 'Too old, too stubborn, too used to the old ways. Every picture's a voyage of discovery, pushing the thing to its limits. I could as soon give up on life itself.'

It was grandly said and he nodded, satisfied, and began at once to elaborate pornographically on the charms of the ladies of the night in Nairobi, as though he had personally fondled each bum, which, as we both knew, was not — never could have been — the case.

We parted on the pavement in Piccadilly. He stood there for a moment, flapping his coat, indecisive, mouth agape to gulp in the air, as though it offered mountain freshness. He made a great business, then, of doing up his coat, fumbling around in the pockets for his cab fare.

'Wife all right?' he said abruptly, not looking at me. I hesitated. There was an opportunity there, to speak. I could have told him that we had survived; that we had lived through an age of darkness before entering an era of calm. That we were constructing a life, day by day, as people did; that I protected her. That we both connived at creating a false, necessary security. That it was possible to love on such impulses too. And if I had said all this to Pie, he would have snorted at it, embarrassed, and looked away. I might even have said that the whole experience had been remarkably character-forming, if it were not ridiculous for a man of my years to imagine that he could both learn and change

— a man who had so thoroughly created himself as Ruffey. He would no doubt have told me that I had too vivid an imagination. Wool-gathering, Ruffey, he might have said; you're getting soft. And I could have told him about the picture, but did not. In due course he would discover whatever it was he needed to know.

'We're both fine,' I said.

'Something I forgot to say.' He was scuffing his shoes against the pavement, looking down — as near as Pie ever came to embarrassment. 'Ridinghouse. Haven't heard from him. Used to drop me the odd postcard. Nothing for months now. Buggered off at last, I think. Odd man. Delusions of grandeur. No loss,' and he spotted a cab then, made a windmill of his arms and broke into an awkward, shambling run. I watched him go, one foot in the gutter, the great head, as always, tipped back a little and pointing towards the stars.

THE WAR AGAINST CHAOS

Anita Mason

THE SOCIETY OPERATED WITH A NIGHTMARE LOGIC. CURIOSITY HAD NO PLACE. NOR DID READING, STROLLING, JUNK-COLLECTING – ALL THE THINGS JOHN HARE RELISHED

He had been upwardly mobile on the ladder of Universal Goods when his wife left him and his career in jeopardy. He seemed the ideal, expendable scapegoat in a powerful company official's much-needed cover-up. And with a trumped-up charge worthy of Kafka, Hare found himself cast into the netherworld of a dreaded population known as the 'marginals'.

What the authorities never reckoned on was the reawakened cunning and imagination of these outcasts. Or the greater threat to them that Hare was to discover – based on self-respect and humour – steeling itself in the bowels of the city.

0 349 10031 4   FICTION   £4.50

ZERO db

MADISON SMARTT BELL

Consider the pitfalls of a would-be streetwise vigilante, a love-sick shrimp fisherman, an officer of conscience at the battle of Little Big Horn. Tune into Manhattan through a hidden mike in a sleazy downtown bar or observe an old widower negotiate the hostile zones of his living room and prepare to do battle.

From the dining halls of Princeton to the hog farms of Tennessee, Bell's vision sets humour against raw and dramatic realities, private ambitions against uncertain futures. The result is one of compelling artistry.

'Considered separately, the stories in this collection are astonishing; considered together, they are even more astonishing, for they indicate a dazzling range of voice'
New York Times Book Review

0 349 10082 9   FICTION   £3.99

The Truth About Lorin Jones

ALISON LURIE

Lorin Jones, an undervalued artist, died of pneumonia contracted from snorkelling in a cold sea. Polly Alter, art historian, feminist and fugitive from emotional chaos, has a mission—to wrest her from her ill-deserved obscurity and reveal for the world's judgement the truth about Lorin Jones . . .

'Alison Lurie's tone is unerring, no word wasted. As slyly cool as Jane Austen, she subjects to pleasantly relentless examination the woman's movement, art and the deep flaws in us all'
Daily Mail

'Miss Lurie's skill and lightness of touch conceal a highly elaborate technique. Her book is funny and shrewd . . . a polished example of the American comedy of manners'
Daily Telegraph

Also by Alison Lurie in Abacus:
REAL PEOPLE
FOREIGN AFFAIRS
IMAGINARY FRIENDS
LOVE AND FRIENDSHIP
THE NOWHERE CITY
THE WAR BETWEEN THE TATES

0 349 10066 7   FICTION   £3.99

Also available in ABACUS paperback:

FICTION

THE TRUTH ABOUT LORIN JONES	Alison Lurie	£3.99 ☐
THE RATTLESNAKE STRADIVARIUS	Teresa Kennedy	£4.99 ☐
THE BRIDE WHO RAN AWAY	Diana O'Hehir	£3.99 ☐
A CASE OF KNIVES	Candia McWilliam	£3.99 ☐
ST HIROSHIMA	Leigh Kennedy	£3.99 ☐
AN IRRELEVANT WOMAN	Mary Hocking	£3.99 ☐

NON-FICTION

RIDING THE DESERT TRAIL	Bettina Selby	£3.99 ☐
THE DROWNED AND THE SAVED	Primo Levi	£3.99 ☐
WHITE BOY RUNNING	Christopher Hope	£3.99 ☐
EASY MONEY	David Spanier	£3.99 ☐
ZOO STATION	Ian Walker	£3.99 ☐
THE PANAMA HAT TRAIL	Tom Miller	£3.99 ☐

All Abacus books are available at your local bookshop or news-agent, or can be ordered direct from the publisher. Just tick the titles you want and fill in the form below.

Name _____

Address _____

_____

Write to Abacus Books, Cash Sales Department, P.O. Box 11, Falmouth, Cornwall TR10 9EN

Please enclose a cheque or postal order to the value of the cover price plus:

UK: 60p for the first book, 25p for the second book and 15p for each additional book ordered to a maximum charge of £1.90

OVERSEAS & EIRE: £1.25 for the first book, 75p for the second book and 28p for each subsequent title ordered.

BFPO: 60p for the first book, 25p for the second book plus 15p per copy for the next 7 books, thereafter 9p per book.

Abacus Books reserve the right to show new retail prices on covers which may differ from those previously advertised in the text or elsewhere, and to increase postal rates in accordance with the P.O.